D1446472

LEVERAGE

LEVERAGE

DAN DOEDEN

FIVE STAR
A part of Gale, Cengage Learning

Detroit • New York • San Francisco • New Haven, Conn • Waterville, Maine • London

GALE
CENGAGE Learning·

LIBRARY OF CONGRESS CATALOGING-IN-PUBLICATION DATA

Doeden, Dan.
    Leverage / Dan Doeden. — First edition.
      pages cm
    ISBN-13: 978-1-4328-2732-8 (hardcover)
    ISBN-10: 1-4328-2732-4 (hardcover)
    1. Private investigators—Fiction. 2. Missing children—Fiction.
3. Mafia—Fiction. I. Title.
PS3604.O335L48 2013
813'6—dc23   2013021222

First Edition. First Printing: November 2013
Find us on Facebook– https://www.facebook.com/FiveStarCengage
Visit our website– http://www.gale.cengage.com/fivestar/
Contact Five Star™ Publishing at FiveStar@cengage.com

Printed in Mexico
1 2 3 4 5 6 7 17 16 15 14 13

LEVERAGE

CHAPTER 1

"I'm gonna ask you one more time," Tony Brassi shouted, voice echoing through the empty warehouse.

Tommy Getti looked up through swollen eyes and spit a mouthful of blood and broken teeth in his direction.

"You tell me now, Bronco and Bobby will finish this quick. You don't, it's gonna be a long night."

"I tole you what I know."

Brassi gestured and Bronco Lucci heaved back again and struck Getti in the face. Getti let out a pitiful grunt and his jaw sprang open like a suitcase.

"Now you done it," Bobby Albanese said. "How's he gonna talk with a broken jaw?"

"He better find a way or he'll never talk again," Brassi snarled.

"Boss," Lucci said, lumbering over, "maybe he don't know. Ain't many guys can take this much."

Brassi reached up from his chair and grabbed the huge man by his blood-splattered shirt, pulling him close.

"And maybe you ain't hurt him enough yet. Didn't I tell you bring the toolbox?"

"I thought it was in the trunk. I forgot to check. Don't worry. I'll make him talk."

"You forgot? You know what happens if I forget? I'm like God, I forget about you, you cease to exist."

★ ★ ★ ★ ★

Frank Via propped his elbows on the bar and watched the reporter named Chizek eat. The fat man was having a grand time slopping Thousand Island dressing onto his salad and chatting up the blonde across the table from him. From the looks of her, she didn't appear to be his wife, or anyone else's either.

Chizek was now into his third course and Via was into his second bourbon, which still wasn't improving his mood any. He hated these jobs, watching other people enjoy themselves, while he sat around inhaling someone else's cigarette smoke. He wanted to forget about the whole thing, but he needed the money and didn't know any other way to get it, legally. Besides, what else was he qualified to do?

He tired of watching Chizek and watched the bartender for a while, a guy who looked like he tended to himself a bit too much, wondering if maybe he could do that. Go to bartending school, become a mixologist, stand around all night choking on cigarette smoke. End up a firsthand alcoholic dying from secondhand lung cancer.

You could still smoke in most places then, Chicago never being the kind of town to discourage people's vices. The smoker was four stools away and Via was giving him dirty looks that didn't seem to be working. He considered going into the restaurant and taking a table in the No Smoking section but didn't want to chance being seen again. He had already tried the fat man in the building where he worked, but the guy made him and squeezed onto an elevator before he could get to him. That was two days ago and his client was growing impatient. So was Via.

He called the bartender over and sent a drink to the smoker, a bony guy wearing a worn-out suit with a face to match.

"Don't get the wrong idea," he said when the guy gave him a queer look. "It's for the cigarettes."

The guy swiveled on his stool. "Want one?"

"I want the whole pack."

The guy glanced at the bartender, who shrugged and returned to washing glasses.

"I beg your pardon?" the guy said to Via.

"You're not going to get it."

The smoker glanced again at the bartender, who said, "Hey, I just work here."

Via was six-foot-plus, with big shoulders and close-cropped black hair salted with gray. He was clean-shaven but his father's five-o'clock shadow cast a coarse darkness against his olive skin. His eyes were dark too, set close to a street fighter's nose, and his chin had a cleft like a dent. He had his mother's mouth, full lips and broad line, which might have softened his appearance, if not for the large scar stitching the corner of his upper lip. It was the face of a man who didn't like debate. The guy stubbed out his smoke.

Via returned to the TV and nursed his drink but could feel the guy's eyes on him and heard his fingers drumming on the bar.

"Hey, don't I know you?"

"Yeah, I'm the guy just asked you to stop smoking."

"You know, I never forget a face."

"Try harder."

"Can't. It comes with the job."

"Sounds like an occupational hazard."

"Stan's a reporter for the *Trib*," the bartender chimed in.

Stan the reporter scratched his head and stared at Via. "Yeah, you definitely look familiar."

Via flicked him the finger. "How familiar is this?"

"Wait a minute," the reporter said, a strained look on his face. "Yeah, yeah, you're that mob lawyer."

Via cut him off with a wave and turned his attention back to

Chizek, who was stuffing filet mignon into his face and trying to impress the blonde with his mouth full. She shifted uncomfortably in her chair and crossed her legs, which were bare and nicely shaped.

"Hey, Pete," the reporter persisted. "You got something of a celebrity here. He's the lawyer kept the Mob out of prison a few years back."

The bartender glanced at him like he'd heard everything in life he cared to, then turned his back and started to inventory his stock.

"Yeah, this here's Frank Via," the guy continued yammering. "Used to strong-arm for Tony Brassi in the old days. Then got smart and went to law school."

"That what you call getting smart?" Pete the bartender cracked.

"You remember Operation Monkey Wrench? Feds wired a booth in the coffee shop in the old Butterick Hotel? Caught a bunch of aldermen and mobsters over breakfast arguing about who was going to pick up the check. Ran the wire for months. Finally had enough to send most of the Outfit's top guns to prison. Plenty of pols, too. Trial lasted for weeks." The reporter thrust a thumb in Via's direction. "Lucky for the Outfit, they had Frank Via here. Got every one of them off. The aldermen weren't so lucky. Yes, sir, this here's a real celebrity."

Pete the bartender twirled a finger in the air and kept on working.

"That's right, isn't it?" the reporter said to Via. "You saved Carmine Delacante's ass, and Tony Brassi's, too."

"Who's going to save yours?"

The reporter got up and moved to the stool next to Via, who was massaging his temple like he was waiting for a headache to pass.

"Ah, come on. I'm just talking. Maybe we can help each

other out here. You'd make a good story. You know, a follow-up, like a 'Where is he now?' kind of thing."

"Get lost."

"Maybe get you some business, get me in good with my editor."

The look in Via's eyes caused the reporter to stop suddenly and put his hands up in front of his chest.

"Oh, shit, that's right. You were disbarred right after Monkey Wrench. Bribed a juror or something?"

Via straightened on his stool and put one foot on the floor.

"Okay, okay," Stan the reporter said. He reached into his jacket and brought out a business card, which he tossed on the bar. "Just in case. I'll do right by you."

"Start by getting the hell out of here."

The reporter put his hands up again and got to his feet. "I'm just saying. Think about it. Have a drink." He told the bartender to put it on his tab and hurried out the door.

Via hunched into his shoulders and watched the waiter moving between Chizek and the kitchen back behind the bar. He checked his watch, flipped through his newspaper, gazed at the Cubs game on the TV again, but couldn't concentrate. He had tried for years to bury the past but some asshole was always kicking up the dirt. At least the cigarette smoke had cleared.

By the time Chizek finally called for his check, the Cubs had lost their pitching and Via had lost his patience. As the waiter came by to collect the bar bill, he pulled the kid aside and waved a twenty in his face.

"I need to borrow your apron and the fat guy's check."

"Don't look at me," the bartender said when the kid glanced over, and went to a far corner to work over his tabs.

Via tied the apron around his waist and extracted an envelope from his jacket, stuck it in the apron pocket, and walked over to Chizek's table. The fat man was finishing his coffee when Via handed him the check and the subpoena.

"Howard Chizek, you have been served."

Chizek choked and set his cup back on the table. "What the hell is this?"

"Looks like some legal thing," the blonde said.

"You're a lawyer now?" Chizek snapped.

"It's a subpoena, right?" the blonde asked Via, looking up with purple painted eyes, a subtle smile on Chianti lips.

"Shut up!" Chizek told her. "This ain't none of your business." He looked at the envelope. "It's a fucking subpoena?" he asked Via.

"What do you think, it's a love letter from your wife?"

"I think you're an asshole, that's what I think."

"Better think again."

An elderly couple at the table behind them watched attentively, sipping liqueurs like this was the after-dinner show.

"This doesn't change our deal," the blonde said to Chizek.

"I told you, shut the fuck up."

"You can't talk to me like that. I'm not your wife." She snatched up the glass in front of her and threw red wine in Chizek's face. He was surprised for a moment, then swung out his fat hand and slapped her hard on the left cheek.

"My God!" the white-haired woman behind them gasped. She touched her husband's arm and began gathering up her things, pulling on his sleeve. He patted her hand, in no hurry to go anywhere.

"You sonofabitch!" the blonde seethed. She rubbed her cheek, but didn't cry. Via figured she'd been slapped before.

Chizek wiped his face with a napkin and tried blotting his shirt dry. "You happy now," he barked at Via, "the trouble you caused?" He mumbled something else under his breath.

Via took a step forward and leaned down to glare into Chizek's fleshy face. "What did you say?"

Chizek threw the napkin back on the table. "I said, you did your job, so now you can get the fuck out of here."

"I think he called you a cocksucker," the blonde said. Her face was scarlet on one side.

Chizek was red, too. He looked up at Via. "What do you want from me? She's a goddamn cunt."

"I want you to apologize."

"What the fuck? It ain't enough you ruined my evening here?"

"No, it ain't."

The fat man looked at him, then over at the blonde, then back at Via again.

"So what the hell? It's over, huh? You're just doing your job. I know that. Forget what I said."

Via started to untie the apron. "Let me ask you something," he said to the blonde. "He look like he's won any fights lately?"

"Not with a man."

Via gave her half a smile for that. Chizek did not.

"All right, all right, I apologize. Okay?" Chizek said, holding up his hand.

"I mean to her," Via said, just to screw with him.

"You kidding?"

"I look like it?"

Behind them, the old woman started to stand, but her husband pulled her back down, chuckling when the blonde said to Via, "Ah, it's okay. He can't help it. All fat men have little dicks. Makes them mean."

"I guess you'd be an expert on that," Via said.

She lost her smile. "Screw you, too."

Chizek spread his arms. "See what I'm saying?"

Via looked to the blonde. "You need to read those personal ads more closely," he said, walking back toward the bar.

"He's right, honey," the old woman piped up. "He's right."

★ ★ ★ ★ ★

When Bronco Lucci shattered Tommy Getti's nose, the rush of blood down the back of his throat was more than his lungs could handle. He slumped forward, gasping for air, but the harder he tried the more blood he sucked into his overworked lungs.

"You die, I'll kill you, you sonofabitch!" Lucci bellowed at him.

"This ain't good," Bobby Albanese whispered, glancing over at Tony Brassi.

"Get some water," Lucci barked.

Getti was coughing up blood, his eyes going white.

Brassi jumped to his feet and ran forward. "Where is she?" He shoved Lucci out of the way and leaned in close to Getti. "You little prick, you better talk."

Getti moaned. Brassi stepped back and kicked him in the chest, knocking him backward in the chair.

Albanese came back with the water and poured it over Getti's broken face. "You better talk," he parroted.

Getti lay on his back, a halo of blood forming beneath his head. He gurgled a deep wet cough, jerked like a marionette, then went still.

Lucci and Albanese stepped away from him, keeping their eyes on Brassi.

But Brassi simply lifted his coat from the back of his chair and said matter-of-factly, "Stupid 'til the end." Then he gathered himself like a theater patron about to leave a boring play.

"You know what to do with the body," he said.

The two men looked at him like they were playing twenty questions.

"Like I said. *Remember?*"

"Oh, yeah . . . yeah, right, I remember now," Albanese stammered.

Brassi thrust a finger at Lucci. "Next time you forget something, Bronco, maybe I forget you. Capisce?"

On the sidewalk outside the restaurant Via took in the cool night air and looked around for a cab. The weather was still mild but the downtown streets were nearly deserted, now that the suburbanites were back home getting their kids ready for the new school year.

The city fathers had done a grand job making the downtown area look safe. There were new green spaces and sidewalk cafés, and the cops kept the streets clear enough of lowlifes to give the illusion the neighborhood folks were just like the folks who were smart enough to move out to the suburbs in the first place.

But Via knew this neighborhood before it was gentrified, when it was the kind of inner-city hell hole suburbanites only saw in movies. His job back then was to collect street taxes from the gangs that ruled these streets and he never came here without security and a gun. Now, pretty people strolled around without either, thinking the chic restaurants and brightly lit signs meant it was safe, unconcerned that just a few blocks west junkies were still cutting lines of crank and each other's throats with razors.

That was the Chicago Via knew, the one beneath the shiny veneer. He had paid his dues in those neighborhoods, doing the dirty work of cracking heads and breaking bones. It was the kind of work any schmuck could do, so when he got a chance to move up and out, he grabbed it. Hell, becoming a Mob lawyer was the best thing that ever happened to him. He felt like he owned the city back then. He was connected. He was family. He felt anchored and secure.

Now, he felt adrift.

Christ, he needed a smoke. He patted his pockets, then remembered he had quit. If Stan the reporter had still been

15

inside, he might have gone back in and bummed one. The nosey little shit. He didn't need to be reminded how far he had fallen.

He sighted a Yellow Cab and was about to hail it when a maroon Buick Park Avenue sounding like a hip-hop funeral rolled up to the curb next to him.

"Hey, Via, things so bad you gotta hoof it now?" Charlie Pignotti shouted, sticking his thick head out the side window. His face was dark and Mediterranean, black hair tied back in a ponytail with a gold band that matched his earring.

"I like the exercise. You should try it some time."

Pignotti reached over and turned down the radio. "You got my money yet?"

"It's not due 'til tomorrow."

"You ain't gettin' no more extensions, Via."

"That's what I said, tomorrow."

The driver, a burly guy Via saw around, leaned over Pignotti and shouted: "You better have it!"

"Still recruiting from the Special Olympics, Pig?"

"He don't like to be called that," the driver yelled.

Via walked over to the car. "Hey, Pig, how about a lift downtown?"

The burly guy reached for the door handle, but Pignotti waved him off.

"You should watch out for yourself, Frank," Pignotti said. "You ain't got no friends no more."

"Geez, and I always thought I could count on you, Pig."

"Sure, you can count on me. Like death."

Pignotti turned up the rap music again and slapped the dashboard and his driver peeled away. "Tomorrow, Via," the Pig shouted, hand extended out the window, fuck-you finger raised in the air.

Via watched him go, wondering how long he would be able to dodge him, and hating himself for worrying about it. There was a time when guys like Pignotti would have to ask permission just to talk to him. Christ, it was time to go home.

He started walking but a voice from behind stopped him.

"You piss off everyone?"

He swung around and saw Chizek's blonde. "Yeah, it's my job."

"I used to have a job like that, but I got divorced."

He gave her the once-over. Better than his first impression. A little fuller than he usually liked, but firm. Good legs and a face that was pretty but would look better with less makeup. Beneath it, he could see she was younger than he had first thought.

"You used to be famous, huh?" she said.

"I don't know what you mean."

"I asked Pete. The bartender."

"He doesn't know me."

"He said you were in the newspaper."

"You shouldn't believe everything you hear."

"I don't. Especially from men."

"Yeah, me neither. Where *is* your boyfriend?"

She glanced back over her shoulder. "Watching from the door. I think he's afraid to come out."

"But not you?"

"Should I be?"

"He won't like it, you talking to me."

"Yeah, that's why I am."

He looked her over again. She didn't look that tough. But with women, you could never tell.

"You don't like him, why are you with him?"

"I'm not with him."

He gave her a wise-guy smirk. "Whatever you say."

She shifted her weight and put her hand on her hip. "It's not what you think."

"What do you care what I think?"

"I just don't like people insulting me before I give them reason to."

"So I should wait until I know you better?"

She poked a finger at him like a gun. "You don't make such a good first impression yourself, you know."

Via glanced over and saw Chizek step back into the shadows of the doorway. "He's still waiting for you."

"He'll die waiting." Her left cheek was still red.

"So why'd you come out here to talk to me, besides sticking it to him?"

"Isn't it obvious? I have poor taste in men."

He squeezed out a half-smile again. "I guess this must be your lucky night, then."

"So it seems."

From the corner of his eye, he saw a police cruiser crawling past, the cop on the curb side gawking at them, looking for something to do on a Sunday night. He kept his eyes on the blonde. She didn't look at the cops either, which he considered a good sign.

"My ex was a cop," she said off-handedly, watching the cruiser's taillights moving away.

"The guy you used to piss off?"

"It didn't take much effort."

"Yeah, I've noticed that about cops." He thought she might smile at that, but she didn't. "Listen, I'm trying to find a cab. Maybe I can drop you."

"I don't think we're going the same way."

"Well, if you want to piss me off sometime, here's my number." He handed her his card, which she held up to catch the light from the restaurant's windows.

"This is what you do? You're a private dick?"

"It's temporary."

"Sure, what isn't?"

She reached into her purse and brought out a matchbook and handed it to him. Her nails were the color of plums.

"Just to show you you're wrong about me. It's where I work, you ever get in the neighborhood. My name's Dee."

He watched her walk away, skirt flicking back and forth like a cat's tail.

At first, Harry Soltis thought he recognized the kid across the table but realized it was just a trick of mind. He interrogated so many gangbangers they were all beginning to look alike to him. This one was no more than fifteen but already carried an arrest record to put Bobby Brown to shame.

The Cook County House of Corrections was the largest jail in the country. It housed eleven jail divisions, a boot camp, a halfway house, a drug abuse program, and a juvenile temporary detention center. Every year, some eleven thousand juveniles like this one found their way there, and Soltis felt like he had interviewed every one of them. This kid was giving him the usual shuck 'n jive and Soltis wanted to reach across and tear the gold ring from his nose. Instead, he called in a cop to guard the kid and went out to throw some water on his face.

The men's room smelled of sewer gas and the walls were the color of urine. The floor tiles had once been white but were now the color of the walls and webbed with cracks. The air itself looked yellow in the light from the overhead bulb, which was caged in a rusty metal net. Water was leaking from somewhere and had puddled beneath the line of faded urinals. He took a stand where the overflow looked most shallow. Standing there with his manhood hanging out, he realized again how much he hated coming here. The whole building reeked of failure.

When he finished, he walked over to one of the stained ceramic sinks, pressed the cold water fixture with his elbow and waited while the dunnish liquid cleared to a murky transparency. This routine, too, was overly familiar. He stared at himself in the milky mirror and pulled a monogrammed handkerchief from his back pocket to dry his hands, knowing better than to try the paper towel dispenser.

"You've been in the trenches too long," he said to his reflection, and felt the truth of it deep in his bones.

He was getting too old for this. If he didn't move up and out soon it would be too late, and he would spend the rest of his career as a Deputy State's Attorney in places just like this.

It was now or never, he told himself, time to run with the big dogs or let himself be neutered.

CHAPTER 2

Nicky Fratelli was reading the morning's *Chicago Tribune* when Via came through the door.

"Mail's on your desk," he said without looking up.

"Coffee ready yet?"

"You'll need to go across the street. The coffeemaker quit. I can make some tea. If the microwave still works."

"The goddamn coffeemaker now?"

The office was your basic cube, configured into two rooms, a main room and Via's small office, both of which were cracker boxes but functional enough, given the state of Via's business. The main room functioned as a combination reception room, waiting room, and kitchen, and was decorated—Nicky refused to use the word—in a style he referred to as Early AmVets. He did his best to dress it up but any new wall art or knickknack he added seemed only to highlight the tawdriness of everything else around it. Finally, he just gave up—Via never noticed anyway—and confined his efforts to the two areas he lived in most, his desk and what passed for the kitchen: microwave, refrigerator, and sink. With Frank Via you took things as they came.

"Any messages?"

Nicky put down the newspaper and pressed a button on the answering machine. It gave off a low hiss. "Just the usual."

"You should have your own sitcom. What about Bitberg? No check yet?"

"You need to call him, he doesn't listen to me."

"Can't imagine why."

Nicky flicked the newspaper with his finger. "Says here Jupiter's in retrograde. Not a good day for financial matters."

"You need the horoscopes to know that?"

"How'd it go last night with whatshisname, the subpoena?"

"Goddamn fat ass. Made me wait in some smoky bar until he finished clogging his arteries, but I gave him a good case of indigestion."

"I know how that feels."

"Why don't you have some tea?" Via went toward his office. "Go ahead and bill the damn job."

"I'm the accounting department now, too? I'm going to need a raise."

"Hey, it's not a good day to discuss financial matters," Via said over his shoulder.

He closed his office door, threw his jacket on a mossy-looking chair, and walked across a matted brown rug that covered the floor like a stain. His desk, which was the kind his teachers had in high school, was mottled with coffee rings and scuffed from his shoes. Above it, someone—Nicky, no doubt—had hung a framed sepia photo of 1940s State Street on the wall, which was last painted about the same time period. It was not the kind of place you would want to spend a lot of time in, which Via didn't.

He sat behind the desk and sifted through the mail, the usual assortment of bills—a second notice on the rent, another letter from his ex-wife's lawyer about overdue child support payments, a couple of pre-approved credit card applications—which gave him an idea.

He went back out, told Nicky he was going for coffee, and tramped downstairs to the Starbucks across the street. He bought a vente regular and took a seat in a corner from where he had a good view of the customers.

The neighborhood was one of those marginal areas where public housing butted up against three-hundred-thousand-dollar townhomes, the suburban kids who bought them thinking they were pioneers, the vanguard of a new prosperity that would somehow create the "unique, urban, mixed-use community" the real estate developers advertised. So far, the mixed-use businesses were this Starbucks, a video store, and the crack whores and drug dealers who were there in the first place.

Via nursed his coffee and watched the stream of customers buying overpriced java on their plastic cards. When he had been there long enough, he went over near the condiment bar, reached into the trash, and smuggled out a large handful of discarded charge receipts, then went back to his office. There he spread the receipts across his desk. After he found five with signatures he could read, he looked up the cardholders in the neighborhood white pages and began making phone calls. On the third try, he found someone at home.

"This is Martin Pitt," he said to the woman who answered, "and I'm calling from the security and fraud department at Liberty Card. . . . Yes, that's right. My badge number is seven four one five. I'm afraid your card has been flagged for an unusual purchase pattern and I'm calling to verify. . . . Yes, Liberty Card. Seventy-four fifteen, that's correct . . . Martin Pitt.

"This would be on your card issued by City One Bank. Did you purchase a blu-ray DVD player for three hundred eighty-five dollars and ninety-nine cents from a Zap Electronics store in Kankakee? . . . No, I don't watch many movies myself, either. So, you did not make this purchase? . . . Yes, ma'am, that is why I'm calling. . . .

"Yes, we will be issuing a credit to your account. The credit will be sent to your home before your next statement. . . . Yes, I have your address," Via said, reading it to her from the phone book. "Is that correct?"

"Good. Now, I will be starting a fraud investigation and if you have any questions, you should call the eight hundred number listed on your card and ask for Security. You will need to refer to Case Number eight nine four three. . . . Yes, that is correct.

"Now, I do need to verify you are in possession of your card and it has not been lost or stolen. If you will look on the back of your card, you will see seven numbers. The last three are the security numbers that verify this card is in your possession. Please read me the three numbers," Via said, writing them on the back of an unpaid electric bill. "Yes, those match our records.

"Now, do you have any other questions? . . . Yes, on your next statement. . . . Well, you are certainly welcome and don't hesitate to call back if you have any further concerns."

He was logged onto the Internet before he finished talking and ordered a new coffee machine for Nicky, a leather jacket for his daughter, and some expensive Scotch for himself. He had them sent to a postal box he kept under a false name. Once the packages arrived, he would cancel the box.

He shopped until the credit card hit its limit, but none of it made him feel any better. This is it, he cursed himself, what he had come to, scamming little old ladies. How the hell was he going to pay Charlie Pignotti like this? He resigned himself to calling Richard Bitberg.

"Look, Dick, we've been through this before," Via said into the phone.

"It's Richard. We've been through that before."

Richard Bitberg was chairman of Chicago Clients Group, one of the nation's largest investment banks. He had hired Via to tail his wife, whom he was certain was having an affair with a local shock jock, but after three weeks Via had found nothing.

Now Bitberg owed him thirty-five hundred dollars and was refusing to pay.

"Richard or Dick, you still owe me money."

"Why should I pay you? You didn't find anything."

"You didn't hire me to find *something*, you hired me to find something *out*. I found out your wife is loyal to you. You should be grateful."

"Grateful you're a lousy detective? I know she's sleeping around, you just can't catch her."

"Well, if she is, she didn't do it on my watch."

"Maybe she knew you were following her."

"Not a chance. Just accept it. Most men would be glad. What's your goddamn problem?"

"My problem is, I want a divorce. And you can't find anything."

"So divorce her, happens every day."

"Without grounds?" Bitberg sounded shocked. "You have any idea what I'm worth?"

"I read the papers."

"Then you can imagine what a divorce settlement will cost me. Why do you think I hired you? Find something on her. I know your background. Manufacture it if you have to."

"Look, you're fucking around and your wife isn't. If she doesn't know, why cause yourself trouble?"

"I told you, I think she suspects me. She finds out first, she'll get everything."

Via could hear Bitberg rustling papers.

"Now Dickie, you're not going to welsh on our deal, are you?"

"That's an ethnic slur, you know."

"Dickie—"

"Welsh, *to welsh*. It implies people of Celtic descent are cheaters. Face it, you're bad at your job."

Via sat back and put his feet on his desk. He *wasn't* much of a detective. But, hell, most of his work didn't require much actual detecting. Mostly, it was serving subpoenas, coercing deadbeat dads, and catching cheating spouses. Occasionally, he did have to find someone and things could get a little dicey, but as long as he had a starting point, someone he could start with, someone who knew something he needed to know, he could usually get it out of him. Because, mostly, it was all about intimidation—which he did know something about—and having the stones to do what most people were too timid to do.

"You don't want to find out what I'm really good at," he said into the phone.

"You don't scare me, Via. I told you, I know about you. You used to be with the Mob, but that was long ago. Now you're just a two-bit hustler with no connections and no prospects. I make one phone call and you're not even a private detective anymore."

Via set his feet on the floor. "Listen," he began, but heard another voice—Bitberg's secretary, he assumed—talking in the background.

"The River Bank Club called, the masseuse can take you at two o'clock," he heard her say.

"Dickie?" he said when he heard Bitberg breathing on the line again. "This isn't some corporate dispute you can hand off to Human Resources."

"I'm a busy man. If you bother me again, I'll have you arrested," Bitberg snapped and hung up.

Via replaced the receiver and reached over and pressed rewind on the old-style tape recorder he had connected to the phone. He listened to the playback with a contemptuous grin. When it finished, he collected the cassette from the machine and opened a desk drawer and took out a sheet of white adhesive labels. He wrote Bitberg's name and the date on one of the labels, peeled it off, and adhered it to the cassette, then put the tape in his pocket. He was still grinning to himself when Nicky poked his head through the doorway.

"Something funny?"

"Bitberg. He's a funny guy."

"I hadn't noticed. Muchado called, says your car is ready."

"About goddamn time. Get me some cab fare from petty cash."

Nicky put his hands on his hips and looked at Via like a teacher appraising a slow student. "Petty cash? I blew all the petty cash on the newspaper."

"Christ. All right, lend me a twenty."

"You haven't paid me for two weeks. I'm the credit union now, too?"

"Hey, I just ordered you a very expensive coffeemaker online."

"Maybe I can sell it on eBay to pay the rent," Nicky said.

Via followed him out to his desk, where Nicky pulled open a drawer and unfolded a tightly creased bill from inside his calendar and handed it to him.

"Twenty bucks isn't going to get you your car."

"Eddie and me go way back. I'll work something out."

"We talking about the same Eddie Muchado?"

Muchado ran the best chop shop in Chicago. Via knew him from the old days. He still did a brisk business in hot cars and hot parts and made a good buck helping the Outfit keep its inventory clean.

"I gave him plenty of business in the old days."

"So what are you going to do, blackmail him?"

"Not him exactly," Via said.

Richard Bitberg felt good. The locker room was empty and he was happy to be alone. In a few hours the River Bank Club would be swarming with expensive suits and even more expensive face lifts and he would already be finished and at the Chicago Union Club enjoying twenty-dollar cigars and twenty-year-old scotch with fellow members of Chicago's business elite. It was good to be rich.

As he stripped off his Hugo Boss suit and Joseph Abboud shirt, he caught a glimpse of himself in the full-length mirror and felt a momentary pang of insecurity. Without his clothes he looked like what he was—a flabby, bald, sixty-year-old with pasty skin and varicosed legs. He wrapped a towel around himself and went for his massage.

Downstairs, Via surveyed the club's lobby, taking in the mix of chlorine and perfume, eyeing the buff women in their spandex outfits. He used to belong to a club like this, back when he was still mobbed up and could afford it. The place was called *Pump This!* and had all the latest equipment, including massage rooms staffed by the best-looking hookers in the city. *Pump This!* was the kind of full-service joint where you could get inflated and deflated during the same visit. The Deputy Mayor, the Superintendent of Police, and the chairman of The Civic Club had all been members.

As Via was casing the check-in procedure, he felt a hand on his shoulder and turned to see a familiar face.

"Hey, Henry. I was hoping you were still here."

"Where else I'm gonna get paid to watch white women shake their asses?"

Via knew Henry Weathers from back when he was bribing cops at the County Courts, before Weathers caught a bullet in the hip and cashed out on permanent disability. He had headed the River Bank Club's security for years and knew all the high-profile members. Weathers knew Richard Bitberg from the time Bitberg parked his car in the club's fire zone and then tried to get Weathers fired for telling him to move it. He was happy to point out Bitberg's silver Jaguar in the underground garage.

"This official business?" Weathers asked on the way back up the stairs. "You don't mind me asking."

"Personal."

"Yeah?"

"I don't work for them anymore."

Weathers put on an innocent look. "Work for who?"

Via took a seat behind a potted palm and waited, sipping a three-dollar coffee and watching women dressed in three-hundred-dollar exercise outfits exchange gossip and divorce lawyers, thinking these were probably the kind of women Bitberg liked, Jewish princesses, the type that made a lot of noise in bed, and out of it.

Maybe that was the reason he wanted to divorce his wife. She seemed to be the quiet type. A tall, wafer-thin woman who spent all of her time at day spas or charity events, which had kept Via hunched in his car for three weeks with an unused Nikon and a sore back. There was no way he was going to let Bitberg stiff him after that.

The overpriced coffee was cold when Henry Weathers came out from the locker room and signaled to him. Via went back down to the garage and settled behind a concrete pillar next to Bitberg's car. A few minutes later, he heard the clicking of someone's heels coming toward him. The sound grew closer, then the car's security system burped and the locks clicked open, and he stepped out and snatched the remote from Bitberg's hand. The chairman of the board shrieked like a five-year-old.

"Relax, Dickie."

Bitberg began peddling backward but Via grabbed him by the lapels. They felt like money.

"I said relax."

"If you touch me—"

"I don't need to touch you to hurt you, Dickie." Via held the cassette tape in front of Bitberg's face. "Recordings of our conversations. Imagine what your wife's lawyers could do with these in court. Imagine what the press could do with them. Just imagine how your shareholders will react when they see your lying, cheating face on CNBC."

Bitberg went white. "You know, it's illegal to record someone without his knowledge."

"Don't be a putz," Via said, putting the cassette back into his pocket. "How's that for an ethnic slur?"

"We have a confidentiality agreement!"

"Grow up, Dickie."

"What do you want, the money?" Bitberg fumbled inside his coat. "Here, I'll write you a check right now."

Via pulled his jacket back so Bitberg could see his gun. "Get in the car. I'll drive."

"Where? Where are you taking me?"

"Get in and shut up."

"I will not! This is kidnapping! You can't just—"

Via snagged him by the ear and dragged him around to the passenger side and pushed him inside. Bitberg seemed to get the point. As they pulled out of the garage, Henry Weathers gave them a friendly wave.

Bitberg squawked while Via drove, threatening one minute, bargaining the next, then pleading to be let out. At one point, Via stopped and reached over and opened the passenger door. Bitberg glanced around at the abandoned buildings and burnt-out cars and was quiet the remainder of the trip. Then, when they finally arrived at Muchado's, he refused to get out of the car.

"What kind of place is this?" he asked, his eyes flicking like a bird's.

The chop shop was tucked away in a dead-end alley in a dead-end neighborhood that butted up against a viaduct on the near West Side. There was only one way in, so Eddie Muchado knew anyone coming down the alley was either a customer or a cop, but when he saw Bitberg's Jaguar pull into the driveway and stop, he didn't know what to expect. He slipped an iron lug wrench beneath his coveralls into the belt loop of his jeans and waited.

"I'm not getting out," Bitberg declared, puffing himself into his suit.

"Sure you are. Either on your feet or on your knees," Via assured him.

Bitberg shrank. "Okay, okay. I'll pay you. I'll pay you right now."

"You know," Via sneered, "I notice rich people scare easily. Your average working stiff—not that you'd know any—he's considering suicide half the time anyway. But you rich pricks, you're having so much fun you want to live forever."

Via went around and yanked Bitberg out the door and pushed him past his white Coupe DeVille parked outside the entrance, the car covered with dust and leaves, the tires low.

"Frank Via," Muchado shouted, arms out, smiling with brown teeth. "Joo make me nervous, man." He pulled the wrench out from his coveralls and tossed it onto the garage floor behind him, the loud clank making Bitberg flinch.

"What's this, Frank, joo jacking cars now?"

"It belongs to him."

"I'm here under duress," Bitberg whined.

Muchado looked him up and down. "Who's this *pendejo*?" He leaned toward Bitberg and sniffed the air. "Smell like a woman."

"He's my banker. What's the bill for the Caddy?"

"I tole joor bitch, Man, eight hundred bucks."

"You hear that, Dickie?"

"Why you have that *maricon* work for joo?"

"All the wetbacks are busy cutting lawns."

"Joo a funny man, Frank."

"The sooner you pay Eddie here," Via told Bitberg, "the sooner you get back to Pleasantville."

"This is coercion," Bitberg stammered.

"Who *is* this *pendejo*?"

"Dickie, write the man a check for eight hundred dollars."

"Man, I don't take no checks. Joo know that. Cash only. I don't trust no check."

"Eddie, you know who this guy is?"

"A *pendejo*."

"Yeah, but rich. Look at his car and his clothes."

Muchado looked Bitberg over again and spat on the ground. "How 'bout I take the Jag? We call it even."

Bitberg was wide-eyed. His eyes ricocheted back and forth between Via, Muchado, and his car. Sweat was speckling on his brow.

"His check is good, Eddie, trust me. He's going to write one to me, too. And, Eddie, if it *does* bounce or gets stopped, you'll have the address of the Jag right there on the check."

Muchado gave him his brown gap-toothed grin. "All right, Frank, I take joor word for it."

"Write," Via ordered Bitberg. "Eight hundred."

"Plus the two joo owe me for last time."

"A grand? You couldn't at least wash my car?"

"Joo think it run better?"

Bitberg fumbled in his suit coat for his checkbook. Via reached in to help him and found his wallet. There were five new one-hundred dollar bills inside, which he removed and folded into his own pocket. "For today's time."

"That's stealing," Bitberg whined.

Muchado rolled his eyes. *"Que culero."*

"A thousand for Muchado, Dickie. That leaves twenty-five hundred for me. Where are the keys, Eddie?"

"In the visor, man."

"You're not worried it might be stolen, huh?"

"Joo kidding?"

"You're not going to get away with this," Bitberg said, handing over the checks. "I know people. Important people."

"Shut up, Dickie," Via said. He handed Muchado the check.

The Mexican ran his thumb over Bitberg's signature and spat again. "Ain't like the old days, Frank," he said, shaking his head. "It don't even feel like cash."

"Get in your car and go home," Via told Bitberg, "before Eddie changes his mind."

"You won't get away with this."

Via pushed past Bitberg and headed over to get his Caddy, but Bitberg followed, saying: "Wait a minute. Wait a minute. What about the recording?"

"Go home."

"I paid you. We're even now."

"We'll never be even, you rich prick. So I'm going to hold onto to this tape for awhile. Who knows, it might interest some of those important people you know."

"That's blackmail!"

"Only if I have to use it," Via said. "Only if I have to use it."

He got into his car and drove away, leaving Bitberg in a cloud of dust.

Driving home in his Caddy, money in his pocket, Via should have been happy, but seeing Muchado had him thinking about the old days again. Jokers like Bitberg never would have dared to cheat him then. What was it Bitberg called him, "a two-bit hustler with no connections and no prospects"? It was just like his old man used to say: *There ain't no percentage in being a civilian.* His old man was always right.

CHAPTER 3

The murder rate in Chicago had recently dropped to six per day, so Tommy Getti's murder only made page five in the *Sun-Times*. His body was found on Lower Wacker Drive, face pulped beyond recognition, the kind of murder the Mob called "buckwheats."

Lucky for the cops, whoever did it left the deceased with his wallet and ID, Getti's name ringing a distant bell in the back of Via's mind. The police were scouring the neighborhood, the paper said, for witnesses and clues. Via knew there wouldn't be any. What the cops found, they were meant to find and it was all they were going to get.

He scooped up another forkful of scrambled eggs and reached for his coffee, but someone grabbed his arm. Looking up, he thought for a moment it would be easy. The guy was as skinny as a swizzle stick and Via figured he could break him with one punch, but before he could throw it, another guy built like a beetle gripped his other arm and helped haul him out of the booth.

"Outside," the round man grunted, and Via felt the skinny guy press something sharp against his kidney. They pushed Via out the back door of the deli and shoved him against a large green dumpster.

"Who the fuck are you, Laurel and Hardy?"

"See if this is funny," the round guy said.

He punched Via in the gut and Via's breakfast came up and

splattered on the skinny man's shoes.

"You're gonna pay for that," the guy swore.

"You got it?" the round man asked.

"Tell him I'll have it by end of week," Via coughed.

"Wrong answer." The guy yanked Via upright and took his .38 from his pocket. "Christ, it's a cop gun."

"You don't like it, give it back."

The skinny man brandished his knife. "Maybe I should cut him, Jolly."

"Maybe you should. That what you want, Ziggy to cut you?"

"Just tell Pig I'll have it."

"He don't like to be called that." The guy named Jolly hit him again and Via bent like a hairpin.

"You laughing yet?" Ziggy jeered. He pushed Via's chin up with his fist, a star-shaped ring pressing into the flesh like a cookie cutter.

"Fuck you," Via gasped and braced for another blow. But it didn't come. He felt the men loosen their grips and looked up to see the owner of the deli staring at them.

"The fuck you looking at?" Ziggy yelled at the guy.

Via yanked loose of Jolly and struck Ziggy in the face. Jolly lunged for him, but he took off running. He heard shouting behind, then footsteps coming fast. He ran north, gasping for air, into an area called Wrigleyville, which he figured he knew better than they did. He had lived there for a short time just after his divorce and he was piecing together a mental street map as he ran. But there were too many new buildings, too many missing landmarks, and as he rounded a corner into an alley he found himself at a dead end. He twisted back around but Jolly and Ziggy were already blocking the way.

He searched the ground and found a piece of discarded pipe, but before he could straighten up the men were on him. He wrestled free and struck Jolly on the arm, then felt a gun barrel pressed behind his right ear. He let go of the pipe.

"You okay, Jolly?" Ziggy asked, a trickle of blood running from his nose.

Jolly groaned, rubbing his wrist. "Sonofabitch. You're lucky The Pig wants his money or I'd kill you right here."

"Let's do him anyway," Ziggy said, wiping blood from his upper lip.

"Nah, I'm just gonna break his legs, so next time he don't run so good." Jolly bent over and picked up the pipe.

"All right, all right," Via grunted.

He reached into his pocket and Ziggy cocked the hammer on his gun.

"Take it easy," Via said, taking out a wad of bills and shoving them at Jolly. "About five hundred. I'll get the rest to him next week."

"Think this is American Express? The Pig don't operate on the installment plan."

"I should at least cut him, Jolly," Ziggy said.

"Maybe you should. Maybe you should."

Ziggy reached for his knife, but something caught Jolly's attention. He held up his hand as a car slid past the alley in slow motion. Then another one passed by.

"You won't be so lucky next time," the round man hissed.

A fist slammed into Via's face and something hard struck him across the shoulders and he fell to his knees.

By the time the limo snaked through the city's near South Side and stopped in front of Via's building, it already had the neighborhood's attention. As the driver got out, he had to push through a gang of homeboys gathered on the sidewalk.

"Hey, man, what you do, took da wrong exit ofta 'spressway?" one of the homeboys called out, and then the others started, too: "Yeah, man, guinea-town be westa here."

The driver cold-eyed them and patted the gun in his coat pocket.

"Hey, motherfucker, what's up wit dat? You got somethin' for us in there?"

The driver squared his shoulders and yanked the wrinkles out of his jacket and walked around to open the rear door.

"What dis, motherfucker, *Godfather IV*?" someone yelled.

Then Tina Brassi slid her long legs out of the back seat and stood there like a Chanel ad and they suddenly went quiet.

"Third floor," the driver said. "I better go up with you."

"I can take care of myself. You'd better watch the car."

The homeboys started in again: "Hey, baby, what you lookin' for I gots right here," but she brushed past them without so much as another glance.

The building was an old Italianate-style tenement, which a century earlier might have looked regal instead of rundown. Tina Brassi went into the vestibule, which was dim and narrow and smelled of sour wine. A bottle of Wild Irish Rose lay broken in a corner and an army of black ants was busy getting drunk on the residue. A battered brass frame was on one wall next to an old-style intercom that had a speaking tube, into which someone had stuffed a used condom. The frame held scraps of yellowing paper adhered haphazardly with bits of tape. She had to bend a bit in her three-inch heels to search through the occupants' names.

She found what she was looking for and started up the stairway, dark even at mid-morning, except for the light sneaking beneath the doors of the businesses behind them—bail bonds, legal aid, community outreach, and, finally, on the third floor, *Via Investigations*. She stood there for a moment trying not to inhale the peeling lead paint and bug spray, then gathered herself and went through the door like Martha Stewart.

Nicky Fratelli was in the center of the room at his small worn desk, talking on the phone. He glanced up, a quizzical look on his face, and indicated he would only be a moment.

"I'm here to see Frank Via," she said.

Nicky put his hand over the phone. "I'll be with you in a minute."

"I don't have a minute."

She appraised him with disdain, eyeing the zircon stud earring and braided leather bracelet, the rainbow tattoo on his upper arm. She surveyed the room and wished she were back in her Gold Coast condo. She drew a cigarette from a gold case in her purse and flicked open a gold lighter.

"Don't light that in here," Nicky said, pointing at the large No Smoking sign on the wall behind her.

She ignored him and lit up.

"I'll call you back," Nicky said into the phone and slammed it down. "I told you, there's no smoking in here."

"I'm not good at obeying rules and I'm not good at waiting, either." She aimed her cigarette at the door behind him. "That his office?"

Nicky pointed to a seedy-looking couch. "Wait over there."

"I don't think so," she said, marching past him.

"You can't go in there."

"Watch me."

"This is a place of business," Nicky yelled at her back, wondering where he had seen her before.

He came around his desk and waved the smoke around with a manila folder, sniffing the air. Cursing, he retrieved a can of air freshener from the desk drawer and began spraying the room as Via came through the door.

"What the hell is that?"

"Morning Mist. My God, what happened to you?"

"Pignotti's boys." Via slammed the door behind him. "For a lousy five grand."

38

"Didn't I warn you?"

"You wanted to be paid, didn't you?"

"Am I supposed to feel bad?"

"It might help."

"Let me see that," Nicky said, looking at Via's face. "Christ, it's shaped like a star. They hit you with a Mercedes?"

Via snatched the spray can from him and set it down hard on his desk. "There's a limo out front."

Nicky poked his thumb in the direction of Via's office.

"A client?"

"Whatever she is, she's trouble."

"More trouble than being broke?" Via stepped around him. "If two guys who look like Laurel and Hardy come through the door, shoot them."

"You need a bandage on that," Nicky called after him.

All Via could see of Tina Brassi were her legs, which he slowly ran his eyes over, and a smog of blue smoke rising from behind the newspaper she was reading.

"I don't know what you're here for, but whatever it is, you're going to smoke, go somewhere else." He went over to open the room's only window.

"Since when did you get so particular?" She lowered the paper. "I remember when you smoked a pack a day."

Something inside him tightened when he heard her voice.

"I used to do a lot of things I don't do anymore," he said, staring at her and trying not to look surprised.

He went behind his desk and slipped his jacket over the back of the chair and switched on a small rotating fan.

"I'm sorry to hear that," she said.

She wore a tailored navy suit with matching hose, chestnut hair cropped to the collar of her crisp white shirt, beneath which a large ruby swayed in her cleavage on a thick gold chain. A

39

matching jeweled bracelet winked from her cuff when she lifted the cigarette to her lips.

"What are you doing here?"

"That's all you can say after all these years?"

"I told you, put out the butt."

"So did your housemaid out there."

"His name's Nicky."

"From the old neighborhood?"

"Look, I'm trying to quit," he said, but didn't know why he felt the need to explain it.

She gave him a derisive smile and uncrossed her legs, then stood and walked slowly to the window. She drew a deep drag, letting the smoke play on her lips, and flipped the cigarette out into the air. Then she smiled again and blew a thick blue cloud back into the room.

"Same old Tina."

"Can't say the same for you, Frank. Used to be the other guy who went home bloody."

He had forgotten the cut and went over to a mirrored medicine cabinet above a small sink in the corner to examine the star-shaped gash below his left eye.

"You here to talk about old times?" he asked, taking a bandage from the cabinet and pressing it against his cheek.

"I need your help."

He stopped what he was doing and looked at her from the mirror. "Now, why would the wife of Tony Brassi need anyone's help?"

"*Ex*-wife. We're divorced."

"Yeah? Welcome to the club."

"My daughter is missing."

That turned him around. "What do you mean, *missing*?"

"She went to school yesterday and never came home. I don't know where she is."

"Back up a second. Your daughter, she'd be, what, in high school now?"

"She was doing her senior internship with Avery Stein."

"That old Jew still keeping Tony's books?"

"She got involved with this guy who worked there."

"Another high school kid?"

"Older."

He went behind his desk again and sat, not liking where this was going, old graves rolling over.

"I'm afraid she ran off with him."

"What makes you think so?"

"Because she would."

Tina Brassi's daughter—he could believe that. "So what am I supposed to do about it?"

"I want you to find her before she does something stupid."

"Maybe they're just shacked up somewhere."

"You don't know her. Seventeen going on thirty."

"Sounds like someone I used to know."

"Yeah, but she's smarter than I was."

"Why me? What about your ex, he can't find her? He's got more resources than I do."

Tina Brassi shook her head, ruby earrings clicking like dice. "I don't want him to."

Via put his palms out in front of him. "Wait a minute. You can stop right there."

"Tony never wanted her," Tina Brassi continued, "she was a package deal with me. He resented taking care of her and she knew it. They never liked each other. If I don't find her first, I might never get her back. She'll marry this guy just to spite him."

"You and Tony have a problem and you want me to get in the middle, is that it?"

"I'll pay whatever you want."

41

"Look, we haven't seen each other for a long time, so maybe you're mistaking me for someone stupid."

"I don't know who else to turn to."

"There are dozens of other private dicks in this city."

"You think they'd do it? Everyone's afraid of Tony."

"Yeah, me too."

"I'm asking for your help."

Now Via shook his head. "Forget it. I haven't been involved with Outfit business since I left. I'm not about to get involved now. You have the wrong guy."

"How much?"

"Forget it."

"Just tell me what you want."

"I want you to hire someone else. I have some competitors I don't like; I'll give you their names."

"Frank—"

He put his hands up again.

"Don't say it. Old time's sake doesn't enter into it. That was a long time ago. Everything's different now. I'm different."

CHAPTER 4

Via's ex-wife, the former Karen McCormick, still lived in the house he lost to her in the divorce. He had bought it just after Karen got pregnant with their daughter, Meggie, a large Tudor with tall narrow windows and prominent gables that looked to him then like something a proper citizen would live in. He liked the house and was sorry to give it up, but he knew Karen deserved it. He had been a lousy husband; she was right to get rid of him.

He had been a lousy father, too, and as he pulled up to his ex-wife's house he recognized in the driveway the black Lincoln Town Car driven by Harry Soltis, his daughter's soon-to-be new father.

Via and Soltis went back a bit, back to when Soltis was an ambitious young prosecutor in the State's Attorney's office hoping to make his mark busting up the Chicago Mob. Unfortunately for him, after Monkey Wrench the Outfit went underground, and when they did, the younger black and Hispanic gangs bubbled to the surface. Suddenly, what a bunch of white goombahs did to one another concerned the voters a lot less than the homeboys who were carjacking their wives and selling crack to their kids. Overnight, one black gangsta in the pen was worth two white gangsters in the bush.

So Soltis changed direction and went after the Latin Kings, Black Gangster Disciples, and Puerto Rican Stones and made a name for himself with a few high-profile convictions that landed him on the front pages where he felt he belonged. Now he was rumored to be a possible candidate for State's Attorney himself.

"Daddy! I'll be there in a minute!" his daughter called from the upstairs window as Via walked toward the front porch.

Behind her, he saw his ex-wife whisper something to her.

"You remembered the tickets, didn't you?" Meggie yelled. "Hey, what happened to your face?" She waved and disappeared.

His ex looked down on him, a familiar look of contempt on her face.

He went up the short stairs and stepped onto the porch. Harry Soltis opened the front door looking like Via remembered him: tall and thin, receding reddish hair, small wire-rimmed spectacles on a nose made for sticking up someone's ass.

"Frank Via," Soltis grumbled, like it was stuck in his throat. "She'll be down in a minute."

"Right, I heard."

Soltis pointed at the bandage below Via's eye. "Trouble on the job?"

"Dropped a dollar on the sidewalk. Had to fight off three lawyers to get it back."

"Still a joker."

"Mind if I come into my own house?"

"It's not exactly yours anymore."

"Lucky for you."

Soltis made a grand gesture and Via stepped past him and into the foyer, which had a scent that smelled foreign to him now. Meggie's dog, Mutt, came wagging at him and he squatted to pat its head, glad at least the dog had missed him.

"You think you could offer me a beer or something?" he asked Soltis, just to get rid of him.

"I probably could," Soltis managed to say. "Wait here." He walked into the kitchen, across the wood floor Via had laid himself, and opened the refrigerator as if he owned it.

Via went into the living room to look around and saw the same pea-green sofa Karen's mother gave them before she stopped visiting, the same sienna-striped wallpaper he had put up with his own hands, the mahogany mantelpiece he appropriated from a tavern owner who couldn't come up with the juice he owed. He ran his finger across the polished wood. No dust. Not like Karen. Soltis was evidently paying for maid service.

The photos on the mantel were still there, too—Karen and Meggie at Disney World, Meggie in front of the dugout at Wrigley Field, Meggie and Karen at Wisconsin Dells—except the shots of him were gone, replaced now by a smiling Harry Soltis, his arms around Karen and Meggie. As if he owned them.

He went over to sit on the green sofa, but it reminded him of Karen's mother, so he walked over to the picture window instead. The neighborhood hadn't changed much, honest, hard-working civilians who never had a clue. Christ, they thought he was respectable. A big shock when he ended up on the front pages. Of course, by then, it was no surprise to Karen.

"Frank?"

She still looked good, like the Phys Ed teacher she used to be, still firm and athletic, but with her hair short and blonde now and her nails a color he hadn't seen before. Still pretty and younger-looking than her thirty-six years. And still with that look in her eyes that the years living with him had put there. He saw her scrutinizing him, his worn sport coat and cheap jeans, his shirt with its frayed collar, comparing him to Soltis in his Hartmarx suits.

"Megan will be down in a minute," she said, as if his visit were scripted, everyone with the same line, keeping the dialogue in control, as if that courtesy was all he was going to get and everyone wanted to make certain he knew it.

"Yeah, I heard that."

"You look like hell."

"I heard that, too." He looked around the room. "House looks good, though."

"It isn't. The hot water heater needs replacing and the toilets all run. Washing machine sounds like beebees in a blender."

"Look, I know I owe you money."

"Megan's tuition is due at the end of the month."

He gestured at the mantel. "What happened to the pictures of me?"

"You hear what I said?"

"What about your boyfriend? He paying rent yet?"

"Don't go there."

"You think it's a good idea, him sleeping over with Meggie in the house?"

"She's been exposed to a lot worse, hasn't she?"

"You think this asshole will make you happy?"

"You're concerned about my happiness now?"

"I'm concerned about Meggie's."

"Too little and too late."

This was her normal tone with him, always there, hostility just below the surface. He couldn't blame her. It was his own fault. His father warned him not to marry her—Karen McCormick, a good Irish-Catholic girl from out of the neighborhood. She didn't know what she was getting into and that was his fault, too. But what was he supposed to tell her? That he was raised to be a crook? That being a mobster was all he knew?

Hell, his father brought him into it when he was just a kid. Just old enough to outrun the cops but still too young to be arrested when he couldn't, the old man used to joke.

At first, he just did errands for the wiseguys that hung around Club Domani, a storefront his father took from some poor schmuck who couldn't pay his weekly vig. He parked their cars, delivered their messages, got them sandwiches from Mr. Beef.

By the time he hit his teens, he had graduated to bagman,

running money all over town for the local *capos.* He never missed a dropoff or a pickup and never came up short. He never asked what he was carrying and never cared. His old man was proud of him; he was a chip off the old block, as he was expected to be. *You show respect, you get respect,* his old man told him. And he did. He also got good money and a good education. He was a big deal with the other kids in the neighborhood.

What was there not to like? He learned more at Club Domani about what really mattered than he did in school. Is that what he was supposed to explain to her?

"The opera starts at seven-thirty," she instructed. "There's a fifteen-minute intermission about eight forty-five and then it's over about ten. With the traffic, you should have her back here by ten-thirty, ten forty-five at the latest."

"I thought we'd get some coffee and pie afterward."

"She's fourteen, she doesn't drink coffee."

"So she'll have a Coke."

"It's a school night. If she could've gotten other tickets, I wouldn't even let her go."

"Look—" he started to say, but Harry Soltis returned with the beer.

"Had to go to the basement refrigerator."

Karen gave Soltis a withering look and he lowered the bottle to his side and stood there like a delivery boy waiting for a tip.

"Aren't you driving?" she snapped at Via.

"It's just a beer."

"It's just your daughter."

Thankfully, Meggie came flying down the stairs in a rush, kissed her mother good-bye, and pulled Via toward the door.

"Time to go," he said over his shoulder.

"Remember what I said," Karen called after him, but he slammed the door and left her standing there with Harry Soltis and his sheepish grin, glad to be saved from that look of scorn on his ex-wife's face.

"Your mother doesn't trust me," Via said to Meggie, walking with her to the car, knowing better than to try to wedge her into the breach between himself and her mother, but doing it anyway.

"She's just trying to impress Harry," his daughter said.

"Think so?"

"I think he's impressed with himself."

He wanted to hug her.

It was colder now and he buttoned the jacket of his only sport coat and looked over at her, wearing a dress barely covering her thighs.

"Does your mom let you dress like this?"

"Daaad!"

"I know, I know. It's just you're getting older—"

"And I should dress like Grandma?"

He counted a beat. "Which Grandma?"

She wrinkled her nose at him. "Daad."

As he drove, he looked at her from the corner of his eye, trying to think of something to say, then remembered he hadn't seen her since she started her new school. So he asked the only thing he could think to: "So, how's high school?"

"Okay."

"Just okay?"

"It's school."

"It's high school. You've been looking forward to this forever."

"Why are you so interested all of a sudden?"

"It's not all of a sudden."

"Seems like it."

He felt that. "Now you sound like your mother."

"Why is she so mad at you all the time?"

"It's complicated. She'll get over it eventually."

She looked away. "Wouldn't count on it."

"Don't worry, I don't," he said, more sharply than he intended.

She went quiet then while he tried to think of something else to talk about, wondering how much his daughter actually knew about what he had done for a living.

"What happened to your face?" she asked after a while.

"It's nothing, just a scratch. I walked into a door."

"It's a pretty big bandage."

"Nicky bought them. You know how he is."

"Yeah," she said, waving her hands, "always a flair for the dramatic."

Via laughed, surprised again at how quickly his daughter was growing up. He only saw her once a month, which was all Karen would allow, and he was always surprised by how much she changed—taller, hair always different, starting to wear makeup now. Mostly, though, it was the way she sounded, more adult, more . . . *sophisticated* was the word. Harry Soltis's influence no doubt. And now the opera.

"So, when did you get interested in opera?"

"Harry. He took us a couple times," she said, shrugging her shoulders.

"No kidding?"

"Mom likes it, too."

"Does she?"

Meggie began fussing in her purse.

"So, tell me again. How did Soltis and your Mom meet?"

She rolled her eyes at him. "You're not going to start again, are you?"

"What?"

"You've asked me that about a hundred times before."

"Yeah, but I can never seem to remember these things."

"Tell me about it. You sure you have the tickets?"

He gasped and frantically patted his pockets. "Oh, geez, the tickets." Then, when he thought he had her, he pulled the tickets from inside his jacket and waved them in the air. "Ta daa!"

"Very funny," she said, grinning.

"You know, I'm not as irresponsible as your mother makes me out to be."

"She doesn't make you out to be anything."

"What's that supposed to mean?"

She raised her eyebrows at him.

"Okay, okay. Just tell me one thing. How did she and Soltis meet?"

"Then can we talk about something else?"

"Anything you want. You can tell me about this opera."

"Republicans for Illinois."

"That's the name of this opera?"

"Daad!"

He was glad he could at least still make her giggle.

Rigoletto was weeping for his daughter and when Via glanced over, Meggie was, too. As far as he could make out, this guy Rigoletto insulted some bigwigs and the bigwigs got even by tricking him into kidnapping his own daughter. Then one of the bigwigs seduced the daughter, killed some guy, and generally dishonored the Rigoletto family name. Not exactly a children's matinee. He whispered into Meggie's ear: "Does your mother let you watch this kind of stuff?" She elbowed him in the side.

When the curtain was finally lowered for intermission he was ready for a drink, but by the time they worked their way to the lobby there was already a crowd at the bar.

"I'll stand in line," he said, "you go ahead," and Meggie went off to the restroom while he stood there sandwiched between two overweight women yapping at their cell phones like Chihuahuas.

He was wondering if he could shoot four fingers of Jack before his daughter got back when he spied two men wearing shiny suits walking toward her. As they got close, one of them dropped something and squatted in front of her to pick it up. The other man said something, while the guy squatting gave her legs a good look over and then showed Via an evil grin. Via started toward them, but the guy stood up and the two men headed his way.

He knew the older of the two, Bobby Albanese, from the old days, before he was sent to become a shyster, back when they were both part of Tony Brassi's street crew. Albanese was not the kind of guy to be interested in opera.

Brassi had sent them together one night to throw some fear into the leader of a street gang called Ebony Nation. The guy had neglected to pay the street tax he owed in return for the privilege of running a small drug operation through the housing projects on the city's West Side. Brassi wanted his money.

From the start, Via knew Albanese, who was called Bobby Bat, was the wrong man for the job. Sure enough, Albanese let his prejudices get the best of him and put a bullet in the guy's brain before they could beat the five grand out of him first. They had to make up some bullshit story about the guy coming at Albanese with a knife, which Via knew Tony Brassi hadn't really bought.

"Hey, Frank Via, long time no see," Albanese said, waddling up.

"Not long enough."

The other man, a younger guy Via didn't recognize, was looking back in Meggie's direction.

"You see that? Madonn'."

Via stepped toward him but Albanese put a hand on his arm. "Don't mind Vito here, Frank, he ain't got no kids." Via brushed his hand away.

51

"She was your daughter?" the guy Vito said, lips thin and feline. "Geez, I didn't know."

"What do you want, Bobby?"

"Hey, we just come to the opera and run into an old friend," Albanese said, standing there like a mook, white dago-T showing through his black polyester shirt, belly melting over his belt like frosting off a cupcake.

"You don't look like opera fans. And we aren't friends."

"No, we ain't," the guy Vito said, smiling with a mouthful of gold teeth. He sniffed loudly and wiped his nose with the back of his hand. His nails were bitten short, except for one pinky finger like a scoop. There was a smell about him, some drugstore aftershave Via remembered from high school, Paco Rabanne maybe. He knew the type: homemade tattoos, Elvis hairdo, the kind of guy who flipped the collar up on his pajamas.

"Tony wants to see you," Albanese said.

"Still pushing numbers to little old ladies, Bobby?"

"Hear what I said?"

"Tell him I don't want to see him."

"You think it matters?" Vito said.

Via's lip curled. "You know, I see guys like you around, but they usually aren't walking upright."

"Tomorrow night, downtown," Albanese said.

"I have no reason to see Tony Brassi."

"I just gave you reason."

"I don't work for him anymore."

"You ain't that stupid, are you, Frank?"

"He looks *real* stupid to me," Vito said.

"Tony's got a job for you." Albanese looked Via up and down. "Maybe you could buy some better clothes."

"Like Vito's here?"

"You just be there," Vito told him. "Tomorrow night."

Via watched them walk away, a feeling in his stomach like a

spring winding. Meggie was heading back and the guy named Vito brushed against her arm as they passed and swiveled around to give her a look. He said something to Albanese and the two men laughed loud enough for Via to hear. The spring wound tighter.

"What did he say to you?" Via asked as his daughter walked up.

"Who?"

"How many guys talked to you on your way to the john? The greaseball in the blue jacket. Before, when he squatted in front of you."

Meggie frowned. *"Greaseball?"*

"What did he say?"

"Nothing. Just said he liked my dress."

"How did he say it?"

"Daad!"

"What did he say, Meggie?"

The house lights signaled the end of intermission.

"Come on, we'll miss it."

"Megan?"

"We're going to miss the curtain." She pulled his arm. "Let's go."

The goddamn opera again. "We'll talk about this after," he said.

But they didn't. He was more concerned about why Brassi's men had followed him there. He thought about that all the way back to drop off Meggie and was still thinking about it when he finally got home and went into his small kitchen and pulled a bottle of Jack Daniels from the cabinet above the refrigerator.

Reaching up, he could feel his spine twisted like a train wreck. Pignotti's goons. He carried the drink into the bathroom and took some Percodans to kill the pain and cursed himself for getting waylaid like some amateur. Tina Brassi was right, it used to be the other guys who went home bloody. Good thing his old man couldn't see him now.

He looked at the star-shaped cut in the mirror, moving his head from side to side, which made his back ache again. He stripped off his clothes, pulling his shirt gingerly over his head, and stepped into the shower. He let the hot water beat on him for a while but it didn't seem to help any.

After he dried off, he wrapped a towel around himself and refilled his drink. He took it back into the bedroom and sat on the edge of the bed. He sat there thinking about Tina Brassi and Tony Brassi, Bobby Albanese and fat Charlie Pignotti, thinking about his father and how much and how little things had changed, thinking while he finished the Jack, thinking until the booze and the Percodans finally kicked in.

Anthony Brazzini, a.k.a. Tony Brassi, parked his Escalade in the underground garage and took the elevator up to the Sears Tower lobby, which was bustling with people. The building was a small city. Some twelve thousand people worked there, presumably for the kind of legitimate companies Como International pretended to be. Good little worker bees, with their foam coffee cups and faux leather briefcases, swarming around making honey for the hive. Brassi looked around contemptuously and swaggered across the lobby toward the newspaper stand, a look of self-satisfied disdain on his Roman face.

Brassi had never had a real job in his life. Like Via, he had been a mobster since he was a kid, even quit high school when he was old enough to become a runner for Louis Calabria, the *capodecina* who ran his neighborhood. His parents didn't complain. Hell, he was earning as much as his father did loading fish onto trucks on Fulton Street. He could still smell the salmon and sweat on the old man.

Most of the guys he grew up with joined the Outfit. It was

what passed for upward mobility in the neighborhood and Brassi moved up fast. He had to do a little killing, of course, but that was the price of success. You were either a made man or a dead one—literally or figuratively. He was made by the time he turned nineteen.

By the time he turned twenty-five, he was ready for greater advancement. The victim was a guy named Jerry Rosetti, who ran one of the largest horse-racing wires in Illinois, which Calabria wanted a piece of, and which Rosetti refused to give up. Brassi volunteered to help influence negotiations in his boss's favor.

But it wasn't just Rosetti's murder that established Brassi's reputation (anyone could shoot a guy), it was the way he disposed of the body, grinding it up in a mix of molasses, oats, and hay, which he then took out to a local racetrack and fed to the thoroughbreds. It was said afterward that those horses went hungry for two full days before they would return to their regular feed.

Brassi had a definite flair for the dramatic, which Calabria mistook for initiative but discovered too late was just insatiable ambition. He gave Brassi his own street crew and, unwittingly, enough backing to amass more power.

It didn't take Brassi long to move on Calabria. To do it, he had to first pre-hit Calabria's underboss, Joey "Fly Boy" Prio, which he also did in dramatic style.

Prio owned a private plane that he kept at Meigs Field and used to make money runs around the Great Lakes for Calabria. Prio thought he was hot shit. He wore a leather flight jacket and white silk scarf around the neighborhood like some World War I air ace. Brassi was more than happy to clip his wings. One night, he paid an airport mechanic to secret a small briefcase beneath the Cessna Skyhawk's pilot seat, claiming Prio was expecting the cargo.

The bomb went off somewhere out over Lake Michigan during Prio's nighttime run. The top half of his body was found a few miles south of Grand Haven, Michigan, by a Canadian fish tug on its way back home. The rest of him and his plane were never seen again.

As Brassi expected, Calabria was too smug to attribute his underboss's death to anything other than an accident. Two months later, Calabria had an accident of his own when he fell on his own knife some fifteen times while being robbed by a "mugger" on the way to his car.

Brassi threw his dead boss one of the largest Outfit funerals Chicago had ever seen.

Harry Soltis watched George Purwell shovel prime rib into his beefy mouth. Christ, the man could eat. At least it gave his mouth something to do besides lecture him on the pitfalls of political ambition.

Purwell had become State's Attorney the hard way. First as a public defender, then as a prosecutor, then decades in the trenches of Chicago politics, nearly thirty years kissing the Mayor's hand until the Mayor finally opened the doors for him to state office.

Now he was ready to retire with the thanks of a grateful citizenry and a lifetime pension that would allow him to keep in trust for his grandchildren the real money he had accumulated over his career from bribes and payoffs. This was the kind of success, he was saying, Soltis could look forward to if he just played his cards right.

"Then you'll back me?"

"Now, Harry, I didn't say that. You know how these things work. I have a reputation to protect. I have to be careful who I put my name behind."

"You don't think I can win?"

"Well, to be honest . . . and you know me, Harry, honest to a fault . . . what's caused me most of the trouble in my life . . . I don't think you can."

Soltis gulped his vodka martini.

"Don't get me wrong, Harry. You're a good prosecutor. Got a few medals on your chest. Lost a few, too, but let's not get into that. And, God knows, I appreciate your loyalty. Hell, that time you took the heat for that, uh, *misunderstanding* about my daughter's pay for running my last campaign. Well, that was real loyalty, Harry, it really was. But you know, my friend, it also got you some bad press—those bloodsuckers—and the voters have long memories, Harry, as you know. It's an obstacle, I'm afraid."

"You know I need your help."

Purwell sighed and speared another piece of meat. "Politics, Harry. It's the art of the practical." He smiled his best campaign smile. Soltis wanted to reach over and stick a fork in his eye.

"So, how do I overcome this *obstacle*?"

"I wish I could tell you, Harry. In the old days there were ways, you know, to arrange things. Something to catch the voter's eye. But nowadays, forget it, too much scrutiny. God-damn media has ruined politics."

"So I need to raise my profile. No problem. I have the right people on board. You know Mickey Finley. He's one of the best in the business."

"Yeah, he's good. Did a great job back then helping Adlai Three look marketable. Little stiff couldn't back it up, though. Still came off like a know-it-all. Reminded voters of their old high school principal."

Soltis studied the olive in his glass.

"No, Harry, image alone won't do it. You need something with meat on it. Something high profile enough to get attention, but juicy enough to mean something to the average voter. Sizzle and steak, like they say, Harry."

"This is your help, George, a cliché?"

"You know how things work. Sizzle and steak, one hand washes the other, you scratch my back and I'll scratch yours." Purwell held up another chunk of beef. "Get yourself some steak, Harry, and maybe I'll help you with some sizzle."

A phone was ringing somewhere and Via tried to get away from it, but the harder he tried, the louder it seemed to ring. He finally gave up and rolled over to answer it.

"Where are you?"

He recognized Nicky's voice. "What time is it?"

"Karen's here with Meggie."

"What? What time is it?"

"You awake?"

Via tried to clear his head. He couldn't read the clock radio. "I took some painkillers."

"You have to come down here."

"What's going on?"

"Meggie had some trouble on the way to school this morning."

He was sitting on the side of the bed now. "What trouble? What happened?"

"She's okay. Some guy. He scared her, that's all."

"Ten minutes."

He slammed the phone down and stood up, the pain in his back nearly forcing him down again. He limped into the bathroom and swallowed a handful of aspirin. He threw cold water in his face, dressed quickly, and drove to the office, cursing himself.

When he pushed through the door, he found Karen and Meggie sitting on the small sofa just inside. Karen jumped up and slapped him. It surprised him and straightened his spine. She always could hit.

"You sonofabitch! This is your fault, isn't it?"

Via looked over at Meggie, who was staring at her knees, and went over and sat next to her.

"You okay? What happened?"

"No, she is not okay!" Karen snapped.

"Mom, you opened his cut." Meggie took a tissue from her backpack and wiped a trickle of blood from his cheek. She was still in her school uniform and looked like a child to him now.

"Some guy stopped her on the way to school and told her to go back home," Karen said, accusation dripping like acid from her lips.

"He said you would understand," Meggie said to Via.

"What did he look like?"

"It was the man from the opera. The one with the gold teeth."

"What man?" Karen asked.

"Did he touch you?"

"No. He just told me to tell you that school's out."

"He didn't touch you?"

"Just told me to tell you that."

Karen interrupted again. "What do you mean, gold teeth?"

"What else?" Via asked his daughter.

"Nothing else. He told me to go home, said he can teach me more than school can."

Karen's ears went up. "He said that! You bastard, Frank! What have you gotten her into?"

Nicky was leaning against his desk. Via motioned to him and he came over and grasped Meggie's hand and led her to Via's office.

Karen watched her go, then spun back and demanded: "What the hell's going on?"

He stood to face her, not wanting her looming over him. "Listen, it's me they want, not her."

"Who? What are you talking about?"

"I'll handle it. She'll be safe."

"You sonofabitch! This is about the Mob again, isn't it?"

She swung at him again but he grabbed her wrist. "I said I'll handle it. You have to trust me. I'll take care of it."

"Trust you? I've already called Harry."

He let her go. "Your boyfriend? Christ, what do you think he can do?"

"Protect her. She's been assaulted, for Christ's sake."

"She hasn't been touched. Even if he could find the guy, what's he going to do, arrest him for talking to her?"

"You don't care about anyone but yourself, do you?"

"Look, you get Soltis involved it just gets worse. You don't know what's happening."

"I know someone's threatening my daughter!"

"They're threatening *me*. They want me to do a job for them and they're using her to pressure me," Via said, trying to make it sound reasonable. "And she's *my* daughter, too. Remember?"

"I remember everything," Karen snapped. Then she slumped on the sofa, her face in her hands.

"I told you, I'll straighten it out."

"Why should I believe you?"

"Because I would never let anything happen to Meggie."

He waited for her to give him that at least, but she only sobbed, a sound that was long familiar to him.

Nicky came back. "Meggie's okay. Just worried about missing school." He put his arm around Karen. "Frank knows what he's doing."

"What he's doing is ruining our lives."

Nicky patted Karen's shoulder. "I know, I know," he said, and that was enough. Via gripped him by the arm and pulled him aside.

"Knock off this sisterhood shit. When Soltis gets here, tell him to go back into his cave."

"Where are you going?"

"To see Tony Brassi."

"Brassi? You sure you know what you're doing?"

"I know what he's doing," Via said, halfway out the door, "that's what's important."

CHAPTER 5

The offices of Como International were on the fortieth floor of the Sears Tower and as Via rode up in the elevator he couldn't help but be impressed by Tony Brassi's success.

C.I., as Brassi's corporation was called, was the legitimate front for all of the Brassi Family's illegal operations. The cash from gambling, loan sharking, prostitution, and drugs was all laundered through the company, which also acted as the laundromat for the other two Outfit gangs, the Salernos and the Delacantes. In return, C.I. extracted a processing fee, which amounted to hundreds of thousands of dollars a year.

"May I help you?" the receptionist asked, not sounding like one of the typical bimbos who hung around Mob joints.

She didn't look like one either, all high breasts, high hips, and high maintenance. She beamed from behind a large cherry desk, *circa* France 1889, so a small sign on the desktop read.

"Frank Via. I'm here to see Tony . . . Mr. Brassi."

"Oh, yes, Mr. Via. Mr. Brassi is expecting you. He's on the telephone. I'm sure he'll only be a minute."

"You always work so late?"

"We just received a large shipment that's a week overdue and has to be catalogued. I'm afraid Milan isn't always as punctual as we might like them to be."

He grinned like a cat. "You know why Italians are always late?"

"No, I don't."

"They like to wait until the shooting's over."

"I'm not sure I get it." She was made of wax.

"Right, me neither." He gestured around the lobby. "All these imported?"

"Indeed. Are you in the business, Mr. Via?"

"Sort of," he said, not sure which business she was referring to. "I used to be a . . . collector."

"Well, maybe you'll see something you like."

He gave her the grin again. "I already have."

She stopped smiling and went abruptly back to her computer. Definitely not one of your typical bimbos.

He strolled around the lobby, which had the look of the legitimate business it was supposed to be, forested with small white columns displaying examples of C.I.'s many imports—an Italian vase, a Persian rug, an English teapot—which he pretended to be interested in.

"You know, I have a daughter in high school who loves this kind of stuff."

The receptionist peered skeptically over her Anne Klein glasses. "Oh, really."

"Yeah, sure. She studies world culture in school. Finds this sort of thing interesting. Hey, doesn't Brass . . . Mr. Brassi have a daughter about that age? She ever come around to check this stuff out?"

"I don't think so."

"You sure? Haven't seen her around lately?"

"I think I would have noticed." Her phone buzzed and she picked it up. "Mr. Brassi will see you now."

Via steeled himself. He wanted to kill Brassi for threatening Meggie. But he had to think of her first. He was in no position to protect her from the likes of Tony Brassi. He took a deep breath before he went through the door.

Like the outer lobby, Brassi's office projected as much

legitimacy as money could buy, all dark oak and leather, with walls the color of old gold and a burgundy carpet that made Via wish he owned better shoes. Against the walls, tall wooden file cabinets stood like sentinels and above them vividly painted Italian noblemen, popes, and kings peered into the room like confidants. In one corner was a tall bookcase stocked with leatherbound books that looked like they had never been opened. Next to it stood a stone statue of Caesar Augustus, decree in one hand, scepter in the other, to whom Tony Brassi felt he had a certain resemblance.

At the rear of the room, the would-be Emperor sat behind a huge wooden desk. In front of him were two large burgundy leather chairs. Bobby Albanese was sitting in one of them and Brassi was going over a list of inventory with him, a pair of peepers perched like a butterfly on his nose. Some guy who must have bought his suits at Big 'N Tall was sitting across the room on a black aniline sofa, pretending to be interested.

"What's going on with the strip clubs?" Brassi asked Albanese. "Revenues are down almost ten percent."

"It's these fuckin' computers. It's all wired-in now. You remember back in the Eighties there was this strip club in New York called Pink's run by Big Charlie Andruzzi?"

"He that guy got whacked by Gotti?"

"Never proven. Anyway, Andruzzi used this club as a training facility for young turks. Back then, the New York Mob used to do all their business from there. Ran it like a goddamn classroom for crime."

"This goin' somewhere?"

"I'm tryin' to explain. See, Andruzzi used the strippers to attract the neighborhood kids to come in to learn the business. See what I mean? Nowadays, they got every kinda pornography on the Internet. So no one needs to see strippers no more."

Brassi shook his head. "Fuckin' kids."

"That's what I'm sayin'."

Brassi ran his eyes over his ledger again. "What about this? Twenty cases from Haifa. Who the fuck ordered twenty cases?"

Albanese leaned over and stared at the page.

"It was a typo. Supposed to be two."

"Two cases? What're we supposed to do with two cases?"

"How many's two cases?"

"What the fuck's it matter? Think you could move one case of menorahs?"

"What's a menorah?" the Big 'N Tall guy asked.

"Like Christmas lights for Jews," Albanese said over his shoulder.

"It ain't even close to Christmas."

"Ah, the Jews always got some holiday comin' up. Always celebratin' the same thing. *They ain't killed us yet. Let's eat.*"

The big man didn't seem to get it.

"Skip the jokes," Brassi snapped. "Contact our guy in Skokie, see if he can lay them off."

"Fuckin' Yids," Albanese complained. "Know how to fix this country? Give every coon a thousand bucks to go back to Africa and the Jews will follow them to get it." He snapped his fingers. "Two birds with one stone."

Brassi picked up a silver pen and threw it at Albanese, hitting him in the chest. "Hey, you hear what I said?"

Albanese lost his smile. "Sure, Boss. I'll take care of it, I'll take care of it." He picked up the pen and set it carefully back on Brassi's desk.

"See what I gotta deal with here?" Brassi said, finally looking up at Via. "Can't make any money in this business."

"Good thing crime pays."

Brassi hadn't changed. Still thick and short, with the personality of someone who spent his life feeling looked down upon. His hair was slicked back and curled over the starched shirt collar at the back of his neck. He wore a gold chain-link bracelet and a diamond pinky ring that matched a multi-carat stud plugged into his earlobe. When he smiled, perfectly capped teeth gleamed from his unseasonably tan face. He reminded Via of the Roman gigolos he'd once seen in Italy who loitered around the Trevi fountain smiling at old ladies carrying guidebooks and lots of lire.

Brassi gestured to Albanese. "You know Bobby Bat."

"The opera fan."

"That right, Bobby," Brassi said with a cold grin, "you a big opera fan?"

"Big."

"I don't think you met Bronco Lucci," Brassi said, pointing toward the sofa. "Bronco, say hello to Frank Via. Used to be pretty good muscle before he became a shyster. Now he's a private dick. One slow slide downhill."

The big man looked like he could give a shit.

"Sit," Brassi said, motioning Via to a chair next to Albanese. He offered a humidor from the desktop but Via shook his head.

Brassi extracted a Cohiba for himself and lit up, polished fingernails glistening in the match light. "You don't mind?" It wasn't really a question. "So, you know why I invited you here?"

"I wasn't exactly invited."

"Hey, there are other ways," Albanese said.

Brassi shot him a look and he eased back.

"You know my stepdaughter, Annette, is missing."

"Do I?"

"Don't play games with me. I know Tina came to see you and I know she asked you to find her."

"You know so much, you know I refused her."

"Yeah, well, she ain't as charming as she used to be. Is she, Frank?"

"You want to talk about old times, too?"

"I want you to find my stepdaughter!"

Brassi's outburst made Albanese flinch. Via gave Albanese a smirk to let him know he noticed.

Brassi sucked on his cigar and blew the smoke in the direction of Caesar Augustus. "Now, let's be smart here. We both know you ain't doin' so good. What's your price?"

"Your wife already tried that."

"Ex-wife," Brassi sneered. "You're on juice with The Pig, you must be pretty desperate."

"This isn't about money."

"That what you told The Pig?"

The guy named Bronco sniggered.

"I can handle Pignotti," Via said.

Brassi pointed at Via's face. "Don't look like it."

"No, it don't," Bobby Bat said.

"You know, I can make your troubles go away," Brassi said. "Just tell me what you want."

"I want you to leave my daughter alone."

Brassi looked over at Albanese, who lifted his chin at Via and smirked back at him.

"Relax," Brassi said to Via. "That was just to get you here. You ain't so stubborn, everything is easier."

"Hey, Via," Albanese said. "Remember that chink over on Wabash wouldn't pay his juice? Now that was one stubborn gook. Hard-headed sonofabitch dented my Louisville Slugger." His eyes narrowed. "I got a new one now."

"Everyone wants to talk about old times."

"You'd be smart to think about them," Brassi said.

"What do you want from me?"

"I told you. Find my stepkid."

"Why don't you have Bobby and Sasquatch here do it?"

Bronco Lucci jerked alert and got to his feet and lumbered over. "That some kinda insult?"

Looking up, Via got a good look at him now, a big boxy face with a flat nose and a prominent brow above eyes the color of slate. His hair was gray, too, cut in a flattop that emphasized his large square head, which sat on massive shoulders like a cinder block. In his gray suit, he looked like a huge cube of concrete.

"See what I'm talkin' about here?" Brassi said. He pinched the bridge of his nose. "Bobby, you and Bronco leave us alone."

"We can find her, Boss," Albanese said. "We don't need this *stonato*."

"I'll decide what we need!"

"Sure, Boss. Sure."

Albanese got up and tapped Lucci on the arm and the two men filed past Via toward the door. They looked like the Green Giant and Sprout. Brassi watched them with a sullen look on his face and waited until they left before he spoke.

"I need someone with brains on this," he said to Via. "This kinda thing can get out of hand. Besides, you've been away long enough to be a civilian now, but not so long you don't still know your way around."

"What's that got to do with it?"

Brassi blew more smoke into the room. "What else did Tina say? She tell you about the boyfriend?"

"The one she thinks your kid ran off with?" Via tried to sound cool, but he knew how this was going to end.

"Fuckin' Casanova. Worked for Avery. Annette thought he was Frank Sinatra, or whoever the fuck makes girls wet these days. I told Tina not to send her to an all-girls school. Avery caught them in the copy room. I should've castrated the little fuck right then, but no, I'm tryin' to be understanding. I sent Bobby to tell him to stay away from her. Of course, she throws a fit. Says she's old enough to make her own decisions. So what's she decide? To steal my books. What I get for being a concerned father."

Via lost his cool facade and straightened in his chair.

"Oh, Tina didn't tell you that, huh? Copied them all on this . . . computer disk. Two days ago. And now she's disappeared."

"You're sure of this?"

"Avery's sure. Said he could tell the files were copied onto her computer. Names, dates, numbers. The works. Little bitch, just like her mother."

"Why would she take your books?"

"Like I said, she's a bitch. We never got along. I don't like her, she don't like me. Thinks I'm a crook."

"Imagine that."

"Let me tell you somethin', that kid's been trouble from the day I took her under my roof. She ain't my flesh and blood, but I been good to her anyways. Bought her anything she wanted, sent her to Europe, to the best schools, got her a summer job with Avery Stein. This is how she repays me."

"But what's she want with your books? She's a high school kid."

"You don't know her."

"Maybe this boyfriend put her up to it."

"See, that's what I need," Brassi said. "I figured that, too. Kid wasn't exactly a Boy Scout. Got caught runnin' a sports line out his college dorm room. Had a pretty good point-shavin' scheme goin' at some of the local schools. You remember Vincent Getti? His grandfather. Had to practically build a new wing just to get the kid graduated."

"I thought that sounded familiar. It's the name of the guy was found on Lower Wacker the other night."

Brassi pushed out his lower lip and shrugged. "Gambling's dangerous business."

"Yeah, newspaper said his face was hamburger."

"Ambitious little prick had big ideas. Planned to sell my books to the highest bidder, take the money and run off with

Annette. Happy ever after."

"He told you this?"

Brassi shook his head. "I never saw the guy." He twirled the cigar in the air. "I heard he was talkin' them around. Fuckin' kid. Didn't know who he was dealin' with. Dumb fuck thought someone was actually gonna pay him for them."

"And you and your ex think she's run off on her own now?"

"Tina and me don't agree on nothin'. Annette might've been planning it, but not no more." Brassi opened a desk drawer, brought out a page of white paper, and unfolded it. *"Don't get nervous. We'll be in touch,"* he read aloud.

"What's this?"

"What the fuck you think it is?"

"You telling me someone nabbed your kid?"

"No, they nabbed this disk. She just happened to have it. But they had to take her, too, didn't they?" Brassi waved the paper at Via. "I would've done the same. What the fuck, she's insurance in case I want to kill 'em before they have the chance to use it. Know what someone could do with that information? They want me gone, they just give it over to the Feds."

"So someone got smart."

"Smarts got nothin' to do with it," Brassi snapped. "The world don't turn on smarts. It turns on leverage. And this disk is a lever. You remember that Greek guy once said, 'Give me a lever, I will move the world?' Well, someone's gonna try to use this disk to move *my* world."

He leaned forward.

"See, there's this thing comin' up. A sitdown, a kind of . . . summit meeting, you might call it. All three families. What it's about you don't need to know. Let's just say there's deals to be worked and whoever has this disk works those deals. That's why you're gonna find it, and my kid, and bring them back to me before this meet."

Via started to speak but Brassi stopped him.

"This ain't no favor I'm askin'. You don't want *your* kid to go missin', you better use that brain of yours.

"This how it is now?" Via said. "You're threatening my daughter? All these years, and you're threatening my kid now?"

Brassi leaned back again and folded his arms across his chest. "Now you see how important this is to me. And maybe now you see how important it is to you, too."

Via could hear his ex-wife's voice in his head: *What have you gotten her into?*

"I do this, you leave my daughter alone."

"You find my kid, you don't have to worry about yours no more."

"This guy Vito goes near her again, I'll kill him."

"I told you don't worry."

Via sat forward, elbows on his knees. There was nothing else he could do and he knew it. He rubbed his eyes with the heels of his hands.

"This note. What about this hostage note?"

Brassi grinned like a skeleton. "Now you're thinkin'. Good to see you still got your priorities straight."

"What's your guess who sent it?"

"Don't have to guess. Only two people got the balls. Al Salerno and Carmine Delacante."

The spring in Via's stomach tightened again.

"Start with Salerno. His take's been slippin' for months. Too much competition on the South Side from the Africans. He's been pushing for a bigger piece of the pie. Besides, your pal Delacante's, what, in his eighties? What's he need it for?"

"Maybe he just doesn't like you."

"Look, you find out. Whoever it is, you tell him I want to deal now, before the meet. I want this resolved. You tell him if anyone suspects I'm being pressured at this meeting, any negotiations will fall apart. He'll understand."

"What if he doesn't?"

"Then you set his head straight. Do whatever it takes to bring my books and my kid back here before this meet."

"Things could get messy."

"You just find her," Brassi snapped.

Via ran a hand across his stubble. "Your kid, what's she look like?"

Brassi opened a desk drawer—"Can't stand to look at it no more"—and withdrew a brass-framed photograph and handed it to Via. Brassi and his stepdaughter. She had long black hair and dark eyes, an Italian princess. He was smiling, his arm around her; she looked solemn and unhappy.

"Taken last year. Parents' Day. Know what that place costs? Should've sent her to a public school. Maybe she wouldn't be so smart."

Via opened the frame and removed the photo and ripped it in half, throwing the half with Brassi's image on the desk. "If she's smart enough to take your books, she's smart enough to know the consequences. Her boyfriend's murder didn't make this any easier, you know. What if she can't be found?"

Brassi stubbed his cigar into an ashtray that looked like something from the Ming Dynasty.

"Then we're both in big trouble," he said.

When Via came out of Brassi's office, the receptionist was gone and Albanese and Vito Tessa were talking to the guy named Bronco Lucci, whose back was to him. Tessa stretched his neck around the big man, grinning and wagging his tongue between his feline lips.

Via made a beeline, shoving past Lucci and knocking Tessa to the floor. He lifted his leg to kick out some of those gold caps, but Lucci stepped in front and seized him by his jacket and tossed him over the reception desk. Via scrambled to his feet and caught Lucci with a foot to the groin as he was coming over, but it didn't seem to slow him any. The big man shoved him against one of the white display columns, knocking a crystal bowl to the floor. Then he grasped him by the throat and drove him hard against the wall and lifted him off the floor.

"I'm gonna kill you!"

Via's face was blue when he heard Brassi's voice.

"What's goin' on?"

"He kicked me in the stones!" Lucci bellowed, hot spittle spattering Via's face.

"You must have big ones, Via," Brassi said. "Don't kill him yet, Bronco. He needs to do a job for me."

Lucci tightened his grip. "How 'bout I mess him up?"

"After. Let him go."

"You sure?"

"I said after."

Lucci released him and Via dropped three inches to the floor.

"I owe you," Lucci growled.

Via staggered to the desk to steady himself, sucking air.

"Maybe you ain't so smart after all, Via," Brassi said.

Via winced at the sight of the cars in front of his ex-wife's house, two blue-and-whites and Harry Soltis's black Town Car, which he parked behind. Before he was halfway up the walk, Soltis came down the front steps to meet him.

"What the hell's going on? What happened to Megan? Karen says it was Tony Brassi."

Via stared at the hand on his arm and Soltis pulled it away.

"What the hell's the Mob want with your daughter?"

"That's right! *My* daughter."

Karen came out on the porch. There were deep, dark circles under her eyes, which were locked on Via. "I don't know what you're involved in, but it's over. You hear me? It's over. I don't want you around here anymore."

"I came here to let you know she won't be bothered again," Via said.

"What, until you screw things up again?"

"I had nothing to do with this."

"Never take responsibility for anything, do you, Frank? You had nothing to do with this? There's a goddamn handprint on your neck."

"What do you want from me?"

"I want you out of our lives!"

"I told you, it's all right now."

The door opened behind Karen and Meggie came out onto the porch, red-eyed and pale.

"You think that's it? You think everything's okay now?" Karen snapped.

Her voice screaked from her throat in a tight, shrill wave that sharpened to a point. Via wanted to reach out and put his hand over her mouth.

"Listen—" he started.

"You're not helping yourself," Soltis told him.

"You mean I'm not helping you."

"Just leave us alone, Frank. Just leave us alone," Karen said.

Soltis touched her shoulder and motioned toward Meggie, who was crying. Karen gave Via a final hateful scowl and escorted her daughter back into the house. The door slammed like a gunshot.

"I'll ask you again," Soltis said.

"Ask all you want."

"Now look, I cut you slack because of Megan."

"I don't have time for this."

"Fuck you don't have time. This is Tony Brassi we're talking about here."

"I told you, she's safe now."

Soltis thrust out his chest. "Listen, Via, you're going to be at my office tomorrow morning to tell me everything you know."

"You don't know what you're dealing with here."

"Don't tell me my business."

"You want to protect Meggie, you'll leave this alone."

"I can take care of Karen and Megan." Soltis tilted his head toward the two cops lounging against their cruisers at the curb.

"You'd better be ready to move them into the spare bedroom," Via said.

"Listen, dickwad, you be at my office tomorrow morning, or I'll send someone to get you. You're lucky I don't take you in right now. If Megan wasn't so upset—"

"Bullshit. This isn't about Meggie, it's about your career."

Soltis got in his face. "Fuck you, Via. Fuck you and all the guinea wops you hang out with. My office. Tomorrow morning."

"Better not let the voters hear you talk like that."

"Don't push your luck with me."

"Why don't you go to bed, Soltis? And try not to do it here."

Walking back to his car, Via stopped to look up at Meggie's bedroom and saw Karen glaring back, hate pouring down on him like boiling oil.

CHAPTER 6

Harry Soltis's office was downtown in the State of Illinois Center, a seventeen-story blue and orange monstrosity shaped like a UFO. It was called the James R. Thompson Center after Big Jim Thompson, who commissioned its construction and was one of the few recent Illinois governors who hadn't been sent to prison. Lucky for him, bad taste wasn't a crime.

Inside, the building was as uninviting as the outside, cold and cavernous and full of people who looked like they would rather be someplace else. Via was one of them. He rode an elevator to the seventh floor and found Soltis's office, where a gray-haired woman guarded the waiting room with a civil servant's air of stale indifference.

"Take a seat. He's on the phone."

He sat under a photo of the President on a hard plastic bench that belonged on a bus and entertained himself thinking of the many times he had come here carrying the promises and payoffs that kept Tony Brassi in business.

Things still worked pretty much the same these days, except for Soltis, who, as far as Via knew, was still squeaky clean. Worse, he still had a thing for the Mob, and now that he was hoping to get his name on the state election ballot, he needed a case that would help put him there. If Via told him what he knew, Soltis would have it.

"Where do I know you from?" the receptionist asked, her eyes like dinner plates behind thick glasses.

"Used to be a lawyer. I did some business here years ago."

"I was here years ago." She adjusted her glasses and blinked her milky eyes at him. "But that ain't it."

"Must be someone else, then."

"Yeah, usually is." Her phone buzzed, but she didn't bother to pick it up. "He'll see you now."

Soltis stood at a window, back to the door, talking on the phone. He turned slightly when Via came in and motioned with an imperious gesture for him to take a seat.

Via surveyed the place, which was sterile and stark like the rest of the building, although Soltis had tried personalizing it with highlights from his career: a law diploma from Loyola University, photos with various politicians and dignitaries, a commendation letter from the FBI. Evidence of a successful life, a life his daughter and wife—*ex*-wife—would soon be part of. He imagined them living in some Waspy neighborhood on the North Shore, Meggie going to prep school, Karen joining the Junior League. He imagined Soltis on the evening news, the State's Attorney-elect, his smiling family behind him beaming from the podium, while he watched alone in his apartment drinking beer and chewing on regret.

"The Mayor's office," Soltis said, hanging up the phone and sitting behind his desk.

"No shit, I would have said hello."

"Skip the wisecracks; you know why you're here."

"I'm here because you threatened to bust me. And if you bust me, you'll fuck up everything."

"*I'll* fuck up everything? Listen, asshole, you're the reason Megan is afraid to walk to school."

"I told you, she's safe now."

"And you expect me to believe you? You think I'm going to trust a two-bit mobster with Megan's welfare?"

"I've been out of that a long time."

"If you were out of it, you wouldn't be here. I want to know why Brassi is threatening Megan."

"He's pressuring me to do a job for him."

"What kind of job?"

"That's my business."

"Who do you think you're talking to? How difficult you think it would be to nail you for obstruction of justice? One of Brassi's boys went and got himself murdered. And that makes it my business."

"I don't think Getti was one of his boys."

"Either way he's dead. Who was he, then?"

"Maybe you should ask Tony Brassi."

"I'm asking you. There hasn't been a Mob hit in this town in a decade. I don't buy it's just coincidence this guy gets whacked at the same time you go back working for Brassi. What's the connection? You know something about Getti's murder? Is Brassi threatening Megan to keep you quiet?"

"It isn't about Getti."

"I don't believe you, and I don't think a grand jury will either."

"You're getting ahead of yourself, aren't you, Soltis? Losing a case against Tony Brassi could hurt your political ambitions."

"Don't piss me off more than I already am. We're dealing with organized crime here. I'll call in the FBI if I have to. I think they might like another chance at you."

"No, you won't. You don't like to share the spotlight. You figure you're finally going to get a shot at the Outfit. And maybe your boss's job, too."

Soltis turned red. "Listen, Dickhead, you had better tell me what the hell is going on."

"I told you; I have to handle this. It's the only way I can make Meggie safe."

"Don't give me this caring father bullshit. I know you, Via."

"And I know you. You want to see your face on the front page, and Karen and Meggie are just part of the plan."

Soltis's lips curled. "You think you've got me figured out? Think you know what I want? Don't flatter yourself; you're not that good a detective."

Via was looking at Soltis's sharp nose, thinking how much he'd like to flatten it. He ran a hand over his mouth and took a deep breath.

"Look, let's assume, for the sake of argument, we both want to keep Meggie safe. And let's assume you're right and I'm still connected, okay, just to make you happy?"

"Sure," Soltis sneered, "and let's assume you're not the kind of lowlife who would say anything to save his own ass."

Via's heart was pounding in his ears. He took another breath and bit his lip. "And let's suppose I'm in the middle of this because of that connection."

"Yes, let's suppose that."

"So, who do you think is in a better position to protect Meggie? Me in the middle, or you on the outside?"

Soltis shifted in his chair and folded his arms across his chest. "You're out of your fucking mind."

"Face it, I'm your best bet. I'm closer to Brassi than you are. Busting me won't get you Brassi and it won't keep Meggie safe."

Soltis rose and went again to the window. He stood there, rubbing the back of his neck, his law school ring glaring at Via like a third eye.

"Maybe you can take Karen and Meggie to your place for a few days."

Soltis jerked around. "You fucking wops are all alike. You're like the kid who killed his parents and then pleaded for leniency because he was an orphan. I don't trust you, Via. You're still a fucking mobster and you'll never be anything else. You only have to think of yourself, but I have to think of Karen and Megan. I want that sonofabitch before he threatens them again. Yeah, I'll give you some rope. I'll give you rope because you're going to hang yourself with it, and I'm going to be there to watch your neck stretch, along with Brassi's. Yeah, I'll give you rope. You just remember I'm holding one end of it. Now, get the hell out of my office."

Via stood and went to the door. "You're doing the right thing," he said, going out.

Soltis reached for the phone. "Not yet," he mumbled to himself. "But I'm about to."

Nicky Fratelli lowered the *Astrology Weekly* and saw two men, one fat, one skinny, looking down at him.

"I asked is Via here," Jolly grunted.

"Do you have an appointment?"

"We're old friends."

"Yeah, just tell him we're here," Ziggy said.

"And you would be?"

"Just say Stan and Ollie," Jolly said, grinning coldly.

"I thought you looked like a couple of comedians."

Ziggy's shoulders went back and his eyes narrowed. He put his hand on Nicky's desk, clicking a star-shaped ring against the wood. "We don't need to ask."

"Ask or not. Either way, he's not in."

"Fuck this flit," Jolly snorted, and the two of them went around Nicky to check Via's office for themselves.

Nicky stayed put, listening to them flipping filing cabinets and banging furniture around. He reached into his drawer with a shaky hand, withdrew a .32 S&W revolver, and slipped it beneath the *Astrology Weekly*. He glanced at his speed dial; the nine-eleven emergency button was number one.

"See, I told you," he sniffed when the two men came back.

"You tell Via The Pig don't wait," Jolly said.

"Sure, that's the trouble with pigs, isn't it? They're impatient. And stupid."

Ziggy lunged for him across the desk, but Nicky brought up the .32 and jammed it hard beneath his chin. Ziggy's eyes became baseballs. Jolly moved to reach inside his jacket, but Nicky cocked the hammer.

"Stanley's brains will be on the ceiling. What little there are," Nicky said. He stood, pushing Ziggy upright with the barrel of the gun.

"You tell Via," Jolly said, backing out the door with Ziggy.

"I'm sure he'll be sorry he missed you."

When they closed the door, Nicky let out his breath. He took a moment to collect himself, then went over and threw the lock.

The office of Stein & Rosen exuded conservatism. No glint of extravagance, no hint of intemperance, its rich wood and sturdy furnishings projected the image of hard work and honesty for which the firm's clients presumed to be known.

Behind this veneer, in the back and out of sight, was a large room where Stein's minions labored in tight indistinct cubicles, monitoring on their computer screens an extensive network of businesses, all of which were Outfit-owned.

The name *Stein & Rosen* was something of a mask, too. Sidney Rosen had died years before but Avery Stein never changed the name. Not out of loyalty to Rosen's memory, but because it continued to lend an air of credibility that attracted clients engaged in actual legitimate businesses, which provided some cover for what the firm was really up to.

Rosen had been an Illinois State Senator, back when that position still carried some prestige, and he had brought his reputation with him when he left politics to join Stein in private practice. Lucky for Stein, the Senator threw a massive cardiac embolism just as the big Mob money began rolling in.

Stein himself claimed to be related to long-dead mobster Meyer Lansky, the so-called founder of the Crime Syndicate. No one knew if it was true but no one doubted his dexterity with numbers. A short wiry Jew, he looked a bit like Lansky except for the shiny scalp and shot-glass spectacles, behind which beady eyes were in perpetual squint. He was a genius with taxes and had spent most of his seventy-plus years managing the Chicago Outfit's finances, finding myriad ways to make large numbers look small, small numbers look big, and the IRS look the other way. When the capos complained about his exorbitant fees, he reminded them it was Capone's tax improprieties that finally brought him down. Among the Chicago Families, Avery Stein was considered *Capo dei libri*, Boss of the Books.

"You here to get help with your taxes?" he said, coming into the lobby, where he had kept Via waiting for fifteen minutes.

"You know why I'm here."

"Of course I know. I'm old, not stupid."

Stein beckoned for Via to follow and led him down a long hallway adorned with photos of Chicago's business elite, none of whom were clients.

"I heard you were back in the family business."

"It's temporary."

"Sure. I've been telling myself the same thing for forty years."

Stein led him to his office and closed the door and told Via to take a seat in front of his desk. He went over to a small armoire and retrieved a bottle of 12-year-old scotch and two crystal glasses, which he set on the desktop. He poured two drinks and handed one to Via, then went around and sat in a forest green leather chair that swallowed him. He pressed his hands together as if to pray and rested his narrow chin on his fingertips.

"So, you want to know about the girl," he said.

"And the disk."

"A thumb drive, probably. Easier to conceal."

"You mean a flash drive?"

"Thumb drive, flash drive. Same thing." Stein reached for his glass and raised it, said "L'chaim," and swallowed a shallow sip. "Doctor says I drink too much. For this he went to medical school."

"So, tell me what happened."

"It was this Getti kid did it. You remember Vincent Getti? His grandson. Graduated from MIT. A wizard with computers. Hired him about a year ago to update our systems. This is how he repays me."

"How much did he get?"

"How much? He got everything. Hacked through the firewall. Got Brassi's books. The *real* books. This information could put Tony away for a long time. A lot of other people, too."

"Which people?"

"You know how Brassi got where he is. Public officials, judges, cops. You think Monkey Wrench changed things?" Stein sipped his scotch again. "I was always sorry about what happened to you."

"Yeah, me too."

"Anyway, the game's the same. It's just the names that change."

"And they're all in this file these kids downloaded?"

"Christ, she was his own daughter. What am I, a babysitter? And Tony vouched for the Getti kid himself, said he owed Vinnie a favor."

"No good deed goes unpunished."

Stein raised an eyebrow. "Know who said that? Henry Ford. Goddamn anti-Semite."

"You know," Via said, "The Getti kid I can understand, but why do you think Brassi's kid got involved?"

Stein gave a world-weary shrug. "What can I tell you? Hormones."

"She and Getti talk to anybody else here? Maybe a friend they might tell about a trip they were planning or something?"

Stein waved the question away. "Those two? Nah. They were like lox and bagels."

"What do you know about the girl?"

"What do I know? She's Tony's daughter; I don't ask."

"She talk about her old man?"

"Like what?"

"Like his business. What he does."

"Not to me." Stein finished off his drink and sighed. "*His* business. Fucking Italians—no offense—think they invented it."

Stein set down his glass. "What's Tony going to do after he finds her? After *you* find her?"

"I don't know."

"Don't know or don't care?"

Via knocked back his drink.

"It was Getti put her up to it," Stein said. "Oily prick. She's just a kid."

"Well, he paid for his mistake. Now she'll have to pay for hers."

"Shame. You think Getti knew where she is, he was protecting her?"

Via shook his head. "You know what Brassi did to him. Nobody's that much in love."

Tina Brassi's condominium overlooked Lake Shore Drive in an area called the Gold Coast. Tony Brassi had bought it for her as a wedding present and, to his profound regret, put the deed in her maiden name because the IRS was giving him a colonoscopy at the time. It originally cost a million dollars and she hoped now to get three for it. Besides her realtor, no one else knew it was up for sale.

The building itself was one of those flat-faced stone high-rises that cordon off Lake Shore Drive like a fence, keeping the view of Lake Michigan all to themselves. Via pulled into the underground garage and rode the elevator up two levels to the bright, Wedgwood blue lobby, then headed to the residents' elevator across white Terrazzo tiles.

"Hey, man, where you goin'?" he heard someone behind him bark. A tall black guy in an olive green uniform was coming out of the janitor's closet.

"Thirty-five," Via told him.

"Not you don't check wit me first," the guy said, marching over to man the security desk.

"Didn't want to pull you away from your work," Via said, coming over.

The guard eyeballed him with the same disdain he might show the pizza delivery boy. "You got business here?"

Via told him and gave his name. The guard called upstairs, all the while keeping his eyes on Via like a department store dick. He hung up and waved the phone toward the elevators.

"You know, I used to work security myself," Via said.

"Gee, no kidding?" the guy sneered.

"Yeah, before I got promoted to doorman."

Via went over and pushed the Up button and bright stainless steel doors opened to a chrome-paneled space about the size of his apartment. Tina Brassi had done all right for herself.

"So, you've changed your mind about helping me?" she said, opening her door.

"Not exactly."

She craned her neck back and forth down the hallway. "Then why are you here?"

"Tony wants me to find your kid."

Her expression changed from confusion to anger. "You're

working for him now?"

"I don't have a choice."

"You know what he did to my daughter's boyfriend?"

"Yeah, and I know about the books, too."

She stepped backward. "What books?"

The look on her face almost made him laugh.

"Look, you want me to find your daughter, we don't have time for games."

A door opened along the hall and an elderly woman shuffled past pulling a small white dog on a leash. She gave them a haughty look and yanked the reluctant animal toward the elevator.

"Come in from the hall," Tina Brassi said, stepping back into her condo.

He followed her along the white marble hall, catching the sweet scent of pears floating on the air behind her. Coming into the living space, he saw that the condo occupied the entire top floor of the high-rise and had views of the lake on three sides. It was all sharp angles, cool colors, and hard surfaces, the look of modern money, minimalist at the maximum price. Definitely a long way from the house on Oakley Avenue and "Little Tuscany" where she grew up.

Then again, she didn't look much like the skinny girl who used to play sandlot softball with the neighborhood boys. Tina Di'Angelo then, a determined kid who always said she was going somewhere. He wondered if she was happy where she ended up.

She sat on a black satin sofa. In her white silk robe and matching pajamas she could have been in an old Bogart movie. He took a seat in a matching chair across from her and told her how he was forced to get involved.

"I'm sorry about your daughter," she said when he finished.

"No, you're not. You're just worried about yours."

"And you aren't?"

"She'll be all right if I can find yours."

"To give her over to Tony?"

"I told you, I have no choice. Your kid got herself into this."

She feigned a contrite look. "Frank, I didn't know about the books when I came to see you."

"Stop lying. There isn't time."

Her gaze shifted to the floor. "I don't know what to do."

"Who're you kidding?"

"I don't."

"Then just do what I tell you."

"What do you think he'll do if he finds her?" she asked, her eyes wet.

"He says he only wants the books."

"You believe him?"

"He killed Getti, didn't he?" He let that sink in, then said, "If you know where your kid is, you'll be better off telling me. The longer this takes, the worse it gets."

"I don't know."

"That doesn't help her."

She got up and went to a bar across the room and filled two glasses with bourbon and brought them back and handed one to him. She took hers over to the window and stood there staring out at the green water, the light through her robe silhouetting those long legs. A beautiful woman. He wished he could believe her.

"Your ex thinks someone might've snatched her."

Tina Brassi turned around, a look of surprise and apprehension on her face. "You mean kidnapped her? Who?"

"Someone who wants those books even more than she does."

"But who would know she had them?"

"Tony thinks Getti was trying to sell them. Word like that gets around fast. Tony has a lot of enemies."

"But who would have the—. My God, you mean Delacante and Salerno."

"Now you're getting the picture."

She stared into her drink, fingers tapping the side of the glass, the situation coming into focus. "Yes," she said. "Yes, I see." She sipped some bourbon. "Do you think it's true?"

"I don't know what's true and what's not, do I?"

"Look, I didn't tell you about the stolen books because I knew you would never take the job if you knew about them."

"You still don't get it, do you? If Tony's right, your daughter's even worse off than you think. You can't protect her now; you can only help me find her."

She raised a hand to her mouth. "My God, what has she gotten herself into?"

"The deepest shit. Now, where's the last place you saw her?"

"Here," Tina Brassi said. "Two days ago, before she left for school."

"Which school?"

"Saint Jude's. In Winnetka."

"The North Shore is a little out of her district, isn't it?"

"It's a special school."

"I bet. How'd she get there?"

"Gabe, my driver, drove her."

"Gabe Court? Christ, that boozer? You trust him?"

"I don't have reason not to."

"Yeah, but he used to work for your ex. I want to talk to him. I also need the school. Address, phone number, who I can talk to there."

"Her class schedule is on her computer."

She walked across the room to a small writing table, set her drink on it, and opened a laptop PC. She slid her finger across the touchpad and a folder opened and then a printer next to the computer began whirring.

Via came over and stood behind her, catching a whisper of pears again. She removed the printout from the tray, wrote Court's phone number on it, and handed the paper to him.

"Don't mind the squiggly letters. Annette says the ink jets are misaligned. She was going to fix it before—"

She lowered her head and began to cry. Via picked up her bourbon and handed it to her and waited while she drank it.

"All right. That's all for now."

"What should I do?"

"Nothing. You get a call, someone brings you a message, you contact me."

"Frank—" she started, but he stopped her.

"Don't trust anyone, including Tony. Especially him."

He folded the printed page into his pocket and followed her to the front door, watching her hips beneath her robe, the white silk flowing across them like cream.

Harry Soltis stared at his FBI commendation and waited for Mickey Finley to say something constructive.

"I said, I think I've found it," he repeated into the phone. He could hear Finley breathing on the other end. "You awake?"

"What case?"

"The case I just told you about."

"Tell me again."

"You listening? The case that's going to get me elected." He heard ice clinking through the wire.

"Oh, *the* case."

"You drinking already? Isn't it a little early, even for you?"

"Hey, I'm a political advisor, not a cop," Mickey Finley said. "In my profession, you can't afford to be too sober."

"Jesus Christ."

"Forget it, can't get the Jewish vote."

"This isn't funny, Mickey."

"Don't worry, Harry, I've gotten more politicians elected drunk than you've thrown in jail sober. Now, tell me about this case that's going to make your career."

CHAPTER 7

Via left Tina Brassi's apartment and rode the elevator back down, looking at his reflection in the chrome walls, wondering how he looked to Tina Brassi. As he stepped into the lobby, the security guard grinned at him like he had just lifted his wallet. Via gave him the fuck-you look and went over to wait for the elevator to the parking garage.

"You boys have a good time now," he heard the guard chirp as the doors opened. He felt a chill up his spine. And then everything went white.

When he came to, he was sitting between Pignotti's goons, Jolly and Ziggy, heading north on Ashland Avenue. Pignotti himself was driving.

"You spend a lotta time unconscious lately, Via," he said into the rearview mirror. "One a these days, you ain't gonna wake up."

"I appreciate your concern, Pig," Via said, trying to clear his head.

"How many times you gotta be told? He don't like to be called that," Ziggy said, and rammed his elbow into Via's rib-cage.

"You're a hard case," Pignotti said. He wore a brown turtleneck that hugged his torso like cling wrap and made him look like a giant Hershey's Kiss. "My associates here ain't as interested in protecting my investment as I am, considering the

91

way you treated them last time. You should be grateful I came along."

"You're a real humanitarian, Pig."

Ziggy punched him in the temple and Via went foggy again.

Pignotti twisted in his seat. "Well, Ziggy, my man, I think you finally shut him up."

"You want I should slug him again?"

"Nah, save it for when we get there."

Via kept his chin on his chest and listened to them talk, laughing and shouting crude remarks to the hookers working the street, having a grand time, while he tried to think straight and figure out what to do.

They caught a red light and one of the hookers sashayed over and stuck her breasts through Jolly's open window.

"Nice," Jolly grunted.

"You want nice, pull over."

"Hey, Pig," Jolly asked, "we got time?"

"I suck your dick 'til your asshole puckers," the whore said.

"Gimme a little feel first," Jolly said, rotating away from Via and toward the whore.

"Hey, me, too," Ziggy said, but when he reached over, Via snapped his left forearm up into Ziggy's throat, then twisted around and slammed Jolly's face down against the window jam, hearing cartilage crack.

The whore screamed and fell backward. Over his shoulder, Via heard Ziggy strangling for air. He reached into Jolly's jacket to take his gun and found his own .38.

Pignotti shouted and hit the gas and Jolly's head thunked back hard against the window frame. Via reached past him and pulled the lock. The car jerked and weaved. Via heard Ziggy choking on air. He opened the door and pushed Jolly out onto the street.

"Goddammit!" Pignotti screamed.

Via leaned forward and pressed the gun against his cheek. Pignotti smelled of garlic and sweat.

"Stop the car, you fat fuck."

Ziggy reached out for Via, but he swung the .38 around. Pignotti slowed the car and steered it to the curb.

"I'd like to kill you, but I'm in a hurry," Via said.

He whipped Ziggy across the face with the gun, then pushed backward out the door and started running.

By the time Pignotti got back to pick up Jolly, Via was several blocks away on Clark Street, an area he knew from the old days when he was working the neighborhood for Tony Brassi. It was cold and he was beat up and he needed a drink. He shoved his hands into his jacket pockets to warm them and found the matchbook Chizek's blonde had given him, a place called *Bistro 30* a couple of blocks away.

It was a place he sort of remembered from the old days, *sort of* because it used to be a dim, quiet, working-class joint, but like a lot of the old places in Uptown had now gone the way of gentrification. Now, it had large picture windows through which he could see people sipping white wine and smiling like imbeciles. He almost went back down the street but saw the blonde back behind the bar and decided to go in.

She was busy setting up and didn't see him, which gave him time to look her over again, see if he'd made a mistake. Watching her move around in jeans that hugged her ass like spray paint, he decided he hadn't.

"So, you kept the matchbook, huh?" she said, looking up at him, smiling through strawberry lips.

"Just in case I take up smoking again," he said.

She smiled again and continued washing glasses, her cleavage swelling from a crisp white shirt opened low to get attention. Her hair was pulled into a ponytail and the purple eye shadow was gone and he could see tiny crow's feet scratching at the corners of her brown eyes. She squinted at the lump forming on his left temple and motioned him to the far end of the bar, saying, "You look like you need a drink."

He followed, eyeing that nice firm ass, that blonde hair flouncing back and forth, silver earrings like tiny zodiacs tapping against her neck. Her nails were red like her lips and so were her shoes, which had toes as sharp as stilettos. "Fuck me" shoes, he'd heard Nicky call them. "Fuck *you*" shoes, he thought, if she ever aimed one at your balls.

She poured him a neat whiskey and he settled himself on a wooden barstool.

"You in the area to see me, or just to get beat up?"

"I can get beat up anywhere."

"So I should be flattered, then?"

While he drank she filled a towel with ice and pressed it against his head. When he reached up to take it, his hand settled over hers and she left it there a moment before sliding it away.

"I just came around to see the old neighborhood," he said, waving an arm in the air. "Used to work around here."

"You mean back when you were a mobster?"

"The bartender told you that, too?"

She shrugged her shoulders. "You know bartenders."

"I'm talking about before it got respectable. This place was a joint called Betty's then. Used to be a jukebox where the salad bar is."

He propped his elbow on the bar to secure the cold towel against his head. The ice was beginning to numb the pain and the whiskey was loosening him up a bit. She poured him another.

"And now you go around serving subpoenas and pissing people off."

"It's a give-and-take kind of thing," he said. "So what were you doing with fat Chizek anyway?"

"I told you, I have poor taste in men."

"So I should be flattered now?"

"That was a pretty nasty crack you made to me."

"Which one?"

Even as he said it, he knew it was wrong. He saw her open face close, her body stiffen, the warmth in her eyes go cold. He softened his tone and tried to manage a grin.

"Don't mind me, it's a joke. I just have a lousy sense of humor."

"You think?"

She bent to reach beneath the bar and he stole a good look at her cleavage. Full round breasts in a thin white lace bra. He considered apologizing again.

She brought up a cutting board and thunked it down hard on the bar. Then she brought up a knife and some lemons and began hacking them into half moons.

"I was with him, so you're wondering if I'm worth talking to, huh?"

He sipped the whiskey. "Something like that."

"You think so much of yourself, or so little of women?"

He raised his hand like a stop sign. "Forget it."

"Bullshit. You don't want to know, you wouldn't have asked."

He set the towel on the bar and nodded. "Okay. You're right."

She stopped cutting and picked up the towel and wiped the lemon juice from her fingers.

"Okay, he's a loan officer at my bank. He's in the middle of a divorce. I'm in the middle of a deal to buy this place. I need a loan. The deal was taking longer than expected."

"So, you were buying some time?"

She picked up the knife again and pointed it at him. "Something like that."

He glanced around the room to avoid her glare. "Bistro Thirty. What's that?"

"The bust size of the current owner's wife. After I buy it, I'm changing it to Bistro Thirty-Six."

He wrenched out a grin. "I hear a business like this can be pretty tough."

"You know a business that isn't? Who beat you up?"

He waved it off, being cool. "Some guys I owe money."

"Well, we have something in common after all." She went back to the lemons. "So, how come you're not lawyering anymore?"

"It's a long story."

Lawyering. He liked the way she said it, like he wasn't just some Mob jamoke. Like he once had some brains, even if he didn't end up in law school by choice. Still, he was glad he did. By then he was already tired of breaking bones and glad to have a chance to move up in the organization, be something besides street crew, maybe look halfway respectable to his wife. He enjoyed it, too, learning about the laws he was breaking, outsmarting the cops and the guys with Ivy League degrees. Smart guys. Smarter than him, but not street smart. Not smart enough to appreciate how things really worked. It took a crook to bribe and threaten and blackmail. It took a crook to truly comprehend that once you compromised a judge you owned him and the law didn't matter anymore.

"Did you like it? Being a lawyer?"

"Sure." He finished his drink and rubbed the knot on his head. "But what did I know? I was young; I thought it was a step up."

Her red lips turned upward. "Maybe you can tell me about it sometime."

"Like I said, it's a long story." He rotated on the stool and stood. "What do I owe you?"

"A long story. Next time."

"You might not like listening to it."

"I'm a bartender. It's my job."

Walking past on the sidewalk outside, he looked in to see if she was watching him, but she was already dusting the bottles behind the bar.

Mickey Finley tamped the tobacco in his pipe and set it ablaze with a Bic lighter. He let out a cloud of Cherry Blend, which almost masked the booze on his breath, and sat back in the chair.

"So what do you think?" Harry Soltis asked from behind his desk.

"You could be right. If there's something to all of this, it could help offset the other problem."

"I told you not to call it that."

"What would you call it? You're dating a mobster's ex-wife and trying to talk tough on crime. We're lucky the press hasn't gotten hold of it yet. But as soon as you declare, they'll be all over it like mold."

"Don't worry, once I nail Tony Brassi I'll be Teflon."

Finley sucked on his pipe. "Maybe so, but how do we do it? We don't know what we're dealing with here, do we? And even if we did, and tried to intervene, we could get some girl killed. So this guy Via says."

"Fuck Via. He's going down with Brassi and the rest of them."

"Sure, Harry, but we have to bust them first, don't we now? And then we have to convict them. And we can't bust them without cause, and we can't convict them without evidence. And the way things stand we're not going to have either."

"I'm not letting this get away."

"It's a pickle, Harry, a real pickle." Finley crossed his legs, bleached and hairless shins showing above his socks. "And you say we can't take it to the police?"

"And tell them what? Besides, I wouldn't know who to trust.

Half the department's on the Mob's payroll."

"And the other half are Democrats," Finley said, smiling at his own joke. "Yes, sir, a real pickle."

Soltis removed his spectacles and pinched the bridge of his nose.

"Don't worry, Harry, I'll come up with something. Relax."

Soltis slammed his palm on the desk. "Relax?"

Finley started like a squirrel. "Jesus, Harry, take it easy."

"We don't have time to take it easy!"

"I'm thinking, I'm thinking."

"Goddamnit, think faster."

Finley was florid. He puffed his pipe and made a constipated face. "There are ways, of course. There are always ways."

"You'd better find one," Soltis hissed. "We need to know what Via's up to."

Finley's face relaxed. He looked like he just passed gas.

"What?" Soltis asked.

"Well, you know, in my business—and I'm not proud of it, Harry—if you want dirt on someone, you just need to follow him around awhile. Everybody trips up eventually."

Soltis put his glasses back on. His eyes were shining.

"It's extremely risky, Harry. If it got out a state prosecutor was—"

"I'll take that risk."

Finley took the pipe from his mouth and used it to punctuate his words. "That's what Bill Clinton said when he first met Monica Lewinsky. You know, he wouldn't have been impeached if he'd been half as afraid of Congress as he was of Hillary. Believe me, you don't want to get your cock caught in your zipper."

"Let me worry about that. Just tell me what we do."

"You don't do anything. I'll arrange it. You won't know anything about it."

"So, who?"

"I have this guy I've used before," Finley said, brushing tobacco from the front of his rumpled jacket.

Soltis came around and sat on the edge of his desk. "A private dick?"

"A campaign worker, idealistic type, but experienced. You remember that guy who ran for senator from Illinois back in two thousand four? My guy is the one found out the would-be senator liked fucking his wife in public places."

Soltis was tapping his lips like a keyboard.

"My guy tails this Via, finds out where he goes, who he sees."

"And he can do this without getting caught?"

Finley drew on his pipe and blew out a smoke ring. "Harry, what did I just say?"

"Where have you been?" Nicky huffed when Via came through the door.

"Chasing hookers on Halsted Street."

"You look like hell. Is that your blood?"

"It's Oliver Hardy's."

"No shit! They found you? They were here, you know."

"Yeah?"

"Look in your office. They tore it up pretty good."

"Shit." Via stepped around him.

"Hey, they were going to do the same to me," Nicky said, following him through his office door.

Via let out a groan and went to an overturned file cabinet. "Think you could give me a hand here?"

"I could have been killed, you know."

They set the cabinet on its feet and Via started picking up papers.

"Did you hear what I said?"

"What?"

"You're not paying me enough for this. In fact, you're barely paying me at all."

"You want me to borrow more money from The Pig?"

"So now you're blaming me?"

"You were here, weren't you?"

"Have you been listening?"

Via went over and set his chair on its feet. "Fat fuck. Had to take a cab back to get my car. Look at my goddamn shirt."

"I could've told you. It's the full moon, you know."

Via waved a hand at him. "Don't start with that bullshit. You've been reading too many of those books."

"Go ahead, believe what you want. But bad things happen during full moons."

"What moon? It's daylight, for Christ's sake."

"It's the lunar cycle. Just because you can't see something doesn't mean it's not there."

"Straighten that lamp, will you?"

"I didn't believe it either, you know, but then I started noticing a lot of bad things happened to me during full moons."

"Right. Like what?"

"Getting this job for one," Nicky said. He picked something off the floor.

"You actually think Pignotti found me because of the goddamn moon?"

"Well, that . . . or because you wrote Tina Brassi's address on this." He tossed Via's calendar to him.

"Sonofabitch."

"So what are you going to do about him?"

"We can't worry about him right now. We have bigger problems than The Pig."

Via told him what Brassi suspected about Salerno and Delacante, and Nicky let out a whistle.

"Jesus Christ. You believe one of them *did* nab her?"

"You better hope not. Or we're in big trouble."

"What do you mean *we*?"

Via found the phone book in a corner and started searching through the pages. "See if I have a clean shirt in the front closet, will you?"

"Where are you going now?"

"To see the patron saint of hopeless causes."

St. Jude Thaddeus was the model of what the Chicago archdiocese thought a Catholic high school should be—white, rich, and insular. Because a school like it couldn't exist within the city itself, it was built on the rich North Shore, where Mother Church lavished it with all manner of money and promotion. There it beckoned like the Sacred Heart of Jesus to the wealthy Catholic parents of Chicagoland's best and not-so-brightest students.

The red brick structure stood on a hill overlooking a capacious green campus. It had huge barrel-shaped towers and cruciform piers that made it look more like a church than a school. Via entered the building through a grand semi-circular arch and into a two-story companionway, where he was met by a tall, thin Franciscan nun whose starched white coif made her face look pinched and sour. She greeted him with little deference and led him up a winding staircase to the third floor, where the school's principal was waiting for him.

"So, how may I help you?" Monsignor Stanley Kochinsky asked, all business after the usual introductory pleasantries.

"I'm trying to locate one of your students."

"You mean the Brassi girl," he said, to let Via know he had connections, too. "Yes, terrible thing. I know her father Anthony. Nice Italian family. She is in our prayers."

He looked more like a prizefighter than a priest, a former middleweight with a buzz cut and a nose that had lost one too many rounds.

"I'll tell her father. I'm sure it'll be great comfort to him."

"You work for Mr. Brassi, then?"

"I work for myself. Brassi hired me to find his daughter."

"And you're here to ask if someone might have seen her," the priest said, as if students going missing was a common occurrence at St. Jude's.

"Or maybe saw something unusual."

Kochinsky gave him a condescending smile. "Nothing very unusual ever happens here at Saint Jude's. Which is the very reason parents send their students to us, Mr. Via."

"I'm sure it is."

"It *certainly* is. And you may also be certain the students here truly appreciate the opportunity they have been given and realize how fortunate they are to be among such a select few."

"Of course," Via said, looking around the principal's richly appointed office. "And not a bad place for a priest to be assigned either, is it?"

The priest smiled again. "The Jesuits are a teaching order. We go where we are needed."

"Don't we all."

Kochinsky folded his hands in front of him and looked at Via as if he were an unruly student. "And what is it you need here, Mr. Via?"

"I need to talk with some of Annette Brassi's classmates. I'd also like to talk with her teachers."

"Of course." Kochinsky pressed his intercom. "Mrs. Farrell, I need a list of one of our students' teachers. . . . Annette Brassi. . . . Yes, as soon as possible, please." He clicked off.

"Annette is one of our brightest students," the priest said. "Something of a firebrand, though. A bit too critical and overzealous. Sometimes students can take the Lord's teachings a bit too literally, I'm afraid. Youthful zeal, I suppose."

102

"You know much about the Brassi family?"

"I've heard the rumors, if that's what you mean."

"Yeah? Which rumors?"

Kochinsky got up and went over to a coffeepot on a small table set against a wall of books bound in black and embossed with gold. Above the table was a large crucifix, the Christ butterflied and stripped, pale sinewy body exposed, except for the thin bloody linen that barely covered him. It had always bothered Via as a kid, this image of a naked man hanging above the congregation; he couldn't understand what it was doing in a church. Nicky had leaned over and whispered some wisecrack about sadomasochism and salvation, which Via didn't understand at the time either.

"Mr. Via," Kochinsky said over his shoulder, "our job is to teach these children. What their parents do, or don't do, is not our concern."

"Render unto Caesar, eh, Father?"

"You are a Catholic, Mr. Via?" the priest asked.

Via watched Kochinsky fussing over the coffee, thinking back to when he was an altar boy, remembering the priest's back to him, chalice extended overhead, the golden reflection sparkling like holy water on his forehead. Back when he was a kid and still believed in something.

"Gave it up for Lent once. Felt so good, I never went back."

"I see. A *lapsed* Catholic, as they say?"

"More like an escapee."

"Yes, that would explain your cynicism," Kochinsky said, coming back with his Notre Dame cup. "I find prayer can soothe the troubled soul."

Mrs. Farrell came in and handed the priest a sheet of paper, giving Via the kind of appraisal he used to get from the nuns—a speck of lint to be flicked away by the Almighty's sacred finger.

"You know, Christ was considered a cynic, too," Kochinsky

said, "but even he recognized, as you say, the need to honor Caesar." He handed Via the list of teachers.

"Sure," Via said, rising to leave, "but look where he ended up."

He heard Mrs. Farrell let out a gasp behind him.

As Via expected, Annette Brassi's classmates and teachers were of little help. If someone snatched her, it seemed to have been a professional job, no witnesses and no leads beyond the hostage note and Brassi's suspicions about Delacante and Salerno. It was looking more and more like Brassi was right.

Walking across the school grounds to the parking lot, he was considering the seriousness of that possibility when he saw a dark blue Lincoln Continental parked behind his Caddy. As he came close, Bobby Albanese and Vito Tessa got out.

"Here to pick up teenage girls?" Via said. "Or just back to finish high school?"

Albanese hiked his belt up over his belly. "Brassi wants to see you."

Via had known guys like Albanese all of his life, guys who worked their way up the ladder until they got their foot caught on a middle rung. They couldn't go up and they wouldn't go down. They hung there in the middle, doing whatever it took to keep from getting pushed off. It was where Via was headed himself before he got knocked up to being a mouthpiece. He would still be there if not for Monkey Wrench. Of course, they were right to disbar him. He did tamper with the jury. If he hadn't tampered with the judge, too, there might have been a retrial, but he had done a good job of preventing that from happening. Not that it did him any good. Brassi got off and he got disowned.

"Tell him I'm busy trying to find his daughter," he told Albanese.

"He wants an update."

"I haven't found her yet."

"You're a real fuckin' comedian," Tessa said.

He wore a pearl gray leather sport coat over a bright red shirt open to his sternum. His black ankle boots had silver buckles that matched the belt holding up his black shark-skin pants. He wore a silver bracelet, too, and a silver pinky ring on each hand. Via wondered if he knew those disco days were over. *The cheaper the hood, the flashier the clothes,* his old man used to say.

"Let's go, Frank," Albanese ordered.

"He wants me to find his daughter, he has to let me do my job."

"That ain't good enough," Albanese said.

Via stepped around him. "Neither are you two."

Tessa reached for him, but Via caught his thumb and forced his wrist back, twisting his arm behind his back and bending him over the hood of the Continental.

Tessa screamed, "Motherfucker!" and Via banged his face against the hood. He wanted to do it again but Albanese pressed a gun between his shoulder blades.

"Enough!"

Via gave Tessa's arm another sharp twist before releasing him. Tessa screamed again and rolled upright trying to hold his elbow in place.

"Get the fuck in," Albanese told Via, gesturing with the gun.

"I already told you."

"We go back, Frank, but this is business."

"Kill the sonofabitch," Tessa groaned.

"That would be real fucking smart," Via said. "What're you going to tell your boss? You came to find out what I know about his daughter, but clipped me instead?" He started toward his car. "When I know something, he'll know something."

"Tony ain't gonna like this," Albanese said.
"Tell him prayer can soothe the troubled soul."

CHAPTER 8

Via met Gabe Court at a Mob-owned strip club, called Freckles, in the city's River North area. It was the kind of place where a man could sit and drink in the middle of the day without feeling like an alcoholic, which Court was. He was at the runway bar where he could be close to the booze and booty when Via took a seat next to him and ordered a beer. A stripper named Champagne was dancing to Yanni and popping wine corks from between her legs.

"And they say Chicago lacks culture," Via said.

Court looked over, unsmiling. "Look, it's my day off."

"Sure, I spend mine the same way," Via cracked, thinking this was probably the pinnacle of Court's day.

Court finished his drink and signaled the bartender for a refill. "There somethin' you want to talk to me about?"

"You know why I'm here."

"Hey, I'm sorry about the kid, but I don't know nothin' about it."

"What time did you drop her at school?"

"I remember you, Via. Thought you was a civilian now."

"What time?"

"The usual time."

"You watch her go in?"

"It's what I get paid to do. She hangs around outside with some other kids, then goes in. That's all."

"See anything unusual?"

Court swiveled toward him. "Yeah, teenagers."

The bartender brought Via's beer and refilled Court's glass. Via told him to leave the bottle.

"Tell me about the girl. What's her name . . . Annette."

"What about her? She's a high school kid, whatta you think?" He shook a cigarette from a pack of Salems on the bar and lit up.

"What about her friends, know any of them?"

"Look, I just drive her. I ain't her nanny."

The stripper danced over and straddled Via's glass and popped a cork into his beer.

"Listen," Via said to Court, "nobody's blaming you. But we're talking about Tony Brassi's kid here. You cooperate, I tell him. You don't, I tell him that, too. Get it?"

"I told you, I don't know nothin'. She's just a kid. Typical stuff. Teenager stuff."

"Like what?"

"Look, she's always been nice to me. Not like her mother, the Dago Princess. No offense."

"Sure, I expect it from a mick. She get along with the mother?"

"Wouldn't know."

Court swiveled back toward the bar and lifted his shot glass, pinky extended like he was at high tea. Via was tempted to reach over and break it. Just one finger, that would be enough to get his attention. He reached over and snatched Court's smoke from between his lips and dropped it on the floor and crushed it beneath his shoe.

"You know the difference between an Irish wedding and an Irish wake?" he asked Court. "One less drunk."

Court didn't seem to think it was funny.

The stripper finished her act and came over naked and squatted in front of Via to fish the cork out of his beer with her hand.

When he looked up, she sucked her fingers and asked, "So, what do you think?"

"Less filling, tastes great," Via said.

He handed her a ten and waved her away, then looked back at Court, who was draining another shot. "Brassi's kid, she talk much?"

"Not to me. She ain't exactly a happy kid. Got that look, you know, like she's pissed off all the time? Kinda like you," Court said.

The music started up again and another stripper strutted past. Court watched her absently with glassy eyes.

"That's all I know," he said. "She don't say much to me, so I don't say much back. Just orders me around like I'm a god-damn servant."

"You think she could've run away?"

"Like where? It ain't enough she's Tony Brassi's daughter?"

"I might need to talk to you again," Via said, pushing away from the bar.

Court poured himself another drink. "Sure, I'll clear my calendar."

Via put a twenty under his glass and went out front. As he opened his car door, he surveyed the street and noticed a beige Volvo sedan parked on an angle a few cars away. When he pulled out, it fell in behind him.

Karen knew Harry Soltis would be angry, but she needed to retrieve her daughter. When he insisted Meggie had to stay with her grandmother, Karen agreed because it seemed like the right thing at the time. Now she wasn't so sure. Her mother wasn't the easiest person to live with in the best of times, and now with her arthritis flaring up she was using Meggie as her nursemaid. Karen could hear it in her daughter's voice; it was time to bring her home.

She backed the station wagon out of the driveway and headed up the street, not noticing the black Escalade ease in behind her as she pulled into traffic at the end of the cul-de-sac. She didn't notice the tractor trailer either, until she heard its horn trumpet next to her and had to jerk the wagon back into her own lane.

She cursed her ex-husband for her preoccupation with the mess they were in, for making her send Meggie away, for making her suffer the abuse she knew would come from her mother when she took Meggie back home. She couldn't remember why she married him in the first place. Probably because her mother didn't want her to, which was reason enough to hate him—he had proved the old lady right.

The thought of her mother's piercing voice made her suddenly remember—too preoccupied again—to stop at the drugstore to buy the arthritis-strength aspirin her mother insisted was the only thing that stood between her and bone-crunching agony. She stopped at the first convenience store she came to.

Besides the aspirin, she bought the *National Inquirer* and *The Globe* and two bags of bite-size Heath bars, which she hoped might mitigate the old woman's disappointment, and her wrath, at losing Meggie.

Behind the checkout, she eyed the child-size bottles of vodka, the kind you got on airplanes, and told the clerk to put two into her bag. She was drinking more than usual lately and this, too, she blamed on Via.

She tried not to think about what happened to her marriage, about the trouble Meggie was in. Better to think about the future with Harry Soltis. Not exactly the kind of guy she would have seen herself married to but the kind she needed now, a single mother facing college costs and middle age. At least Harry was ambitious, and as long as his ambition included an instant family, she was willing to provide it. It was time to get on with her life.

She paid the clerk and noticed him looking her over, a glum-looking guy with sparse, heavily gelled hair that looked like plastic.

"You gonna drink these alone," he asked, putting the liquor into a bag, leering at her with greenish teeth.

"No, with pretzels," she said.

On the way out she caught a glimpse of herself in the glass door as it swung open and felt thankful she had kept her figure. She could still hear her mother criticizing everything she ate.

She walked to her car thinking about the vodka now—one here in the parking lot, the second when she got there. She set the groceries on the passenger seat and pulled the door closed and sensed immediately she was not alone.

"Easy," Bobby Albanese said from the back seat. "I just wanna talk to you."

She kept her eyes on him in the rearview, afraid to turn around.

"You ain't changed much. Still a good-lookin' broad, you don't mind me sayin' so." When she didn't answer, he said, "Don't remember me, huh? That's okay, I remember you."

"What do you want?"

"Your daughter takes after you. On your way to visit her again?"

She turned then to look at him.

"That's right," he said. "We been watchin'."

"Yes, I remember you."

"Yeah? I was thinner then. But you, you still look good."

"Get out of my car."

"Listen, I know this ain't your fault. You just hooked up with the wrong guy. Trust me, this will all blow over. Maybe we can get together or somethin' after."

"Get out!"

"Hey, I understand. It's not a good time. I'll be in touch. You tell your ex we talked."

He got out then and she watched him walk to a black SUV. She waited until he pulled away before bursting into tears.

Via was met by two beefy guards when he got out of his car at the Delacante Family compound. They patted him down and led him through big studded oak doors into the orange brick mansion that served as Carmine Delacante's home and headquarters.

The guards marched him down a long dim hallway and left him in a large anteroom with a vaulted ceiling, from which hung a massive Venetian crystal chandelier. Ornate gilded sconces with hand-blown glass shades bathed the room in a soft amber glow. On the walls were deep green and red Italian tapestries and on the floor was Travertine marble the color of terra cotta, each tile of which was emblazoned with a small, yellow, three-legged symbol Via recognized as the Sicilian *Trinacria*.

At one end of the room was an enormous fireplace framed by heavy wrought iron scrollwork, and at the other end was a huge mahogany table laden with earthenware, statuary, old photographs, and art objects, all of which looked like they belonged in a museum. One object in particular, an elaborate sterling silver espresso machine, caught Via's eye.

The machine had been a gift to Delacante on his sixty-fifth birthday from Dominic Galanti, the night before Delacante had him killed. It was meant to be a token of respect, a peace offering, really (the thing cost fifteen grand), which Galanti hoped might gain him some consideration in the power grab he correctly suspected was coming. Unfortunately for him, Delcante partnered with Tony Brassi and Al Salerno to wipe out Galanti and his crew, along with the Franzi and Morrelli gangs, in a war that lasted less than two weeks.

Via had been at that party as part of Brassi's security. He was too young then to do the heavy lifting, so he spent the following days shuttling the big muscle all over town and disposing of bodies at night. He kept his cool—"Johnny Via's kid"—well enough to get his own street crew afterward. He had never felt so pumped in his life.

He learned quickly, anxious to impress his old man, even more anxious to earn big money. He was arrested here and there on chump charges—car theft, assault, arson, breaking and entering—but nothing stuck. He had never been indicted or spent more than a few hours in jail, thanks to Brassi's chief counsel, Benny Boninno, a smart and crooked lawyer with a degree from Northwestern University and the connections hobnobbing with those wealthy Wasps had gained him. It was those connections that eventually landed Boninno a County Court judgeship and the wherewithal to help out his fellow *goombahs* whenever they needed it. Boninno had helped grease Via's way into law school, and he became a role model for the kind of success Via hoped to achieve for himself.

But it was that night at Delacante's when things first began to come together, and as he stared at the memories reflected in the espresso machine, he tried not to think about the way things had actually turned out.

Down the hallway from which he had come, he heard the uneven clicking of someone's heels and went out to see a man limping toward him from the dark end of the hall. As the guy drew closer to the light, he saw the familiar face of Jimmy "The Razor" Rizzo. He knew Rizzo, too, from the old days. He had given Rizzo that limp.

Rizzo was thin and short—shorter on one side than the other was the wiseass joke—with an angular face, sharp and rigid, as if cut from stone. His eyes were hard, too, and when he glared at Via the hate came off him like heat.

As usual he was wearing a suit and tie, the gentleman mobster, hair combed with Vaseline and parted with a knife. He brushed past Via and limped into a room just off the foyer, leaving behind a trail of Old Spice.

Rizzo was *sottocapo* to Delacante, and Via knew he had ambitions to be more. If the Delacante Family had kidnapped the Brassi girl, Rizzo was likely the one behind it. Talking to the old man with his underboss in the room would make things more difficult.

After a few minutes, Rizzo opened the door and grudgingly waved Via in.

"He ain't well."

"You don't look so good yourself, Jimmy."

"You wouldn't be here, it was up to me."

"Sure. But it isn't, is it?"

"You finish fast and get the fuck out."

"I'll finish when the Don's finished."

Rizzo led Via toward the old man, who sat near a window in a large, tan wingback chair looking out at the grounds of his palatial estate. Sitting there in a worn brown sweater, liver-spotted hands folded in his lap, he looked more like a retired waiter than the boss of Chicago's second-largest crime family.

Rizzo motioned for Via to stop and went over and bent to whisper something in Delacante's ear. The old Don listened impatiently, then brushed him away. Via waited while Rizzo skulked to a far corner of the room.

The old Don hacked a wet cough and reached for a tissue on the table next to him and spit into it. Then he directed Via to the chair across from him.

"Don Delacante. Thank you for seeing me."

Delacante squinted through clouded eyes. "Frankie. It's been a long time."

"Yes, Don Delacante."

"You look older. How long has it been?"

"Too long."

"Yes, then I must look older, too," the old Don said, a faint smile on his lips. "The years can be cruel, don't you think?"

"They can, but I'm glad to see you looking so well."

"I look like shit!" Delacante said in a surprisingly strong voice. He flicked a weathered hand in Rizzo's direction. "They think because my body is weak, I am weak. But my mind is a diamond, so don't use false flattery to try to get what you want from me." The old man wagged his finger. "Capisce?"

"Si, capisce."

"And you did come to ask for something, didn't you? I don't see you all this time and you suddenly drop by for grappa?"

"Your mind *is* a diamond, Don Delacante."

"I warned you about flattery." Delacante motioned for Via to move closer and whispered to him. "How does Rizzo look to you? Impatient, no? He can't wait for me to die."

Via glanced over and saw Rizzo staring back, rocking slowly on his heels.

"You remember how he got that limp? I think he would like to see you dead, too. No?"

"The feeling's mutual," Via said.

"Still a hard-ass like your old man."

Via began to speak, but the old Don raised a hand to silence him. "We talk while we walk."

Delacante summoned Rizzo, who brought him a cane and helped him up, giving Via a surly look as he did. Then he went back to his corner to sulk. The old man slipped his arm under Via's and they stepped out onto the porch and descended some stairs to an expansive lawn as smooth as a putting green.

"The doctors say I have to walk. My constitutional, my

daughter calls it. I tell her the only constitutional I know is the one the Feds tried to nail me on back in ninety-nine."

"I remember."

"Wasn't for you, they might've done it. You was a good lawyer, Frankie. Too bad, I could use you again."

"You have problems?"

"Remember Johnny Fish?"

Via didn't.

"Johnny Fischetti," Delcante reminded him. "Twenty years ago. Went missing."

"Oh, Fischetti, sure. Nobody knew what happened to him."

"Nobody still don't. But it ain't stopped the cops from wondering about it. So now what happens? His little brother, Joey, gets nabbed buttlegging smokes from Canada. Small-time shit, but he's already carrying some assault warrant, so he's looking at some time. Thing is, this old-time copper remembers about Johnny and wants to know what Joey knows about it. Joey don't know nothin'—Christ, he was ten years old—but he's gotta tell the cops something to save his ass. And this old-time cop is coaching him, so he says maybe Carmine Delacante was involved."

"They're sniffing around again?"

"Like a dog in my ass. Ancient history. They ain't got enough to do, they gotta dig up the dead?"

"You know the statutes. Murder lasts forever."

"Yeah? Maybe someone should tell that to Joey Fischetti."

The old Don led Via across the lawn into a lush garden of flowers so perfect they might have been plastic.

"See this? A Carmine rose," he said, pointing to a pink flower with his cane. "My daughter's invention." He waved the cane in an arc. "All this. Breeds them like the children she never had. It's a sad thing not to have a son, but not to have a grandson is a *tragedia*."

"Yes."

"You have children, Frankie?"

"A daughter."

"A girl," Delacante said, rubbing his chin as if contemplating some great mystery. "Well, daughters are good in your old age."

"Don Delacante, I came to speak with you."

"Yes, yes, we can't talk all day about flowers like a couple of *fanooks*, can we? So tell me before age takes me."

"Tony Brassi asked me to see you."

"Brassi!" the old man barked and spit on the ground, his avuncular facade now gone. "You're on record with him again? You want back in the business, you should come to me."

"It's only temporary. He hired me to represent him."

"*Represent* him," Delacante sniffed. "Rizzo used to represent me, now he makes deals on his own. Thinks I don't know."

Via glanced back at Rizzo, who was still stone-faced behind the glass outer door.

"Lorraine Lee," Delacante said.

Via grunted like he cared.

"That one," the old man said, pointing to a rose with his cane. "Beautiful, no?"

"Yes, beautiful."

"So you speak for Brassi?"

"Only on this matter."

"Then you should speak now. I have no time for Tony Brassi, even when he speaks through you. I shoulda clipped him years ago."

A deep cough shook the old Don's body and Via felt a bony hand tighten on his arm.

"Brassi also has a daughter, Don Delacante."

"And what is this Brassi's daughter to me?"

"This is what he wants me to speak to you about."

Delacante reached out to another rose bush and broke off a

dead twig. He held it up to his spectacles for a moment and then tossed it away.

"His daughter is missing," Via said.

Delacante shrugged. "Maybe she ran away."

"He thinks somebody snatched her. He's looking for . . . information."

"Information?"

"Anything you can give him."

Delacante stopped walking and bent stiffly to smell a white rose. "And why does Brassi think I have such information?"

"You're a powerful man, you have many connections."

"My connections are well known to Brassi. He should ask them himself."

"He asks for your help out of respect."

"Respect." The old man spat again. "From Brassi? He has no respect." He plucked the white rose and stuck it through a buttonhole in his sweater.

"Information," he scoffed. "He thinks I nabbed his daughter, no?"

"Because of the upcoming negotiations."

"Negotiations? You still talk like a shyster. Since when did you ever see Tony Brassi negotiate? All he knows is threats."

"That's why he thinks maybe you have her," Via said, wondering if Delacante knew about the books.

Delacante waved a feeble hand in the air. "I don't need no threats to deal with Tony Brassi. Only a shitbag like him would nab someone's kid to get what he wants."

The old man began coughing again and Via helped him to a nearby bench.

"Jimmy Razor," the old Don said, pointing toward the house, "thinks like Brassi. Confuses muscles with brains." He straightened up, his breathing shallow. "I hope you are wrong about this kidnapping. This would destroy the peace between the families. Then where are we? It ain't like the old days, Frankie. Everyone wants a piece of the pie now. The spics, the niggers, even the kikes. We ain't alone no more. That's why the three families divided it years ago. It's the only way we can keep what we got. It's our heritage. Maybe we each gotta settle for just a piece, but at least it's an Italian pie. This, even Brassi should understand."

"They say Salerno is hungry, too."

"Yes, hungry men do foolish things."

A constricted sound came from Delacante's throat and he wiped his mouth with the red kerchief around his neck. He surveyed the garden with chalky eyes. "Roses in September," he said, "all of this will be dead soon."

The meeting was finished.

"It was good of you to see me, Don Delacante."

The old man shrugged. "I know nothing of this girl, this Brassi's daughter. Only that she is unfortunate to have such a man for a father. This you may take back to Tony Brassi."

"As you wish." Via felt his options narrowing, not knowing if it was a good thing or not.

"This is dangerous business, Frankie. Especially you're a civilian now. You remember what your old man used to say? 'You ain't connected, you ain't protected.' Watch I don't have to send flowers for you."

"Maybe you'll have to send them for Brassi."

Delacante removed the rose from his buttonhole and handed it to Via. "For your daughter," he said.

Via left the old Don in his garden and headed back toward the house. Jimmy Rizzo was still waiting inside the doorway.

"You come here to say your good-byes? Or you got something else on your mind?"

"That's between me and your boss."

"Still the hard ass, Via."

"Some things never change."

"Some things," Rizzo said. "Others are changing as we speak. You got business with the Don, you see me first. I handle his business now."

"That's not what he says."

"He don't always know what he's saying. That's why you come to me first." Rizzo shepherded Via back to the front door. "I don't expect to see you here again."

"We'll see each other again, Jimmy," Via said, stepping outside. "I look forward to it."

"Stick your nose where it don't belong, you're gonna lose it." Rizzo slammed the door behind him.

Via sat in his car in the gathering darkness, sorting things in his mind. Delacante could be ruthless but he followed the old ways, children were off limits. It was clear he didn't have the girl. Rizzo, however, was another matter. And Delacante was right about Salerno—he was capable of anything.

He started the Caddy and pulled out and saw the beige Volvo again in his rearview. It was laying back about ten car lengths, not a smart thing, leaving too much room to get through an intersection on the yellow if it had to.

He made a left at the next street without signaling and was actually forced to slow so the Volvo didn't lose him when it made the turn. A fucking amateur.

Via increased his speed, sticking to the side streets. It was getting dark, but he didn't turn his lights on. Neither did the Volvo, but it was still back too far. Finally, Via took a sharp right and then another into an alley and waited while the tail went by. Definitely an amateur.

CHAPTER 9

Tony Brassi sat behind his desk, chin jutting like Mussolini.

"What news you got for me?"

"Delacante doesn't have her," Via said.

"What makes you so sure?"

"Nothing in it for him. He's old and sick and knows he hasn't much time left. I don't think he's interested in negotiating a bigger piece to leave to Jimmy Razor."

Brassi grinned and reached into a drawer and brought out a bottle of cognac, his Movado glinting like a mirror, reminding Via of the one he had to sell on eBay so he could pay child support.

"You saw Rizzo, huh?" he said, filling a crystal glass halfway. He called over to Bronco Lucci, who as usual was sitting on the sofa, shovel feet on the coffee table in front of him. "Hey, Bronco, you know Jimmy Razor?"

"Fuckin' gimp."

"You know, your boy here gave him that limp."

"Fuck him, too."

Brassi smirked at Via and sipped his cognac. "So Delacante? What, he's dying?"

"Rizzo thinks so," Via said.

"Whatta you think?"

"Jimmy's counting on it."

"You think Rizzo's got the balls to snatch my kid without the old man's okay?"

121

"He's ambitious. Maybe the old man doesn't know."

"Maybe? More fuckin' maybes? *Maybe* I send Tessa to visit your kid."

The mention of Meggie brought Via's blood to a boil. "What do you want from me? Am I a fucking mind reader?"

"See if you can read mine," Brassi growled.

"Look, we don't know anything for sure."

"So what're you doin' sittin' on your ass then? Take Bronco and go bring Rizzo. Bronco, get Tessa in here."

Lucci slid his feet off the coffee table. "He's home with a broken arm, or somethin'."

"Oh, yeah, that's right," Brassi said, glaring at Via.

"You don't even know if Rizzo has her, for Christ's sake," Via said.

"That's why I'm gonna find out."

"You rush into it, you could get her killed."

"You think I give a shit about that little bitch!"

"You care about your books? If Rizzo has her, he's got the flash drive. Why hasn't he used it yet?"

"The fuck do I know."

"That's what I'm saying."

"I ain't waitin' for nobody. Especially some piss-ant like Jimmy Razor. I let that fuck blackmail me, might as well spread my cheeks and bend over."

Brassi was up and moving now. Lucci's eyes followed him like a tennis ball.

"When I find out, whoever it is, he's dead. I don't care who it is."

"I'll take care of him," Lucci said.

Brassi stopped pacing and spun on him. "You have to find him first!" He glowered at Via. "What the fuck you still doin' here?"

"I need some money to spread around," Via said, hoping he

122

sounded matter-of-fact about it. "Nobody talks for free."

Brassi threw up his hands. "I knew it. This little bitch just keeps costing me."

He went to a painting of the Capitoline hills on the wall beside Caesar Augustus. He pulled it back and opened a safe and withdrew some packets of cash, then tossed the bound bills to Via, who stashed them inside his jacket and got up to leave.

"Hey. I expect return on my money," Brassi said.

"Sure, I'll get receipts."

Brassi thrust a finger at him. "You bring the books, asshole. You bring the fuckin' books."

"What do you mean, you lost him?" Harry Soltis demanded.

Billy Carlyle cowered in a chair before him, twisting a Red Sox cap in his hand. Mickey Finley stood against a far wall, nipping from his flask.

"I told you," Carlyle squeaked.

"I know what you told me. I want to know *how.* How the fuck did you lose him? How many ten-year-old, white Coupe DeVilles are on the goddamn street?"

"Harry, he's not a gumshoe," Finley said.

"I think it's a Two Thousand Four," Carlyle said.

Soltis threw his hands up. "Jesus Christ."

He went across the room and stood looking out the window so he wouldn't have to look at Carlyle. The sun was setting and he glanced at his watch. There was something happening out there, something that could get him on the ballot, maybe get him elected, and he couldn't do anything with it. He was running out of time. Three candidates had already declared. By the time he got in, the big donors would already have chosen sides.

"Billy's doing the best he can," Finley said, going over to the kid.

Soltis twisted around. "You get back out there and find him!"

Billy looked at the floor.

"You hear me?"

"Hold on, Harry," Finley said. "Billy? What's the matter?"

"It's just . . . well, this guy isn't . . . I mean, what's he doing talking to gangsters? He almost twisted some guy's arm off."

"How do you know they were gangsters?" Soltis demanded.

Finley put his hand on Billy's shoulder. "Like I told you, the kid's smart."

"I didn't sign on for this, Mickey," Billy whined. "I have a Masters in Political Science, for God's sake."

Soltis folded his arms across his chest and scowled at Carlyle. "Christ, he's scared."

"Billy once faced down Hillary Clinton," Finley said. "This boy is no coward. Are you, Billy?"

"But they're crooks."

"Don't be naive, Billy. You know politicians."

"But they don't kill people."

"Billy, someday I'll tell you how old Joe Kennedy won young Jack's first senate race."

"Nobody's going to die," Soltis barked at Carlyle. "But you don't keep an eye on that sonofabitch, you'll wish to hell you had."

Nicky stared at the pile of cash on his desk, trying not to go giddy.

"You robbing banks now?" he asked Via.

"It's bribe money."

"How much?"

"Fifty gees."

"This is what fifty thousand dollars looks like?" Nicky ran his hands over the money like it was mink. "This Brassi's money?"

"Used to be."

"Jesus."

Via reached in and picked up a handful of hundreds and put them in his pocket. "Take out your back pay. Then take the rest of it to this address." He flipped a matchbook on top of the cash. "Give it to a woman named Dee. Ask her to put it in her safe. I don't want it here if The Pig's boys come back."

"Why don't you just pay him now? Get him off your back."

"Fuck him. I don't like being strong-armed. You respond to that shit, it just gets worse."

"You should know."

"That fat prick's the least of my worries. I've got bigger problems with Salerno."

Nicky was already counting out the money, but stopped abruptly. "What about Salerno?"

"Looks like it's come down to him."

"You think he has the girl?"

"Brassi thinks so. It's as good a guess as any."

Nicky set the money aside, started to speak, stopped himself, then cleared his throat and started again. "I know a guy works for Salerno."

"Lots of guys work for him. So what?"

"So maybe I can help."

"Help what?"

"This guy owes me."

Via shook his head. "Won't help anything, both of us getting killed."

"I'm worried about Meggie, too, you know."

"Forget it. This isn't musical theater."

Nicky jumped up. "Fuck you." He went over to the new coffeemaker and poured himself a cup.

"Look," Via said. "This is Al Salerno we're talking about. This is serious shit here."

"You think I'm not serious? I couldn't live with myself if anything happened to her."

"You do this, you might not live to regret it."

Nicky turned to face him. "I already regret it. But I'm going to do it anyway."

"You don't know what you're getting into."

"If I knew, I wouldn't be doing it."

"No, you wouldn't."

"So, you'd better take the offer before I smarten up."

Via waved a hand in the air. "Don't say I didn't warn you."

"Do I ever complain?"

"Christ. How well do you know this guy? You tell him what we're doing, we could all end up dead."

"We partied together a few times."

"He's gay?"

"What do you think?"

Via pinched the bridge of his nose and rubbed his eyes. "Christ."

"Look, he's not out. He's got as much to hide as we do."

"He's a closet fag?"

The blood rose in Nicky's face. "Yeah. I guess Salerno's not as open-minded as you are."

"All right, all right," Via said. "So, why does this guy owe you?"

"Because he came out to me. Haven't you been listening?"

"I don't get it."

"Trust me, you don't have to."

Via took a seat in Nicky's chair. "Look, Brassi's impatient, he wants Rizzo too."

"That's what I mean. We need to work both ends. Maybe I can get my guy to snoop around Salerno while you deal with Rizzo. Might speed things up."

Via ran his hand across his chin. "Yeah, maybe so. I've been thinking about a way to make that happen, too."

"With Rizzo?"

"Listen. He's Delacante's bag man, right? And Como International washes money for Delacante, right?

"So?"

"So Rizzo makes a delivery to C.I. every week. When he makes the next one maybe I can get Brassi to tell him he's canceling the big sitdown. Get Brassi to tell him his daughter's missing . . . no, he thinks she ran away . . . and he won't do anything until he finds her."

"I don't follow."

"Rizzo can't wait indefinitely, can he? He knows Brassi's sniffing around. If he has the kid, he has to use her soon."

"And you think delaying the meeting might force him into the open?"

"It might. He's the anxious type. Either way, I don't have a better idea and the longer this takes, the longer Meggie's in danger. I figure it's worth a shot."

"So is my idea," Nicky said. He poured another cup of coffee and brought it over and handed it to Via. "When do we start?"

CHAPTER 10

Via left Nicky to call his Salerno contact and went out to his Caddy, which was parked behind a CPD cruiser, which wasn't there when he pulled in. The two uniforms got out as he reached for his door.

"You Via?" the taller of the two asked.

"Which Via?"

"Yeah, I heard you was wise."

"What's this, a Two Thousand Five?" the other cop asked.

"What're you, a collector?"

"Yeah, we're collectin' you," the tall cop said. He looked like his feet hurt. "Prosecutor's office wants you downtown."

"What kinda mileage this thing get?" the shorter cop asked.

"The expensive kind."

"You can ride with us or follow us," the tall cop said.

The shorter cop was peering in at the Caddy's interior. "Leather upholstery, huh?"

"Forget the car," the tall cop said to his partner. Then to Via: "What'll it be?"

Via held up his car keys. "I'll take the leather upholstery."

"Hey, Carl, how 'bout I ride with this guy?" the short cop said.

The tall cop gave him the death look. "I told you, forget the goddamn car."

★ ★ ★ ★ ★

Harry Soltis didn't bother to look up from his computer screen when the cops brought Via in and left him standing on the Seal of the State of Illinois carpet.

"You know, Via, you have a thicker file than Courtney Love. Can't figure out why you were never convicted, all the shit you were into."

"You bring me here to talk about incompetence in the prosecutor's office?"

"How'd you ever get a law license?"

"Same way you did. Connections."

Soltis pulled his glasses off his ears and jabbed a finger at Via. "You're on thin ice here and you're going to fall through. It's just a matter of time."

"Everything is," Via said, being cool. But he knew Soltis was right; all it took was one slip up and his skating days were over.

"You know, Via, I don't give two shits about you. You die tomorrow, the world's a better place. But you're playing with Karen's and Megan's welfare here, and that I do definitely care about."

"Think I don't? I'm doing everything I can to keep them out of it."

"Are you, smartass? Ask Karen if she thinks you're doing enough."

"What's this about?"

"A friend of yours. One Bobby Albanese, a.k.a. Bobby Bat, a.k.a. Bobby the Slugger."

"What about him?"

Soltis put his glasses back on and leaned forward in his chair. He told Via about Albanese's visit to Karen, growing more agitated, more red-faced, until veins were popping from his forehead and he was standing over his desk shouting: "So don't tell me you're keeping them out of it!"

"Tell Karen it won't happen again," Via said. Goddamn Albanese. Another hard-ass with a hard-on. Brassi behind it, keeping him on his toes, reminding him what was at stake.

"Fucking right it won't. I'm ready to pull in the whole guinea lot of you."

"That'll just get Karen and—"

"Can that shit. I don't believe you. You'd better get this closed out in forty-eight hours, or I'm taking you down with Brassi and the rest. I figure you're already an accessory to crime and I'm damn sure I can find worse to pin on you."

"Look—"

"Get out of my office. You're wasting time. In two days you're just another greaseball in the fire."

"Whose money is it?" Dee asked, frowning into the open briefcase on the bar.

"He just wants you to keep it for him, put it in your safe."

"Keep it for him? What am I, a bank?"

"Don't worry, he knows how to return a favor."

"That's what this is, a favor?"

Nicky shrugged. "I'm just the delivery boy."

"You work for him, huh?"

"I think of it as my karma."

"Why me?"

"What can I say? He trusts you."

"He doesn't even know me."

"Yeah, but the people he does know, he doesn't trust."

"That makes a lot of sense."

"Welcome to my world."

"He always do stuff like this?"

"What do you expect? He's a Capricorn."

"Oh, well, that explains the stubbornness and authoritarian attitude all right."

Nicky broke into a wide smile. "I'm an Aquarius, myself. Incurable romantic."

"Try getting married. That'll cure you."

"I bet you're a Libra."

"Sagittarius with Libra rising."

The front door opened and a guy wandered in. Dee watched him closely as he went to a seat at the far end of the bar. She closed the briefcase and set it next to her on the floor.

"This makes me very nervous," she said.

She went along the bar and tended to the guy, taking her time, slowing things down while she considered what she was getting herself into.

"This is a nice place," Nicky said when she came back. "Could use some greenery, though."

"I don't think your boss liked it. Said the old place was better. Back when he used to work in this neighborhood, I guess."

"He told you about that?"

"He only mentioned it. I figured there was more to it."

Nicky rolled his eyes. "You don't know the half of it."

"I'm not so sure I want to know.'

"Ah, he's a stand-up guy. Trust me. When I came out, my parents, my sister, all the other cousins . . . well, Frank was the only one in the family stood by me. Always watched out for me when we were kids, too. Let me work on his street crew, even though the Don didn't like it. Got me out of a lot of scrapes. Believe me, I could tell you stories."

"Oh, yeah? You like whiskey sours?"

Nicky smiled again. "How about rum?"

"Rum sour coming up."

While she mixed the drink, Dee asked Nicky more questions, starting general then working into the particulars. She filled a large glass and he took a good swig, and when he set it back down she topped it off from the blender, then did it again, until

Nicky was answering her questions like an old school chum.

"It was a long time ago. Back then, this neighborhood belonged to the Brassi Family and the Delacante Family. Their territories butted up against each other right here at Halsted Street. Poor neighborhood but good for prostitution and gambling, numbers mostly.

"To keep the peace, Brassi and Delacante divided Halsted Street right down the white line. Frank was running a street crew for Brassi on the west, and a guy named Jimmy Rizzo was running one for Delacante on the east. Both just kids, really.

"For the most part, the crews and numbers runners respected the boundaries, but the pimps and whores went wherever the money was. One summer Rizzo's numbers were running bad and to make up for his losses he decided to raise his kickback from the pimps. Well, they wouldn't have any of that and moved across the white line to Frank's side to ply their trade. This of course didn't set with Rizzo, and one day he got fed up and grabbed this whore who crossed the line, one I think he was sweet on anyway, and started roughing her up, screaming for her to get back over to his side. She wouldn't, so he pulls out this straight razor and starts slashing the poor girl right there in the middle of Halsted Street, like he's Jack the Ripper. The whore is screaming, Rizzo's screaming, the whole neighborhood is hanging out their windows."

"Jesus Christ."

"Frank happens to be making his rounds just then, hears the commotion, and comes running. He sees Rizzo out in the street slicing this poor girl like filet and pulls out his piece and orders him to stop. Needless to say, this kind of thing is bad for business."

"Bad for the whore, too."

"So Frank tells Rizzo two, three times, but Rizzo's crazy. He's Sweeney Todd. There's blood flying everywhere, people running around screaming. So Frank does the only thing he can do—shoots Rizzo in the foot."

"He shot him?" Dee's eyes were wide.

"Yeah, but Rizzo deserved it."

"Sure, because of the whore."

"No, because he almost got himself and Frank both clipped." She arched her eyebrows at him.

"Yeah, the Dons got very upset about the whole thing, one Family blaming the other. Like I said, bad for business. Brassi wanted satisfaction because Rizzo nearly brought down the whole operation, and Delacante thought he was owed because one of his good earners was crippled now. Finally, to keep the peace, they make a Solomonic decision and decide since the incident happened in the middle of Halsted Street, on the white line more or less, it was in neutral territory. Then, to prevent any reprisals, Delacante sends Rizzo to Vegas to learn the casino business, and Brassi pulls Frank off the street and sends him to work with his counsel, Benny Boninno. Well, Boninno takes Frank under his wing, one thing leads to another, and Frank ends up in college. He does good, so Boninno decides he'd make a good lawyer, uses some local judges he owns to get him into law school."

Nicky set his empty glass on the bar and Dee filled it again.

"That's how he became a Mob lawyer?"

"He didn't have a choice. That's the way it works. You get something, you give something. But he became a good one. Came to represent all the Families. Had a good run, made some good money."

"So what happened?"

"You remember awhile back the Feds busted a bunch of aldermen with Outfit connections, some cops, too?"

"Operation Monkey Wrench," Dee said, remembering what the bartender told her the night she first met Via.

133

"Right." Nicky took a sip and patted the foam from his upper lip with a bar napkin. "Well, the Feds busted some of the Outfit's most prominent members, who just happened to be some of the most guilty, too. Chicken shit charges, though—bribery, extortion, influence peddling. The kind of stuff makes Chicago 'The City that Works,' but illegal nevertheless."

"And Frank represented them?"

"Did a hell of a job. Feds had them dead to rights on RICO, but Frank argued they had been wiretapped illegally and the jury agreed. Problem was, afterward there were rumors about tampering. Threats, bribery, that kind of thing. So the Feds naturally suspected somebody who worked for the Outfit. Frank was an attractive target because he beat them in court. They never could prove anything, but they raised enough questions to get the attention of the Bar Association, which wasn't difficult since its chairman was one of the Monkey Wrench prosecutors Frank embarrassed in court."

"That's quite a history," Dee said.

"You can look it up."

"I mean his."

"You don't know the half of it."

CHAPTER 11

Adam's was the kind of place where a man with a certain desire for discretion could feel comfortable and safe. More restaurant than bar, it was tastefully modest from the outside, but inside it was dim, neo-classical, and ostentatious, with private cabanas in the bathrooms and heavy gold drapes across the doorways. At nine o'clock at night it was packed and Via hoped he wouldn't see anyone he knew.

"And what are the chances of that?" Nicky said, as they waited to be seated in the bar. "Or is there something you haven't told me?"

Via was wearing a white t-shirt and jeans with black work boots and hoped he didn't look like one of those guys from the old Village People. The maitre d' came over and handed him a blue blazer festooned with the club's logo, an abstract symbol he didn't want to try to decipher.

"I told you to wear a sport coat," Nicky said. "Now don't you feel out of place?"

"That a trick question?" He felt like a dog in a room full of cats.

"Come on, relax. There are more tough guys here than a Bears game."

"Guys with the Outfit?"

"Why not, Sonny Cheeks is. Everybody needs a place to go."

Via eyeballed him. *"Cheeks?"*

"It's not what you're thinking. His name's Sonny Cicci.

135

Sonny *Cheeks.*"

A booth opened in the bar. Nicky ordered a daiquiri, Via ordered Jack straight up.

"So you've been here before?" Via asked, just to make conversation.

"Used to come here all the time when I was still managing at Saks."

"Oh, before the, uh . . . incident . . . with your boss's husband."

Nicky gave him a withering look. "Back when I could *afford* it."

Via rolled his eyes. "Listen, I'll make it up to you. We find Brassi's daughter, maybe I can get some more money out of him."

"If we're still alive."

That set a silence between them. They drank quietly while Via studied the crowd and Nicky watched the door. After a few minutes, Via got up to go to the men's room but two guys strolled by arm-in-arm headed in the same direction and Via decided he could wait.

Nicky grinned. "Want me to hold your hand?"

They both gazed around the place some more, like they might find something in common they could talk about.

"So, how are things with Karen?" Nicky finally said. "She calm down yet?"

"What do you think?"

Nicky sighed. "Sometimes you just can't please them."

"Things a bit rocky between you and your . . . partner?" Via asked, just to change the subject.

"Craig. Why is it you can't seem to remember that?"

"Maybe because there's a new one every month."

"Oh, so, we're going to compare relationships now?"

Via put a hand up. "Fuck it, ignore me. I'm in a bad mood."

"I usually do. And you always are. Have you ever considered talking to someone? You know, you have anger issues."

"And I thought I was just pissed off."

"I'm serious. I have this great therapist. You wouldn't know it, but I used to have anger-management problems, too."

Via swallowed some Jack. "I don't have a problem. I just know a lot of assholes who do."

"See, that's a problem right there—denial. The first step dealing with an illness is admitting you have it."

Via glared at him over his glass. "So, now I'm sick?"

"Well, not sick. But you have to admit you don't exactly have a healthy lifestyle."

"Like yours, you mean?"

"See, there's that anger again. Don't worry, I don't take it personally. I used to be angry all the time myself. But since Dr. Melman put me on Paxil . . . well, I still have problems with low self-esteem, of course." Nicky sipped his drink. "Probably why I still work for you."

Via couldn't keep from grinning. "I sense some hostility in your tone."

"There you go. Just talking to me, you're already more in touch with your feelings."

"Yeah, now I feel like having another drink."

Nicky looked around for the waiter but someone else caught his eye and he jumped up, waving and calling across the room.

Via watched a tall, gaunt man in a white Italian knit shirt and black leather jacket coming toward them. He had a sallow, pocked complexion and greased-back hair the color of licorice, too perfectly black to be natural—Via put him in his mid-forties—and wore large black-framed sunglasses with someone's gold plastic logo on the temples. When he removed them, Via noticed a glazed, distant look in his eyes. He settled next to Nicky and peered nervously about the room.

"You didn't tell me he was gonna be here," Sonny Cheeks said, his gaze settling on Via.

"What's the problem? We're all friends, aren't we?" Nicky touched his wrist and Cheeks jerked away.

"I remember you, Via. Used to be a shyster. Now what, you're a security guard or somethin'?"

"Now, Sonny," Nicky said, "you know Frank's a private investigator."

Cheeks stuck a cigarette in the middle of his goatee and searched his pockets for a light. "So what're you investigatin', the homosexual lifestyle?"

"Yeah. Your boss hired me to root out any queers on his payroll."

"Ignore him, Sonny," Nicky said, glaring at Via. "It's all in confidence."

Cheeks looked away. "Can I get a drink here?" he shouted at a passing waiter. "Stoli, rocks."

"Listen, Sonny, we'd like your help with something," Nicky said.

"That's what you said on the phone. You also said there's money."

"Yeah, well, here's the thing. We're looking for a girl."

"There's a switch."

"This girl is special," Via said.

"She always is."

"I'm not talking about some hooker here. This is a young girl, a kid."

The waiter brought the Stoli and Nicky snatched some matches from the tray and lit Cheeks's cigarette.

"Old, young, in-between. We got 'em all," Cheeks said, raising the glass to his lips.

Via noticed needle marks on his wrist. "Well, this kid's missing."

"No shit. They all are. New picture on the milk carton every day."

Nicky signaled the waiter for another round and then spoke again to Cheeks. "Sonny," he said, glancing at Via, who nodded assent. "The missing girl? It's Tony Brassi's daughter."

Cheeks's eyes widened and he put his head back against the booth.

"That's right," Via told him. "And he'll pay real money to find her."

"Brassi's daughter? Man, it's a fucked-up world." Cheeks dragged on his cigarette.

"No one knows about this," Via said. "Word gets around, I'll make sure Brassi knows it came from you."

Cheeks pushed out his lips and filled the space between them with smoke.

"You hear what I said?" Via growled.

"Yeah, yeah." The waiter arrived with the second vodka and Cheeks gulped it down. "So what do you want from me?"

"We want you to ask around," Nicky said. "Brassi thinks one of the dons might've snatched her."

"You mean my boss? What the hell for?"

"Let us worry about that," Via said. "You just see what you can find."

"Fuck this. You think I'm gonna cop on Al Salerno? I look like I got a death wish?"

Via reached over and clasped his wrist and pushed up his sleeve. "What do you think this is?"

Cheeks jerked his hand free. "Fuck you."

"We're just asking you to snoop around," Nicky said. "If your boss has her, someone around him must know."

"I need a drink."

"Ten grand could buy a lot of fairy dust," Via said.

"What's with this asshole?" Cheeks said to Nicky.

Via considered reaching over and slapping the shoe polish out of Cheeks's hair. "Ever eat a lit cigarette, Sonny?" he said.

"This guy's a real ballbreaker," Cheeks complained.

"Forget him. I'm asking you to do me this favor," Nicky said. "What do you say, Sonny?"

"Fuck favor. Gimme the ten now. More if I find something."

"Half now and the rest when you give us something we can use," Via said.

"The fuck do you care? It's Brassi's dough, ain't it?"

"Yeah, but I don't like you."

Nicky gave Via the bug eye. He withdrew an envelope from his breast pocket and set it in front of Cheeks. "Don't take it personally, Sonny."

"Fuck you both."

Cheeks stood and crushed his smoke on the floor, put his sunglasses on, and slipped the envelope into his pocket.

"Don't spend it all in one place," Via said.

Nicky watched Cheeks leave, then snapped at Via: "You ever hear about catching flies with honey?"

Via dropped Nicky home and drove to his apartment. Coming up the street, he spied the tail again, sitting about half a block from his front door. He parked and went into the lobby. There was a back door that led out behind the building and he went through it and down the dark alley and came around the corner behind the Volvo. He kept low behind the cars along the curb, cut between them to the street side, and inched along the side of the car toward the driver's door. Stretching up, he could see the guy's head resting back against the seat.

Behind him, he heard a car approaching. He crouched back behind the bumper until it passed, slowing as it did, some guy inside gawking from the passenger seat. He watched until it went around the far corner and then eased out his .38 and slipped up to the side window and tapped sharply with the gun.

The driver jumped like a squirrel and let out a gasp Via heard through the glass. He motioned for the guy to lower the window.

"Don't kill me!" The guy's voice reminded him of the soprano in *Rigoletto*.

"Who the hell are you?"

"I didn't do anything."

"You've been tailing me."

"Please!"

Via reached into the guy's coat and pulled out his wallet. "Put your hands down. This isn't a stick-up."

He got a good look at him then. Skinny, baby-faced, scared as an altar boy caught sneaking the holy wine.

"Who do you work for?"

"What?"

He pushed the gun against the kid's pink cheek.

"Mickey Finley!"

"Who's he?"

"Just a political consultant. That's all."

Via slapped the Red Sox cap off the kid's head. "Who does *he* work for?"

"Don't. Please. The prosecutor's office. Harry Soltis."

"Soltis? No shit?"

Via put the gun away and slipped the kid's wallet into his jacket pocket. He stepped back, about to order him to get out, when he saw a car speeding toward them. He jumped beneath the Volvo's front bumper. Gunfire exploded and chunks of asphalt kicked up around him. The car's rear window shattered and the side mirror exploded. He heard metal piercing metal and a tire burst, then the car squealing into the distance.

He waited a few minutes to make sure the shooters were gone and then stood up to check himself.

"Hey, it's over," he shouted at the kid.

There was no answer. He heard sirens and saw lights blinking on in the buildings around him.

The CPD district station was like every police station Via had ever been in. The cops were the same, too. Like always, in a hurry to bring him in, slow to take his statement, and indifferent once they had it. Now they had him waiting for the watch commander to take his turn.

The desk sergeant motioned to an empty seat across from him and Via sat next to a woman with eyes like glass who was mumbling to herself, cursing someone named Chanteal. He closed his eyes and rested his head back against the wall and knew immediately it was a mistake. He jerked forward, not wanting to think about what might be congealing in his hair. The glass-eyed woman reached into her sweatshirt through the neck, digging around for something he hoped wasn't moving. When she brought her hand out and sucked her finger, he got to his feet.

The sergeant eyed him. "Hey!"

"Don't worry, I'm not going anywhere."

"You got that right." The sergeant squinted at him. "Don't I know you?"

"I've been around."

"I bet."

The station was filling up with the usual suspects. Via found a spot next to a file cabinet and leaned back to watch the circus and pass the time.

First, the drunk and drugged were dragged in, filling up most of the benches, playing musical chairs whenever someone got sent to the tank. Next came the whores, who lounged against the walls looking like they were still on duty, flirting and blowing kisses to the cops. Then the gangbangers were brought in and immediately shoved into holding cells, where their lawyers passed them advice and cigarettes through the bars. Finally, one by one the average citizens appeared: a Latino guy caught with a concealed handgun, some sullen teens nabbed driving a stolen car, a battered wife who stuck a serving fork into her husband's throat while he was sleeping.

Somehow the coppers managed to keep it all under control until some homeless guy trying to get locked up for the night threw a cursing fit and the entire crowd joined in. It took the cops several minutes to quiet the place, by which time the profanity reached a level that made even the desk sergeant wince. Via couldn't keep from smiling.

"Something funny?" the sergeant asked.

"Private joke."

"You know, I never forget a face."

"Yeah? Me neither."

"Where have I seen you before?"

"You don't want to know."

"I don't want to know, I wouldn't be asking."

Via scratched his head and smiled to himself. *The only difference between a cop and a gangster,* his old man always said, *is a badge.*

"You a wise ass or something? I asked you a question."

"You used to be in the 14th," Via said. "Worked the street back then. Busy district. Drugs, hookers, numbers. The holy trinity. Lots of money passed around." He let it sit there.

The sergeant dead-eyed him. "What the fuck do you know about it?"

"Just know a lot of cops who were on the take back then."

"What the hell you talking about?"

"Hey, it happens. No big deal. As long as no one finds out."

The cop reached into his shirt pocket and retrieved a pair of drugstore peepers. He balanced them on his nose and looked Via up and down again. "You kidding me?"

"Look at this face. What do you think?"

The front door banged open and a uniform with a lot of brass burst through. The sergeant jumped to his feet.

"Evening, Lieutenant."

The lieutenant looked around the crowded squad room. "Christ, what is it about full moons?" He removed his cap and wiped inside the brim with a handkerchief. "Which one's Via?"

"I am," Via said.

The lieutenant ignored him and ordered the sergeant: "Put him upstairs."

"Oowee. You is fucked," the woman with the glassy eyes yelled out to no one in particular. "Chanteal, you done fucked yo'self this time."

The sergeant led him to an interrogation room, ordered him to sit, and left. The room was empty except for a cold metal table and two metal chairs. The walls were a color that might once have been green and the ceiling was crossed with patched pipes spattered with a reddish sweat. The floor was scuffed and brown as dirt. At one end was a lone window of wired glass, shattered from the inside, a cobweb of cracks radiating from a point of impact about the height of a man's head. On the wall beside it someone had scrawled: *Cops . . . the largest street gang in America.* At the other end of the room, a smudged one-way mirror reflected Via's own battered image.

He wondered why it was cops always put you in this kind of box when they wanted you to talk. When the Outfit wanted something from a guy, they took him somewhere comfortable, wined and dined him, got him loosened up. This place made your sphincter tighten.

Next, they'd make him wait again, let the stark reality of broken plaster and cracked concrete sink in, maybe watch a cockroach crawl across the table, think about how it would feel to spend the remainder of your life in a place like this. He had come close more than once.

Like the time he chased some Latino guy off the roof of a five-story walk-up. Tony Brassi owned a string of restaurants back then and the guy had been dumb enough to rob one of them. Unfortunately for him, one of the busboys recognized him from the neighborhood and ratted him out for a hundred bucks and whatever goodwill he thought it might earn him.

Brassi told Via to take care of it, so he waited for the guy one night in the lobby of his apartment building, but the guy made him when he came in and sped off up the stairs like a scalded dog. Via chased him up the five flights, which almost killed him, until he finally cornered the kid on the roof. He was wheezing so hard he couldn't get to him before the kid tried to jump across to the building next door and, as luck would have it, landed in front of a squad car cruising the alley below. Via had to shimmy down a drain pipe, cut through backyards, and jump half a dozen fences to get away. He quit smoking for the hundredth time right after.

"Fucking Frank Via," the lieutenant said when he finally came in and sat across from him. "How the mighty have fallen." His voice was strained and roupy with fatigue.

"I already told downstairs what I know."

"Yeah, now tell me."

The cop crossed his legs, pants creased like a newspaper, shoes like chrome. He leaned back in his chair and gazed at Via with eyes that had seen it all before.

"It's in my statement," Via said.

"Fuck your statement. What about the victim?"

"What about him?"

"Who is he, for starters."

"Like I told them, some guy's been tailing me."

"Some guy?"

"Never saw him before. What's this about? Am I a suspect, or

145

you guys just get lonely on night duty?"

The lieutenant closed in, garlicky breath in Via's face.

"I don't know what you are. But let me tell you what I do know: I got a dead man behind the wheel of a car he appears to have been driving without a license, a wallet, or any other form of ID. I got a state prosecutor on his way here to talk to some ex-wiseguy he shouldn't care about, about some drive-by he shouldn't know about, because I also got some spy in my command who must've called him. I got two shooters driving around in a vehicle you can't identify because you were busy shitting your pants. And worst of all, I got heartburn from having my late-night dinner interrupted by all these things I suddenly got I don't know what to do with."

"Harry Soltis is on his way?"

The cop cocked his head. "You know how many prosecutors we got in this city? How'd you know it's Soltis?"

"Lucky guess."

"I know your record, Via. You ain't that lucky."

The lieutenant sparred with him awhile and Via played along, not cooperating exactly, but not challenging the copper's right to try to make him. The trick was to let the lieutenant feel like he was actually doing something—professional pride and all. That was the thing with cops, especially one the lieutenant's age, who knew by now it was all about just getting through the day, but his Boy Scout training wouldn't allow him to keep from trying to do his job along the way.

"You think you're a hard case, Via? Few nights in the drug tank, you'll go soft enough."

Over the cop's shoulder, Soltis's face appeared in the window in the door. He tapped on the glass and waved the lieutenant outside. The two talked for several minutes, Soltis doing most of it. Then the cop left and Soltis came in alone.

"You have every cop in the city on your payroll?" Via said.

"Only the ones in your neighborhood."

"So what is it, Harry, that gets you out of my ex-wife's bed this time of night?"

"You know why I'm here," Soltis said, sitting across from him. "You're done running this by yourself. I want to know what's going on. And don't give me that bullshit about protecting Megan. There's a gang war to deal with now."

"What gang war?"

"There are greaseballs shooting up the street in front of your place and one of them ends up dead. What's that look like to you?"

"Ineffective neighborhood policing?"

"You've got about thirty seconds before I charge you for withholding evidence."

"I don't think so, Harry."

Soltis got in his face. "Well, you'd better think so, asshole. I'm through fucking with you. I should've never held off in the first place."

"You should've never put a tail on me, either."

Soltis blinked and backed off a bit. "What are you talking about?"

"The kid you hired to follow me, Harry."

Via reached into his pocket, brought out Carlyle's wallet and tossed it on the table, and Soltis stopped blinking.

"Go ahead. Check the driver's license."

Soltis opened the wallet and the color drained from his face.

"The Department know you're working out-of-pocket, Harry?"

Soltis stared at the license and the air seemed to go out of him. Via waited, wanting it to last.

"This means nothing," Soltis huffed.

"It will when your boss finds out Carlyle was working for you."

"Who says he was working for me?"

"He did. Before he was killed doing your legwork. And one Mickey Finley can corroborate it."

"Don't count on it, Finley's old school."

"Yeah, me too. When I was mobbed up, I kept payrollers at the *Tribune*. I still keep in touch." He showed Soltis the business card the reporter had left on the bar the night he served fat Chizek.

Soltis's color was rushing back. He ran his hands through what was left of his hair. "You think anyone's going to believe you? You're a crook."

"Yeah, but you're a politician." Via got up to leave. "The thing about voters, Harry? If they can't believe the facts, they tend to believe the rumors."

Downstairs Via passed the desk sergeant again, who pretended to be busy with some papers, and left the station for home. The cops had brought him in a blue-and-white, so he flagged a cab. He ordered the cabby to circle the block before he got out but didn't see anything suspicious. The bullet-riddled Volvo had been towed away for evidence and now there was only space where Billy Carlyle breathed his last lungful of earthly air. There was no indication he had been there or what happened, except for the bullet divots in the asphalt outlined in white. Via figured the body was already being toe-tagged at the city morgue, just another gunshot victim without a name. He was certain Soltis wouldn't give Carlyle's wallet to the cops.

"Neighborhood's gone to hell."

Via's landlord, an elderly guy named Warren, was standing on the sidewalk wearing a tattered, blue terry cloth bathrobe, pale shins protruding below like sticks of chalk.

"Couldn't sleep after all the commotion. Phyllis is very upset," Warren said, meaning the tiny brown Schnauzer yanking the leash in his hand.

"Don't worry about it, it's over. Should be quiet the rest of the night."

"Better be. Can't have my tenants ducking stray bullets."

Via moved past him and up the front walk. "Go to bed, Warren."

"Can't have their girlfriends banging on my door all hours of the night, either."

Via stopped.

Warren hacked up a ball of phlegm and spat it on the sidewalk.

"Yep, she's up there," he said, wiping his mouth with the back of his hand. "Banged on my door and wouldn't take no for an answer. Some friends you got."

"Upstairs?"

"You get shot in the ears or something?"

Via moved down one step. "Don't get in the habit of letting people into my apartment when I'm not here, Warren. It could be dangerous."

Warren waved him off. "She don't look exactly dangerous."

"I mean for you."

Warren went even whiter and pivoted abruptly and dragged Phyllis back along the sidewalk.

Via hurried up to the second floor and put his key in the lock and opened the door. He heard a noise in the kitchen and when he got there Dee was standing on a chair trying to reach something in the cabinet above the refrigerator.

She was dressed in those tight jeans again and a short black sweater that rode up as she stretched and revealed the smooth creamy crescent of her hips. Her hair was put up in a casual way, held with a butterfly clip from which fine strands of saffron hair danced across the back of her neck. She nearly fell when he spoke.

"What are you doing here?"

"Trying to get a drink."

He helped her down and reached for the whiskey. "You know what happened?"

"Your landlord told me some guy got shot. There were cops all over the street when I got here."

"That doesn't scare you?"

"Hell, yes, it scares me. Why do you think I need a drink?"

He reached up again and got two glasses and poured them each two fingers. She threw hers back like a pro.

"You haven't answered my question," he said.

"You give me a suitcase full of money and you wonder why I'm here?"

"Look, it's not safe. Those guys were aiming at me."

"Think they'll be back?"

"Not anymore tonight."

Her shoulders relaxed. "You really have to stop pissing people off. I brought Chinese and beer. You have plates?"

He helped her set the table, liking the way she moved, those stiletto-toed shoes kicked into the corner, her toenails painted red. Liked her red lips, too, the lipstick ring they left on the bottle of Tsingtao, and the way she ate, no dainty nibbling like most women, not trying to impress him, eating like they already knew each other.

"You know who it was?" she asked between bites.

"Just a couple of guys don't like me."

"The guys who beat you up?"

"Don't worry, it's not their money."

"Whose is it, then?"

"It's better you don't know."

"I have this cash in my safe, but I'm not supposed to ask questions?"

"It's just for a short time."

"Yeah, well, that's how long we've known each other, so I guess we're past the small-talk phase."

"You're not in any trouble, if that's what you're worried about."

"I don't mind a little trouble, but I do mind being kept in the dark."

"I can't tell you anymore about it."

"Nicky said they threatened your daughter."

"Nicky talks too much."

"Ah, don't be too hard on him, I got him liquored up." She handed him another beer. "It's what I'm good at." Her eyes were as bright and brown as bourbon.

"A bartender with breasts. Just what every man needs."

"Except Nicky." She smiled at her own joke.

They chatted while they ate, Dee doing most of it, talking about nothing in particular, helping him relax. When they finished they left the mess and went to sit on the sofa in his small living room with some brandy Nicky had given him for Christmas. He put his head back against the cushions, the beer and brandy like a balm.

"If you want to talk, I can listen all night," she said.

"I told you, I can't."

She drew her legs up beneath her. "Say something nice, then."

His head was swimming with the booze and the smell of her hair. "Like what?"

"You forget how to sweet-talk a woman? Tell me I'm beautiful."

He lifted his head and moved toward her. Her lips were like one of Delacante's roses.

"You are."

"Well," she said, moving closer, "now we're getting somewhere."

CHAPTER 12

Harry Soltis lay on the sofa in his office, arm over his eyes, Billy Carlyle's wallet clutched in his hand. Mickey Finley sat in a chair staring off into space and gulped another snoot from his flask.

"Jesus Christ, Harry. Jesus Christ."

Soltis didn't move.

"My God. Why did they have to kill him? He's just a kid."

"They're mobsters, Mickey."

Finley shook his head. "You should've warned me. This isn't my area. You should've told me. I'm a political consultant, for God's sake."

"Shut up, Mickey."

"What am I going to tell that poor boy's parents?"

Soltis sprang upright, his Florsheims hitting the floor hard.

"His parents? What the hell are you talking about? You can't tell anyone anything. The press finds out about this, I'm ruined."

"How can you think of that at a time like this?"

Soltis was crimson. "How can I think of it? It's *your* job to think of it. What the hell am I paying you for!"

"Now, Harry, getting upset won't bring the poor lad back."

"Listen, dickhead, you'd better get your head straight. What do you think is going to happen if word gets out Carlyle was working for you when he got bumped?"

Finley's eyes saucered.

"Think about it. You'll be lucky to get a job passing out political pamphlets."

"Jesus Christ, Harry, this is a terrible mess."

"Tell me something I don't know."

"Mother of God. Poor Billy."

"It's time to worry about yourself, Mickey."

Finley cupped his chin in his hand and closed his eyes. After a minute, he got up and poured himself some coffee from a carafe on Soltis's desk. He added a healthy shot of whiskey from his flask, tasted it, added more, and then went back over and slumped into the chair again.

Soltis glared at Finley, twisting his law school ring and tapping his foot. "The body isn't getting any warmer," he hissed.

Finley lit his pipe and smoked pensively, sipping his coffee between puffs.

"Patience, Harry, patience," he finally said. "We have time. As long as Via doesn't say something they probably won't identify the body anytime soon. And, even if they do, they have no way of tying it . . . him . . . Billy, to you. Even if they can, we'll spin a story about, uh . . ."

"I'm on the edge of my seat."

Finley drank more coffee, a smile slowly forming on his lips. ". . . about this, this young crusader, working . . . voluntarily . . . undercover for this office."

Soltis put up his hand. "No, not for this office. For you, not for me. Remember?"

"Right, right. But not for me, either. Not at my direction. No, on his own. An ambitious, passionate young crusader, against his own boss's, my, advice. Trying to help the one man— you, Harry—he believed could stem the tide of drugs engulfing America's youth."

Soltis listened, jaw set, rubbing his hand across his chin.

"Sacrificing himself, Harry. A martyr for the cause."

Soltis rose slowly, his head bobbing like a rooster. "A hero."

"A *tragic* hero." Finley raised his cup like a salute. "A misguided but heroic effort. A tragic death *you* will make certain did not happen in vain." Finley beamed. "To this, you will pledge your campaign."

"Jesus. It might work."

"Might? Someday I'll tell you about LBJ's Texas campaign back in '54."

Jimmy Rizzo parked in the underground garage and rode the elevator up to Como International. He carried a bright metal briefcase, inside of which was a week's worth of laundry, just over two hundred thousand dollars.

It would be laundered now through one of C.I.'s legitimate businesses and come out the other end ten-percent lighter to cover Brassi's fees, a levy Rizzo considered insulting.

If it were up to him, things would be different. Old Man Delacante was wrong to put up with it, afraid to challenge Brassi, gone delicate and frail like one of his cherished roses. Well, soon he would go the way of roses. And Brassi would go, too. Soon everything would change. After the big sitdown, everything would be different.

When he pushed through C.I.'s polished wood doors he couldn't help but be envious again. The whole goddamn set-up was impressive, like the offices of some tycoon. Fucking Brassi. Rizzo knew him when he was just a street-level button man. Now he was living in the clouds like Donald Trump.

He limped toward the receptionist, Gail, he remembered, straightening his tie.

"Mr. Rizzo. How nice to see you again."

"I told you, call me Jimmy." He flashed a smile. "Would you let him know I'm here?"

"He's just finishing a meeting. I hope you don't mind waiting a few minutes."

"With such a beautiful view," he said, smiling again, "I don't mind at all."

She raised a tweezed and painted eyebrow and went back to her work.

Rizzo limped over to the waiting area, self-conscious now, and sat with the briefcase on his lap. Sitting there, he wished he had something to read, sitting there like a goddamn . . . delivery boy. He wondered if Brassi was actually in a meeting or just making him wait. He imagined him with his feet up on his big desk, laughing with Bobby Bat about how he had Jimmy Rizzo waiting like a school kid outside the principal's office.

He stood and strolled around the lobby, past the crystal and ceramics, the porcelain and jade, wanting to smash them into pieces, wanting to show Brassi he wasn't afraid of him, give him something to think about before the summit meeting.

He was staring out at Lake Michigan and wondering how far out you had to go to avoid the Coast Guard, when the receptionist's phone buzzed. She answered it and giggled and he thought he saw her glance at him when she did.

"Mr. Brassi will see you now," she said, still grinning.

Brassi was looking over his invoices when Rizzo came in. Bobby Albanese was standing off to the side like a soldier awaiting orders. Rizzo set the briefcase in front of Brassi and sat in his usual chair.

"How much you bring me?" Brassi asked, flipping the latches and thumbing through the bills.

"Two hundred and change."

"Not bad. Things'll pick up during the Series next month. Want a drink while you wait?"

"I'll pass."

"Count this," Brassi said to Albanese, who carried the case to a table across the room. "What? Too early for you?" he said to Rizzo.

Rizzo shrugged.

"I got some twenty-year-old scotch."

"I told you, I don't want it."

"You're refusing my hospitality now?"

"I gotta drink just so's you're not insulted?"

"Hey, Bobby, I think Jimmy doesn't want to drink with me."

"Have a drink," Albanese said, unpacking bills.

"Can we just get this done. I got things to do," Rizzo said.

Brassi drummed his fingers on the desktop. "Yeah, I bet you do."

"What's that supposed to mean?"

"What do you think it means? What're you so touchy about?" Brassi offered the humidor. "Have a cigar. Relax."

Rizzo waved it away.

"Don't drink, don't smoke," Brassi said, rolling a cigar between his fingers. "It's good you're worried about your health. Man worried about his health avoids doing stupid things."

Rizzo folded his arms across his chest and shifted in his chair. He called over to Albanese: "Hey, Bobby, what're you doin', countin' like a Jew?"

"You want it faster, next time bring more C-notes."

"Yeah, that reminds me, Bobby," Brassi said. "How'd things go with the guy in Skokie?"

"Ah, you know the Yids. Always wanna negotiate. I gave him a choice between the goods or the Louisville Slugger. Guess which he chose?"

Brassi chuckled. "Don't want to get on the bad side of Bobby Bat," he said to Rizzo, who looked away.

"Hey, Jimmy, know why the Jews wandered the desert for forty years?" Albanese said. "They heard someone lost a quarter out there."

Rizzo tugged at his tie. "We almost done here?"

"Can't wait to get out of here, huh?" Brassi said.

"I told you, I got things to do."

"Well, relax. I want to talk to you about somethin'."

Rizzo spread his hands. "So talk."

"You know, Jimmy, you got a bad attitude."

"That what you want to talk about?"

Brassi lit his cigar and struggled to stay calm. "I got a message for the old man. The sitdown's off next week."

Rizzo uncrossed his legs and sat forward. "What do you mean off? You're changin' the date?"

"Somethin' like that."

"To when?"

Brassi blew smoke at him. "Until I get my daughter back."

He watched Rizzo, looking for a sign, holding back from killing him right there, reminding himself he had to find Annette first.

"What're you talking about?" Rizzo asked.

"You sayin' you don't know?"

"Know what?"

"My daughter is missing."

Rizzo showed his palms. "How I'm gonna know? What, she ran away?"

"That what you think?"

"What're you askin' me for? I told you I don't know nothin' about it."

Brassi held himself in his chair.

"Hey, I understand you're worried," Rizzo said, sensing the tension. "But she'll turn up. You know kids."

Brassi fixed him with a menacing glare. "She'd better."

"So what're you gonna do?"

"I told you. Cancel the meet."

"What, until you find her?"

"You don't think I got good reason?"

"Sure, sure. But the old man ain't so understanding. He ain't gonna like this."

"Yeah, well, you explain it to him."

"Sure, but what about Salerno?"

"What about him?"

"You can't just change things sudden like this. What about the plans?"

"What plans?"

Rizzo calmed himself. "You know what I mean."

"Sure."

"So you're gonna make another date?"

Brassi jabbed the cigar at Rizzo. "You know, Jimmy, you're an insensitive fuck. I tell you my kid's missing, and all you can think about is this fuckin' meetin'."

"Hey, I'm—"

Albanese closed the metal briefcase with a loud click. "Two hundred thousand, four-hundred twenty."

"Give him a receipt," Brassi barked.

"Listen, Tony, there somethin' I can do?" Rizzo asked, trying to sound sincere.

"You can get the fuck out of my office."

"Listen, I'm sorry," Rizzo said. "About your kid, I mean."

"Yeah, well, somebody's gonna be," Brassi said, motioning for Albanese to show Rizzo to the door. "Sorry don't cover it."

Via waited outside the Sears Tower in Nicky's six-year-old Honda Civic. He figured Rizzo was up there getting the news from Brassi and hoped to hell he was right—that Rizzo would panic and lead him to wherever he had stashed the girl.

He felt better when Rizzo came up from the underground garage in his black Crown Vic and sped up the street and north onto Lake Shore Drive, all the while making calls on his cell. At the north end, Rizzo merged onto Sheridan Road and continued north for about forty minutes until he came to an area called

Highwood, an old working-class Italian enclave, out of place on the ritzy North Shore.

When Rizzo finally made a left on a residential street, it was dusk and beginning to rain. Via went past and turned to come back around the block. He found the Crown Vic parked in front of an old church with several other cars just as much out of place in the neighborhood. He circled the block to check for stragglers and then parked in the alley behind the church.

St. Anthony's was one of those old cathedrals built, back when there were parishes, to be the center of the community. Back when there was enough religious zeal and money to maintain the frescoes and mosaics and gold inlays that made the working-class parishioners who paid for them humble in their presence.

As Via approached he saw the basement lights were on. It was raining harder and he moved clumsily through the shrubbery and mud along the church's outer wall, not used to the cat-and-mouse, catching a faint scent of incense on the autumn air, thinking he could almost hear the murmur of whispered prayers.

A car came around the side of the building, headlamps like searchlights, and he put a hand on the gun inside his jacket until it passed. Then he inched forward to a small rectangular window in a dark corner looking down into the basement. Crouching, he could make out about a half-dozen men in Italian wool, some of whom he recognized.

At one end, Jimmy Rizzo was talking with Gino Marcelli, the capo who ran things north of the city for the Salerno Family. Marcelli was called Gino Mercedes because he only drove German cars. He was also called The Kaiser because he had the personality of one. At the other end of the room, Vito Tessa stood, right arm in a sling, bouncing from foot to foot, jazzed on being a tough guy.

With Tessa, Rizzo, and Marcelli in the room, there was a representative from each of the three Families present. Who the others were Via didn't know, but figured them for foot soldiers along as back-up.

Rizzo's cell phone rang and he went off to a corner to talk. Gino Marcelli went over to Tessa and put a hand on his shoulder. Via saw Tessa shake his head and Marcelli shove a finger in his face. Then Marcelli clutched Tessa by his good arm and pulled him over against the wall directly beneath the window. Tessa pulled loose and moved away, mouthing something Via could see Marcelli didn't like. Jimmy Rizzo heard it and pocketed his phone and limped hurriedly over to Tessa and grabbed him by his shirt.

Via moved in closer, straining to hear what they were saying. Behind, something brushed against the bushes.

When Via opened his eyes, Rizzo was standing over him holding his .38. He tried to lift his head, but the pain in the back of his skull laid him flat again.

"You shoulda hit him harder. Now we still have to kill the sonofabitch," Rizzo said.

"Ain't no trouble," a familiar voice said.

Then somebody else chimed in: "The fuck you talkin' about? You can't even squeeze the trigger."

"Use your imagination," the familiar voice said.

Via realized it was Vito Tessa. He pushed up on his elbows, trying to focus on the circle of men standing over him.

"I want to do this myself," Rizzo said.

"Come on, Jimmy, you got more important things to worry about," Gino Marcelli said. "Vito owes him."

"Not like me."

Rizzo looked down at Via: "You're one dumb fuck, you know that. You should've stayed out of this when you had the chance."

"Out of what?" Via said.

"Get this *cazzo* out of my sight. I don't want to see him again."

Marcelli started giving orders to some guy named Artie and another guy called Craps, who pulled Via to his feet and yanked his arms behind his back and bound his wrists with someone's belt.

"I don't care how you do it," Rizzo said, tossing Via's gun to Artie, "but don't get careless with the body. We already got enough heat because of Tommy Getti. Fuckin' Brassi."

Tessa and the two men pushed Via up the basement stairs and out to a black Chrysler 300. They shoved him into the back seat, Artie and Craps sitting on either side of him, Tessa behind the wheel, groaning as he stretched over to turn the ignition with his left hand. "I'm gonna enjoy this one." He snapped the car into gear and headed back south.

When they finally merged onto I-57, Via knew they were going to Calumet City. In the old days, the Cal-Sag Canal was used so often by the Mob they called it the Cal-*Sack,* because so many body bags were dumped there. He used to joke that the bodies were the only biodegradable trash in the water. It didn't seem so funny now.

"Whatsa matter, Via, you got nothin' to say?" Tessa mocked over his shoulder.

"Looks like he's thinking," Artie said. "I can see the veins in his head."

"Maybe he's just got gas," Craps said. "That the problem, Via, got an upset?"

"He'll be shittin' his pants when I start on him," Tessa said.

Artie and Craps laughed like madmen.

"Hey, Vito," Artie said, "let me do him."

"Not a chance."

"Aw, come on. How I'm gonna get made, I don't clip someone?"

"Don't worry, we do this thing with Jimmy Razor, you'll be made in the shade."

Via stared at the back of Tessa's head, noticing the way his oily hair hung over his shirt collar, the way he combed it back into a duck's tail, sorry he wouldn't have the chance to put a bullet between the feathers.

Craps leaned forward over the back of Tessa's seat. "Yeah, but Rizzo says the sitdown's off. How we gonna get all three dons in one place now?"

"We can't," Tessa said, "then we hit 'em one at a time."

"How you gonna arrange somethin' like that?" Artie asked.

"What's the problem? We clip 'em, that's all. It's just all gotta happen at the same time. Otherwise there's chaos, everybody trying to grab everybody else's."

"Lemme have one of 'em," Artie pleaded.

"Talk to Jimmy Razor and The Kaiser. It ain't up to me."

Via couldn't believe what he was hearing—they were planning to whack the heads of all three Families.

"You're out of your fucking minds," he blurted. "You'll never pull it off. Brassi already knows something's up. You think these guys got where they are being stupid? You can't keep something this big under wraps, too many people already know."

"No shit. That's why we're gonna kill you," Tessa said.

Artie and Craps broke up again.

"What do you think you're going to get out of it?" Via asked Tessa.

"Well, I think I'm gonna get a lotta pleasure out of it."

Artie and Craps nearly wet themselves.

"What did Jimmy Razor promise you? You think you're going to take Brassi's place? You think Rizzo's going to share power with a *stonato* like you?"

"Yeah, I'm gonna really enjoy this."

A state trooper cruised by in the oncoming lane and they went still, only their eyes following him. The air in the car smelled of cheap cologne and garlic and sweat, and Via wished someone would open a window to let in the rain. He felt Craps' and Artie's shoulders crowding him and was almost anxious to get to wherever they were going to do him, just to get out into the air. Funny, he thought, the things you think about when you know you're going to die. Not your life passing before you, not remorse for what you've done, but sorry for what you won't be able to do—like killing these motherfuckers dead.

When the car finally stopped, Tessa left it running and Artie and Craps forced Via onto his knees in front of it, the head-lamps casting his shadow at Tessa's feet.

"You know, when I finish here," Tessa said, "maybe I'll go visit that kid of yours. She's gonna need some comforting, if you know what I mean."

"Fucking scum," Via spat.

Tessa reached into his pants pocket with his left hand and brought out a long narrow switchblade.

"Pull his head back," he ordered Craps. "Grab his hair."

"What am I, just along for the ride?" Artie said. "Ain't there somethin' I can do?"

"You can shut the fuck up," Tessa barked.

Via heard the knife snick open, felt his head yanked back, the rain patting on his upturned face.

"Let's get this done," Craps said, "these shoes cost me two hundred bucks."

Tessa managed one step forward before his chest exploded. Then there was another gunshot and Via felt Craps release his hair.

Artie had his gun out now, but took a bullet before he pulled the trigger. He landed in the mud in front of Via with a slap, looking surprised to be dead.

Via started to stand but Bronco Lucci appeared over him and pressed a hot gun barrel to his cheek.

"You wanted me dead, you could've just waited five seconds longer," Via said, breathing heavily.

"Almost did. You're lucky Tony wants you livin'."

"How'd you get here?"

"Think I don't know how to run a tail?"

"So, you're my shadow now?"

"Tony don't want you dead. Yet."

Lucci lowered his .45 and freed Via's hands. Via picked up his .38, which Artie had dropped next to him, and Lucci raised his gun again.

"Don't get any ideas. I'm supposed to keep you alive, but I ain't gonna die doin' it."

"Don't get excited," Via said, his own blood racing.

He got to his feet and went and stood over Tessa, who was moaning and pleading for help. Tessa raised his good arm, like he was reaching for someone's hand. Via shot him in the face.

They dragged the bodies back to the car and opened the trunk. Lucci grabbed the spare tire and tossed it into the water like a Frisbee. Then they crammed in the three bodies—Lucci broke Tessa's neck to get him tucked inside—and drove the car into the canal.

That done, they headed back down I-57 in Lucci's Ford Excursion, the big man silent as an undertaker while Via told him what he had heard. For once, Lucci had no trouble grasping it.

"You know, once Rizzo knows you ain't dead, he's gonna realize the word is out on him. Maybe he still tries to hit the dons before they hit him."

"Alone? We just floated his friends."

Lucci frowned and scratched his flattop. Via imagined rusty

gears churning in place. "Yeah, but maybe he's got more on the inside," Lucci said. "We gotta find out who else was with him."

"No time, even if we could. Let your boss worry about that. We still have to find his stepdaughter."

"Tony ain't gonna like this. He's gonna want to kill someone."

"Yeah, he usually does."

Lucci seemed to find that amusing but got over it when he looked over at Via again. "Hey, you're bleedin' on my seat."

CHAPTER 13

It was well after midnight when they got Tony Brassi out of bed. He lived in one of those old brick manors from a former age, a large stately house, imposing on a block of stately houses. It dated from a time when Chicago's moneyed elite actually lived at street level, before the upper classes moved to the upper floors of security-heavy skyscrapers to escape the men, like Tony Brassi, who came to control their streets. Brassi now thought of himself as one of the elite, a man among men, the *capo di tutti capi.*

He came downstairs wearing a yellow sport coat over a black shirt and trousers and showed them into his living room, which looked like Versace on steroids. From the marble nymphet in the corner pouring water from a jug, to the fake Caravaggio above the gold-leaf fireplace, everywhere Via looked something was vying for attention.

Lucci went over and stood against the golden mantel and began cleaning his nails with Tessa's knife. Via went over to an uncomfortable-looking purple chair, holding a bloody bar towel to the back of his head. Brassi took a seat on a red tufted loveseat across from him and listened intently while Via told him what happened.

When Brassi had heard enough he stood and walked slowly to the bar and poured himself a whiskey, which he drank in silence. Via watched him, imagining a lit fuse burning low. When it reached the bottom, Brassi exploded.

166

"What the fuck you been doin', Bronco!"

Lucci snapped to attention like a plebe.

"My daughter's been snatched and Jimmy Razor's plotting to whack the whole fuckin' leadership!"

"Boss—"

Brassi cut Lucci off with a sharp wave. "What the fuck's goin' on? First my kid and now this."

"I don't think they're connected," Via said, taking the towel from his head and staring at the blood.

"You forget the way things work? You've been a civilian too long."

"Think about it. Why would Rizzo need your daughter if he's planning to clip you?"

"Fuckin' insurance. In case it didn't work out."

"Yeah, but he was planning to whack Delacante and Salerno, too."

"Why not? I'd do the same."

"It just doesn't add up."

"I'll find out what adds up. You bring Rizzo here. And Marcelli. Who else you see there?"

"Bunch of guys I didn't recognize."

Brassi slammed his glass down on the bar. "You didn't recognize? What the fuck did I give you fifty gees for? I want names. Names. This kind of shit is cancer, it's gotta be cut out."

"I was thinkin' the same thing," Lucci said.

"Don't strain yourself. You just find 'em."

"That's not the deal," Via said. "I'm supposed to find your kid."

"You ain't makin' the deals here. You bring Rizzo and Marcelli. They'll tell me where she is."

"If they know, she's their only chance. They won't give her up."

"They'll fuckin' talk."

167

"Like Getti?"

"Fuck Getti."

Brassi started pacing, his soles shushing across the Persian rug.

"If we don't find her first," Via said, "Rizzo and Marcelli can use her against you."

Brassi stopped and fixed on him. "Use her? Those flat dicks are dead already. They just ain't been buried yet."

"We need to find the books. You can do them after."

"After ain't soon enough."

"We need to get your kid first. And the books."

Brassi arched his eyebrows, a scornful smile on his lips.

"*We?* You hear this, Bronco? He thinks he's one of us now."

"Won't keep me from killin' him."

"You still got a taste for it, huh?" Brassi said. "Things ain't so easy out there for civilians, are they, Via?"

"Let's just do what we have to do here."

"What? *We* again?"

Via stood and went to the door. Lucci followed.

"*We* better find my books," Brassi shouted. "You hear me! *We* better find my fuckin' books!"

Jimmy Rizzo sat on the edge of his bed and loaded the Ruger 97. The bullets snapped into the magazine with a surety that helped relieve his nerves. He was troubled by hanging threads; his men should have reported back hours ago.

It wasn't like Artie and Craps not to call. Tessa he could understand, the dickless fuck never could be trusted. But Artie and Craps would be too scared not to report in. Or not answer their cell phones, which Rizzo had tried several times. It could mean only one thing, but he refused to believe it—there was no way Via could have done all three.

He should have killed Via right there in the church. Should

have killed him long ago. Or maybe just cripple him, a bullet in the spine, let him feel what it's like to drag around a weight. Fucking Via. Always thought he was smarter than everyone. A big man for a short time. A disgraced shyster, broke and alone. Fucking loser had to be dead.

Rizzo ran scenarios through his mind: Maybe they were busted somewhere along the way and the cops wouldn't let them make their one phone call. Maybe the spot at the Cal-Sag wasn't right and they went further out. Maybe they had a wreck.

The more he thought about it, the more agitated he became. He had called Gino Marcelli at home at 3 a.m., but The Kaiser hadn't heard anything either.

"What do you mean, they're not back?" was the first thing Marcelli said.

"What the fuck don't you understand?"

"Maybe they went out to celebrate. Probably layin' around drunk somewheres with some broads or somethin'."

"They ain't that stupid."

"Ah, you know Artie and Craps. They ain't exactly high school graduates. And Tessa, shit, can't rely on that *mamalucco*."

"It don't wash."

"The fuck do you know? Maybe they got car trouble or somethin'."

"They have phones, Gino."

"Yeah, but what? How's this Via gonna do all three. It ain't possible."

"So, what else then?"

Marcelli was silent.

"See what I'm sayin'?"

"Let's not get excited here," Marcelli said. "Okay, let's say you're right. What's he do? Tell Brassi?"

"Maybe Delacante and Salerno, too."

"Motherfucker."

"What I'm saying is, we can't be sure."

"This figures. This fuckin' figures. Forty years kissing the boss's ass. Fuckin' figures."

"We gotta find out about Via, Gino."

"Fuck that, I ain't waitin' around."

"What're you gonna do?"

When Marcelli didn't answer, Rizzo asked again.

"Scuse me, Jimmy, but if things are like you say, I ain't tellin' nobody nothin'."

Now it was 9 a.m. and Rizzo still hadn't heard anything. He checked the phone again for a dial tone. He snorted more cocaine to keep his head clear.

At 10 o'clock, he began counting money. He pushed the bed aside and withdrew the stash beneath the floor boards. He pulled a wad of cash from inside the bathroom heat vent. Finally, he opened the safe behind the back of his liquor cabinet and laid the bills with the pile on his bed. About two hundred thousand. Enough to get out quickly if he needed to, but then what would he do?

He needed more. He wasn't going empty-handed after half a lifetime kissing Delacante's ass. Fucking Via, if he was alive then the dons would know everything. But Marcelli was probably right; Via couldn't have capped all three. No, something happened. A car accident, maybe. But what if Via survived? He needed more cash.

Old Man Delacante's medications usually kept him asleep until noon. Maybe he could get into Delacante's safe, take what he needed, and lay low until he knew what really happened. He snorted more cocaine and felt confident he had made the right decision.

He dressed in a brown suit, pink shirt, and maroon tie, put the Ruger in his pocket, and went out to the Crown Vic in the driveway. He got in and reached over to start the car but saw

Bronco Lucci pull his truck across his path. He fumbled in his pocket for the gun but Via rose from the back seat and stuck his Smith & Wesson into Rizzo's ear. "Don't be stupid."

Lucci left his truck and lumbered up the driveway and got in next to Rizzo like a bear crawling into a rowboat.

"You comin' or you need convincin'?" he asked.

"Comin' where?"

Via reached over and collected the Ruger from Rizzo's pocket. "To try to save your life."

Rizzo looked at him in the rearview.

"Brassi wants to talk to you. You give him what he wants to know, maybe he gives you a pass."

"Who you kiddin', I'm already dead."

"You was dead, we wouldn't be havin' this conversation," Lucci said.

"Look," Via said, "right now only Brassi knows what's what. You work with him, maybe your boss and Salerno are kept out of it."

"Big *maybe*," Lucci said.

"So, what? He wants me to rat out the others?"

"Can't have anarchy in the ranks, Jimmy," Via said.

"Brassi tell you this? About the pass?"

"I'm telling you. You give him what he wants, maybe you can buy back your life."

"What's it to you, I'm alive or dead?"

"Not a goddamn thing. But I figure you give up the others, maybe one of them leads me to Brassi's kid. You give him names and he gets her back because of it, who knows, maybe we both get out of this alive."

"*Big* maybe," Lucci said.

Rizzo seemed to be thinking.

Via cocked the .38 to help him. "You can take the chance, or you can take the bullet," he said.

Brassi was waiting in his empty office when Via pushed Rizzo through the door. Via was surprised to find him alone, but then realized Brassi wouldn't want his own men to know what Rizzo had been planning—no sense giving them ideas.

"Back for that drink, Jimmy?" Brassi jeered.

Via took the Ruger from his waistband and tossed it on Brassi's desk. Brassi picked it up and sighted down the barrel at Rizzo.

"This what you were gonna use on me?"

Lucci shoved Rizzo into a chair in front of Brassi and went around and stood behind it. Via stood off to the side, out of the line of fire.

Brassi set down the gun and stroked it absently while he spoke. "You got nothin' to say, Jimmy?"

"About what?"

Lucci slapped Rizzo on the head.

"Jimmy, Jimmy," Brassi sighed. "This the best you can do? Guy with the ambition to whack the entire leadership."

"I don't know what you're talkin' about."

Brassi slammed his fist on the desk so hard the Ruger bounced. Rizzo lost his smug look.

"Want me to make him talk?" Lucci volunteered.

"Oh, he's gonna talk," Brassi said. "You're gonna give me chapter and verse, Jimmy. You're gonna talk, you're gonna sing, you're gonna dance if I want you to."

Brassi came around and stood over Rizzo. "This ain't just business, Jimmy. If it was, I might just put a bullet in your brain. But for this, I'm gonna get creative." He slapped Rizzo hard. "Where's my kid?"

Rizzo's eyes were watery, and a red handprint glowed on his

cheek. "I got nothin' to do with your kid."

"Yeah, that's what Via here thinks. But it ain't his kid that's missin'." Brassi gave Via a menacing look. "Not yet."

"Why would I nab your daughter, I was gonna clip you?"

"Motherfucker! You admit it!" Brassi backhanded Rizzo across the mouth, splitting his lip.

Via jumped up, his. 38 in his hand, and shouted, "Tell him who else was in on it!"

"I'm no rat," Rizzo said, squaring his shoulders.

Via shot him in the foot and he curled, screaming and cursing, into a ball.

"Was that the good one or the other?" Via said.

"Goddamn!" Brassi yelled. "Just like the old days, ain't it, Frank?"

Via aimed at Rizzo's other foot.

"Wait, wait! I know who's got the kid!" Rizzo squawked.

Lucci pulled him upright by his hair and Via jammed the gun beneath his chin.

"Where is she?"

"I don't know where."

Via cracked Rizzo on the nose with the gun barrel. "Think again!"

"Salerno. I don't know where. On my mother's grave."

"How do you know?"

"Gino Marcelli."

"How's he know?"

Rizzo was slow to answer so Lucci rapped him on the back of the head again.

"He said he saw her."

"He *said* he saw her?" Via demanded.

"He *saw* her."

"Fuckin' Salerno," Brassi mumbled.

Via straightened and looked at Brassi. "Don't tell me you

believe this shit."

"I ain't gonna bet my life on it," Brassi said. "But I'll bet Jimmy's." He pointed at Rizzo. "If you're right and Salerno's got her, you give up the other assassins, maybe I'll let you live."

"Salerno's got her, I swear."

"There's no way he can know," Via insisted. "Salerno's not going to let something like that slip."

"That's your job to find out!" Brassi snapped. "You and Bronco get the fuck movin'. Find Marcelli. I'll learn what Jimmy here knows. All of it."

He stepped on Rizzo's bloody foot, making him scream again. "Bobby, get in here!" he shouted toward the door.

Albanese came in as Via and Lucci were going out. He tried slipping past, but Via grabbed him by the lapels and shoved him against the door frame.

Lucci grasped Via by the collar and yanked him backward. "The fuck you doin'?"

"He's still got a hard-on for his ex," Brassi jeered.

Albanese snapped his sport coat straight and shot his cuffs. "This is a cashmere jacket."

Via lunged toward him but Lucci wouldn't let him go.

"Take it easy, I didn't touch her," Albanese said.

"Keep this asshole away from my family," Via told Brassi.

"Your family? You forget you gave all that up? You're alone in the world, Frankie. Me and Bronco's the only friends you got."

"Yeah, and we don't like you," Lucci snorted.

"We have a deal."

"Yeah, well, you ain't found my daughter yet. So I figure you might not be tryin' hard enough."

"Your ex still looks good," Albanese cracked, and Via tried to get at him again.

"Don't get distracted," Brassi ordered. "I'll curb Bobby. But you better find my kid soon, or I'll let go of his leash."

Chapter 14

The Chicken Vesuvio was getting cold and Al Salerno was getting angry.

"They can't bring the wine with the food?" he complained, looking around for the waitress. "These broads from the old country. Bring 'em over straight off the farm. Whatta they know about the restaurant business? She didn't have good tits, I'd send her back myself."

"You want I should go get her?" Sonny Cheeks asked from across the table, scraping back his chair.

"Where you goin'? Sit. I ain't payin' you to manage the help."

Cheeks settled back and played with his salad. The restaurant was empty except for Salerno's two bodyguards seated at the bar near the entrance.

"You know why you're here?" Salerno asked.

Cheeks shook his head.

"What're you, nervous?"

"I just never ate lunch with the Boss, with you, before."

Salerno plucked some bread from the basket between them and tore off a hunk. "No, you ain't. Normally, I don't give two shits about you. But today you're lucky, because I wanna know somethin'."

"Anything I can tell you, Boss."

Salerno barked over his shoulder at the waitress loitering near the kitchen. "Hey, sweetheart, the Amarone, huh?"

"What can I do for you, Boss?" Cheeks asked.

Salerno shoved some bread into his mouth and mumbled, "I don't know. What *can* you do? I'll tell you, I don't hear much good about you."

"Anything you need, Boss. Anything."

The wine arrived and Salerno pulled the waitress down by her open shirt collar and whispered in her ear. She smiled broadly and touched him on the shoulder, then padded back toward the kitchen.

"See what I mean about the tits?"

Cheeks took a deep gulp of wine.

"Oh, I forgot. You don't swing right-handed, do you?"

Cheeks got pale and stared at his salad.

"Relax. Think I didn't know? Don't mean shit to me. We ring up maybe half-a-mil a year from fudge-packers. Hell, I hear you're one of our best customers."

The waitress brought more bread and Salerno swatted her behind as she turned to leave.

"Sex is big business, don't matter where it comes from. No, what I'm wonderin', given your . . . predisposition . . . is why you're suddenly so interested in young girls." He stuffed more bread into his mouth.

Cheeks glanced at the men at the bar.

"You think I don't know you been askin' around?"

"Boss, I—"

Salerno stopped him with a raised hand. "Before you say somethin', you should know I got no patience for bullshit. You lie to me, I'll find out. I find out, you ain't fuckin' man or beast no more."

Cheeks told him everything then. While he talked, Salerno bent over his plate and attacked his meal like a shark, pausing only to drink some wine or slather butter onto a piece of bread.

When Cheeks finished, Salerno sat back and belched, patting his belly like a sack of cash. "You tellin' me Tony Brassi's kid is missing and he thinks I snatched her?"

"I thought you'd want to know, Boss."

"Sure you did. I hear Jimmy Razor's gone missing, too."

"Yeah, I heard that. Think they're connected?"

"Who knows? Maybe you was snoopin' round trying to find out, you'd be some use to me."

Cheeks gulped more wine. "You want me to check it out, Boss, I can do it for you."

Salerno reached into his jacket pocket and brought out a cigar and lit it. He blew smoke into the air and stared at it like an apparition.

"Maybe this is good. Jimmy Razor's missing, Delacante might as well be, and Brassi thinks I got his kid. Yeah, maybe this is good."

Cheeks relaxed a bit. "So, you don't have her?"

"Wish I did."

"What're you thinkin', Boss?"

"Ain't none of your concern."

Salerno pushed his plate aside and put his elbows on the table. "You wanna do something for me, you tell this Via I got her. You tell him I wanna work a deal. You tell him I'll only deal with Brassi. No go-betweens. Tell him I want to set up a meet. No, tell him he can set it up, but someplace neutral."

"Sure, Boss. When?"

"He'll want it soon. Tell him not to get too anxious. I find anyone else snoopin' round," Salerno said, fixing Cheeks with a cold stare, "ain't gonna be nothin' to deal with. Capisce?"

"Sure, Boss, sure. But what about Via?"

"What about him?"

"He's trouble."

"What kinda trouble?"

"The kind don't listen. And Lucci, too."

"Fuckin' Bronco Lucci." Salerno pulled on his lower lip.

"Maybe you got a point."

"I can help you, Boss. Whatever you need."

"I told you what you can do." Salerno pulled the napkin out of his collar and tossed it on the table. "You'da come to me instead of sneakin' behind my back, maybe I could find somethin' more for you."

Cheeks's foot was tapping the table leg like a woodpecker. "I fucked up. I know that. Just gimme a chance. I wanna help you, Boss."

Salerno pushed his chair back and the bodyguards jumped to their feet.

"I don't think so," Salerno said.

"I'll take care of Lucci and Via for you!" Cheeks blurted.

Salerno's eyebrows went up, his black eyes glistened. "You hear this shit?" he said, looking over at his men. He settled back in his chair and signaled for them to do the same.

"I can do it," Cheeks said.

"Don't make promises you can't keep."

"Gimme this chance, I won't disappoint you."

"Nobody disappoints me twice, Sonny."

"You can count on me, Boss. You'll see."

Salerno scratched his temple. "What the fuck. You wanna do this, I'll give you this chance to redeem yourself. I'll even give you some of my men. Hell, maybe you can pull it off. You people are supposed to be creative."

"I can handle it, Boss. I'll take care of everything."

Salerno reached out and crushed his cigar in Cheeks's salad. "You better do that. You better do that," he said, sitting back again. "Now get outta my restaurant."

Cheeks got up and started backing toward the door. "You won't regret it," he said. "You won't regret it."

"You do good, Sonny," Salerno called after him, "and maybe I forget you're a fuckin' faggot."

CHAPTER 15

"Maybe Marcelli already skipped," Lucci said as Via got into the big man's truck.

"Then we're fucked."

"You believe Jimmy Razor?"

"Doesn't matter what I think."

"You got that right." Lucci started the truck and pulled into the street. "Now we gotta find Marcelli."

Via hadn't taken orders in a long time and he didn't like it, especially from a dumb fuck like Lucci. He had known guys like this his whole life, not as big, but just as stupid. The Outfit seemed to attract them, guys with capacities too limited for work that was legitimate, but with skills enough for the kind that wasn't.

"Find a drugstore first," Via said.

"We ain't got time for that."

"You want to find Marcelli, find a drugstore."

Via had to explain it so Lucci understood. When they finally found a Walgreen's, Via went inside and bought some bottled water and aspirin, four tablets of which he popped into his mouth standing in the aisle, washing them down with the water.

When he got in line to pay, some tall guy with big biceps and big tattoos jumped ahead of him, saying, "I was here first," pointing at some smokes already on the counter, tossing some Tic Tacs next to the Marlboros.

He looked to Via like the kind of guy who let his size do his work for him, showed it off in those tight clothes, probably daily workouts at the gym. The kind of guy who thought a threatening look was enough to win a fight.

"You got a fuckin' problem?" the guy asked when he noticed Via staring at him.

"Nah, no problem," Via said, grinning through his teeth.

He grinned while the guy took his time pinching pennies from the *Take-A-Penny* dish so he didn't have to break a buck and try to squeeze ninety-seven cents into the pocket of his skinny white jeans. He grinned, too, as he watched the guy strut out the door, and grinned when he paid and went over to the pay phone and yanked the plastic-covered phone book from its security chain. The chop-haired kid at the cash register grinned back at him and saluted him with a raised fist. Via grinned then, too, and told him to get fucked.

Outside, the Marlboro Man was back behind his red Sebring, fussing in the trunk. Via tossed the water and aspirin in next to Lucci and marched over to the guy, still grinning, and whacked him on the side of the head with the phone book. The guy stumbled sideways but righted himself, so Via hit him flat in the face. He went down this time and didn't try to get back up.

"What the fuck is this?" Lucci shouted out the side window.

Via kicked the guy in the kidneys a couple of times and then went back and got into the truck.

"What? You know that guy?" Lucci asked.

"Just reminds me of someone."

Lucci didn't get it. "He looks queer to me," he said.

Via set the phone book on his lap and riffled through the pages, running his finger down the M's.

Lucci snorted. "Think it's gonna be that easy?"

Via tossed the phone book on the floor. "He's across town on Morgan Street. Near the expressway."

"He's listed? Just like that?"

"Just like a regular citizen."

"Shit, don't pay to be respectable."

Lucci backed the truck out, craning his neck at the guy on the ground. "That blood ain't never gonna come out of those jeans," he said.

Marcelli lived in Little Italy, or what was left of it. The old neighborhood didn't look so old anymore. Gentrification had painted over most of its character and the city had demolished the rest when it expropriated the property to build the University of Illinois at Chicago campus in the 1960s. It was now three hundred acres of concrete and colleges where the children of Chicago's labor classes could get the remedial education they needed to learn the basic skills the city's public high schools failed to provide them.

Via used to come to this neighborhood as a kid. His uncle, his old man's brother, owned an IGA grocery store back then and his mother came here to shop. He could remember the smells in the air and his mother's hand around his, but he couldn't quite remember his uncle. *Because he was a loser,* his old man said, which it turned out he was. He lost his store, his home, and his livelihood to eminent domain. He eventually lost his life, too—from heartache, his mother always said. *From eating other people's shit,* his old man would sneer back at her.

It was dusk when they found Marcelli's row house. The lights were on and they could see him moving around through an upstairs window. Lucci wanted to kick in the door.

"You ever do anything the easy way?" Via said.

Lucci snorted. "You'll be easy." He took out his .45 and checked the clip.

"Look, before we wake the neighbors, let's see where he's going."

"Whatta you think, he's dumb enough to lead us to Brassi's kid?"

"Probably to the airport, but it'll be easier there. No telling what kind of firepower he's got in there."

"What're you worried about? You ain't got that long to live."

It sent a chill down Via's spine. How the hell was he going to handle this huge sonofabitch? Guy was like a goddamn dinosaur. The question was how to cause his extinction. The only way was with a bullet. But the odds were against getting the opportunity to do it. Hell, the odds were against him period. Even if he could kill Lucci, where would that leave him? Where would that leave Meggie? Brassi would come for her for sure. Whatever happened, he had to keep her safe.

He glanced over at Lucci, wondering what went on inside that big square head, wondering if maybe he had some ambition tucked away in a corner there. If he couldn't get to Lucci with a bullet, maybe there was another way.

"So, what's the plan?" the big man asked as if he had read Via's mind.

"Plan? You think there's a plan? This is your boss's idea, ask him. Maybe he's got a goddamn plan."

"Yeah, that's what I thought. You got nothin'. No plan. No connections. No dough. Just another fuckin' loser."

"Who you kidding? I remember what it's like," Via said. "How much money you pull down? How much does it take to keep you eating your boss's shit?"

Lucci lifted his chin and grunted. "I don't take shit from nobody."

"That what you tell yourself?"

Lucci reached over and tapped ashes onto Via's lap. "Hey, I ain't the one takin' money from street trash like Pignotti."

"No, you're taking it from Brassi. You think he's different? You think you're important to him? You think he's going to look out for you?"

Lucci dragged on his smoke. "I look out for myself."

"Well, you'd better look out for yourself real good," Via said. "Because when the shit comes down, you're going to end up under it."

"Why don't you shut the fuck up."

"Let me fill you in on something—the state prosecutor is watching my every move."

Lucci peered at him from the corner of his eye.

"He wants to know why I'm working for your boss again. And if he's watching me, he's watching you. He wants me for past sins, but he wants your boss even more. And when this is over, he's going to want you, too. You're going to need something to give him. You're the one who needs a plan."

"I ain't givin him nothin'."

"Wise up, Bronco. This is more complicated than you think. The Feds are planning to take down the whole operation and you're going down with it. Brassi's books could save your ass."

Lucci's jaw was set like concrete.

"Of course, it will take some negotiating. With the Feds, with the heads of the other families, for whatever you want in return."

"What I want is you to shut the fuck up."

"Think about it. The Feds could wipe your slate clean. Brassi's books could be your ticket out from under. But you'll have to be able to make the proper deal, and you'll need help to do it."

"Help like you?"

"Face it, you'll need someone who knows how to lawyer. You're not smart enough to do it on your own."

Lucci flipped the lit butt at Via's head.

"You're gonna look out for me, huh? How you gonna do that when you're dead?"

A dinosaur, all right. Big everywhere except the brain.

Via gave it up and waited silently in the dark, watching Marcelli moving back and forth, watching the lights upstairs go out, watching a trail of new lights moving downward, until finally a light came on in the attached garage and the door went up and The Kaiser backed out in a silver Mercedes CL550 and headed up the street. When he headed onto the Kennedy Expressway to O'Hare, Via knew he was right.

Lucci followed, keeping back, his eyes locked on Marcelli's bumper while he worked on a new pack of smokes. He reached over and pushed the button for the CD player and Sinatra floated from the speakers. He smoked and drummed along on the steering wheel, cruising along like he was on vacation.

"You hear this guy? Fuckin' Sinatra. Giancana almost clipped him, that shit with the Kennedys. Could've done it easy. Lucky for him, Momo liked his singin'. See what I'm sayin? It ain't hard to kill nobody."

Something caught Lucci's eye in the mirror and he suddenly tapped the brakes. From behind, a police interceptor flew past, lights like fireworks. The Mercedes slowed, too, and Lucci tapped the brakes again to keep his distance. Via put his hands on the dashboard, watching the cops recede into the rain. He let out a deep breath.

"What's the matter, you nervous?" Lucci mocked. "Tell me somethin'. You happy being a civilian?"

It was still raining when Gino Marcelli pulled into the airport's short-term parking lot. He wanted to be as close to the terminal as possible, even though the car would probably be found sooner here. Not that it mattered, he wasn't coming back for it anyway, which pained him deeply. He loved this car and hated the thought of it being impounded and eventually auctioned off to some *moolie*—blacks being, in Marcelli's mind, the only ones who bought cars at auction—who would trick it out with lots of chrome and oversized tires and a chain link steering wheel. A hundred grand car. Still, it was better than trying to drive it to Portland or, worse, ending up in the trunk.

The parking lot traffic was fairly slow this time of night. The rush-hour flight delays had cleared out and airport security, as usual, was nowhere around. In the rearview mirror he saw a Ford SUV come up the ramp and he kept his eyes on it until it drove past to the far end of the aisle and pulled into a handicap parking space close to the elevator. Another cheap-shit domestic car; he wouldn't drive one if it were free. He waited a few more minutes, enjoying the smell of cashmere leather, running his hand over the car's gleaming dashboard and walnut wood shifter, sitting there admiring the jewel-like instrument cluster, until the Ingenieur clock told him to get moving to catch his flight.

He got out and tucked the key into the sun visor—at least that would keep the towing company from having to tear up the steering column. He opened the trunk, retrieved a small carry-on, and slipped the strap over his shoulder. He had sent the money ahead to his sister's bank in Portland and there was plenty enough to buy new clothes. And another Mercedes, too, if he wanted. Hell, maybe he'd get himself one of those 4 × 4s to drive around the mountains there. Maybe he would drive to California, find a place of his own to stay after things cooled off.

It wouldn't be so bad. Not as good as if things had worked out, but, hell, he was getting too old for this shit anyway. Maybe it was even a good thing; he wouldn't mind trying retirement. He reached into his breast pocket to double-check for the tickets—bought under the name of George Martin—and felt the touch of cold metal against the back of his neck.

"Ain't this a kick? Couple minutes more, I'da been gone."

"Sure, timing's everything," Via said.

"Go ahead, do me here. I ain't goin' nowhere."

"No shit," Lucci said.

Via came around in front and patted him down.

"You think I'm gonna try to get on a plane with a weapon? What am I, stupid?"

"You're not on it, are you?"

"So, you ain't dead yet, huh?" Marcelli said to Via.

Lucci grabbed Marcelli's arm. "Forget about him. Let's go."

Marcelli pulled away. "I told you."

"How 'bout I drag you by your balls?"

"Be smart," Via said, gesturing to Lucci's SUV, "get in the truck."

Marcelli regarded the vehicle with contempt. "What's that, a Ford? I'm being taken for a ride in a fuckin' Ford? Christ, have some respect. At least take the Mercedes."

"Nazi piece a shit," Lucci said. He reached out and scraped the barrel of the .45 along the back fender.

Marcelli got in his face. "Goddammit! You don't need to do that!"

Lucci cracked him on the forehead with the gun butt. The Kaiser buckled but didn't crumble, so Lucci hit him again, and he did.

"You kill him, it doesn't help," Via said.

"Hard-headed fuck."

They bound Marcelli's hands and tossed him into the back seat of the truck. Via tossed the carry-on behind the seat and climbed in next to him.

"Where now?" he asked Lucci.

"West Side. C.I.'s got a warehouse there."

Marcelli moaned and opened his eyes, blinking away the blood dripping onto his trousers. "Motherfuckers. This is a thousand-dollar suit."

"You'll look good at your wake," Via said.

"What the fuck you doin' here? I thought you was out of the business. Hey, Bronco, what's with Via here?"

"He's just hired help."

"What the fuck? A freelancer? You gonna let a freelancer do me? This ain't right."

"Don't worry, I'll handle it myself," Lucci told him.

The C.I. warehouse was a huge corrugated steel structure with a single steel door and painted gray windows behind heavy steel grates. Surrounding it was a muddy lot littered with the usual flotsam of discarded tires, broken bottles, and abandoned cars. It was the kind of place long forgotten and seldom used, except for the business they were there for.

They dragged Marcelli out of the truck and Via kept a gun on him while Lucci fumbled with a large combination lock. Then they shoved him through the heavy steel door into the large warehouse space, empty except for some old tarps and ropes and a couple of wooden chairs. The air was still and stale. Via noticed a dark stain on the concrete floor.

"This where you did Getti?"

"Get my toolbox outta the back of the truck," Lucci ordered.

"Fuckin' toolbox," Marcelli sneered. "Think I don't know all the tricks?"

Lucci shoved him toward one of the chairs. "Think you're too old to learn new ones?"

Via went out to the truck in the rain and pulled the red metal toolbox from the hatch, surprised by the weight of it, the handle straining, squeaking like a cemetery gate.

Coming back through the door, he saw Marcelli stripped to the waist and tied to a chair. Lucci's jacket was off and his shirtsleeves were rolled over his elbows.

"Bring it here," Lucci ordered.

Marcelli wasn't exactly a tall man—who was next to Lucci?—

but he was built like a bunker, with a barrel chest and bulky arms impressive for a guy past sixty, one of those guys who'd be working the docks or shoveling ore if he wasn't mobbed up. Via figured he'd be tough to crack. He brought the toolbox over and leaned in close to Lucci.

"Look, a guy like this, you shoot his dick off, he might spill. But you hurt him in bits and pieces, it becomes a contest. The dumb fuck thinks he's got something to prove."

"What's the matter, ain't got the stomach for it no more?"

"We don't have the *time* for it."

Lucci reached in and removed a pair of pliers. "Don't worry, this won't take long."

Via went over to Marcelli. "Look, we know you're a tough guy. We're all tough guys here. But you're the one tied to a chair. You can tough it out, but you'll die trying. Why don't you get smart and tell us what we want to know? Tell us, and you can go back to the airport and catch the next flight to wherever the hell you were going."

"Fuck the both of you."

"You ain't gonna be fuckin' no one no more," Lucci said.

"I guess you're as stupid as you look," Via said to Marcelli.

"Hey, Bronco, do me a favor," The Kaiser said, "don't let that *cacchio* get my Mercedes."

Via went outside, across the dirt lot filled with muddy pools like oil. The rain had slowed but the wind had risen and he went over to the truck and got in on the passenger side and hunkered into his jacket. It smelled like an ashtray in there.

A pack of Camels and a lighter lay on the driver's seat and he grabbed them and tapped out a coffin nail and lit it, watching the smoke glide across the windshield like a ghost. He pulled the nicotine deep into his tobacco-starved lungs, felt it fill him up and exhaled through his nose. He took another deep drag and let it numb his nerves, then stubbed the cigarette out in the overflowing ashtray and rested his head back against the seat.

He closed his eyes and tried not to think about was happening inside the warehouse, tried not to think about Lucci or Marcelli or the Brassies. But the more he tried not to think, the more he did, and he drifted off thinking of Tina Brassi.

He thought back to the old neighborhood, back to happier times, back to Festa Pasta Vino, when Tina was the festival Queen, waving to the crowd, attracting everyone's attention, while he sneaked behind the food booths and stole whatever he could get his hands on.

Later, they hid in the basement of Mrs. Trafficante's three-flat, settled against an old ringer washing machine, talking and drinking a bottle of Chianti he had snatched. They talked about the future like the world was full of possibilities, as if their lives weren't already set by fate. He pulled someone's blanket off the clothesline and Tina lay on it, her white Queen's gown billowing about her like a cloud. He lay next to her and felt like he was floating. She smelled of something sweet and he was about to taste her lips when she suddenly pushed up wide-eyed, a loud voice bringing him back to earth.

"Via, what the fuck you doin'?"

He opened his eyes and checked the dashboard clock. Only twenty minutes had passed. "Get the hell in here," Lucci shouted.

Via went back through the door and saw Marcelli slumped in the chair, chin on his chest, trousers and socks soaked through with blood.

Lucci picked up Marcelli's shirt from the floor and wiped his hands on it and began gathering up his tools. "He wouldn't talk."

"So try again when he comes around."

"He ain't gonna be."

Via went over to get a closer look. "He's dead?"

"Stubborn fuck."

"You killed the sonofabitch?"

"I think his heart quit."

"Jesus fucking Christ. Did he say anything?"

"Not about the girl."

"You stupid bastard! You know what this means?"

"Hey! Who you talking to!"

"Now all we have is Rizzo's word."

"He knew something, he woulda told me," Lucci said, bending over his toolbox.

"That what you're going to tell your boss?"

Lucci straightened up. "What I tell him is my business. You get it?"

"You're fucked, Bronco. Rizzo convinced him Marcelli knew where she was."

"I told you, he didn't know nothin'."

"Tell your boss. Now he's only got Rizzo's word."

The big man walked over to a stack of tarps and sat atop it. He took a cigarette from his shirt pocket and tamped it against his thumbnail.

"If I'm in the shit, you're in it with me," he said, but it lacked conviction.

"What if Salerno doesn't have Brassi's kid and your boss goes after him? Think about it. A lot of people are going to end up dead. You think that's good for you when Brassi finds out you fucked up with Marcelli?"

Lucci's head swiveled toward him like a tank turret. "How's he gonna know that?"

"You think if I'm dead, it makes a difference? Your boss is going to have to blame someone."

Lucci lit his cigarette and pretended to be thinking, the smoke swirling around him like a fog.

"Listen," Via said, "my guy Nicky's got a guy inside Salerno.

If we can buy some time, maybe he can come up with something. Maybe that something makes you a hero with your boss."

"What guy? What're you talkin' about?"

"A guy works for Salerno. My guy knows him."

"This guy he knows a faggot, too?"

"You think it matters? He's inside. Another twenty-four hours maybe it gets easier."

Lucci was still for a moment, then got up and stood over Marcelli. "What about him?"

"We tell your boss he skipped. We never found him. How's Brassi going to know?" Via said.

Lucci scrutinized the body like a carpenter measuring a plank of wood. Via watched him cautiously, wondering what was going through his flat head.

"There's this industrial furnace out back," Lucci said. He crushed the cigarette beneath his shoe. "Don't think this buys you anything with me."

They untied Marcelli, rolled the body onto a tarp, and Via gathered up the dead man's clothes. He removed the United Airlines ticket portfolio from the jacket and threw the clothes on top of the body. Then they folded the tarp over and secured it with rope. Alive, Marcelli weighed over two hundred pounds. Dead, he felt like a VW Beetle. Lucci lifted him like a toy.

"You clean this shit and don't forget the toolbox," he said, then went out the door carrying the body like a movie monster.

It was late when they got to Brassi's house. He was not happy to be disturbed.

"You two can't talk to me except the middle of the night?"

He wore a red silk robe over black pajamas, his feet in blue velvet slippers. He was wearing glasses now, large black horn rims with gold temples and lenses tinted yellow, which made his eyes look wolfen. A thin gold chain hung from his neck. Attached to it was what appeared to be an ancient Roman coin, and on his wrist was a golden bracelet shaped like a crown of laurel leaves. The modern Caesar in his palazzo.

He walked over to the bar and made a drink while Via waved Marcelli's ticket receipt at him and told him the lie.

"We found his car at O'Hare. Left this on the seat."

Brassi snatched it out of Via's hand. "Portland. Now I gotta send someone to fuckin' Portland? This rat fuck is costing me money."

Lucci glanced at him nervously. "You gonna send someone after him?"

"I'm goin' after Salerno first."

"You want me to cap him, Boss?"

"Shut the fuck up."

"Listen, Salerno could've made a dozen copies of your books by now" Via said. "You kill him, how do we know?"

He let Brassi think about that for a moment.

"We have to find out if he's got your kid first. You go in there like Tony Montana, you could get her killed."

"You think I'm worried about her? She ain't dead, I might kill her myself, this shit she caused me."

A young woman wrapped in an emerald-colored sheet suddenly appeared on the stairs over Brassi's shoulder.

"Tony, I'm lonely," she said in a slight voice.

"Go back upstairs. I got business."

"Toe-nee."

"Upstairs!"

The girl stamped her bare foot and swiveled around and slithered up the stairs, her naked backside playing peekaboo through the sheet.

"Listen, we have someone inside Salerno," Via said, when he had Brassi's attention again. "Give it a couple days, maybe he pays off."

"What guy?"

"A fuckin' swish," Lucci chimed in.

"Some queer?"

"Some friend of Via's secretary. Another fuckin' faggot. Via here's got more fag friends than Madonna."

"This *frocio* works for Salerno?"

"He works for us now," Via said. "Maybe he learns something that makes things easier."

"And maybe he don't." Brassi swallowed his drink. He rolled his shoulders and stretched his neck from side to side. "This is what she brings me to, this ungrateful little bitch?"

The girl's voice came from upstairs again: "Toe-neee."

Brassi thrust a finger at Via. "You'd better fucking find her." He turned toward the staircase. "You're running out of time."

CHAPTER 16

Windy City Bar was full of hard hats just off work from the nearby loft and condo conversions dotting the near West Side. When Via walked in with Nicky Fratelli and Sonny Cheeks, he knew Nicky had been right.

"I told you we should go to Adam's," Nicky said, looking around.

"Maybe you could have worn something more conspicuous," Via said, gesturing to Nicky's tight blue jeans and red fishnet top, through which his nipple ring was showing.

"My horoscope said red's my lucky color today."

Via gestured toward the construction workers at the bar. "Did it also say you'd find yourself in a bullring?"

Sonny Cheeks put his elbows on the table. "We come here to talk about fashion?"

A waitress came over to take their drink orders and Via made it a point to run his eyes over her halter-top and spandex shorts, in case some of the hard hats were watching. He unconsciously checked for the gun inside his jacket.

When the waitress left, they got down to business, Cheeks telling them Salerno had the girl, how he heard it from Salerno himself, that she was okay but scared.

"What's he want?" Via asked.

"That's between him and Brassi."

"Salerno tell you why he snatched her?"

"Like I said, that's between him and Brassi."

"He can deal through me, that's how Brassi wants it."

"You think Salerno's gonna do business with some *cazzo* like you?"

"No need to get nasty, Sonny," Nicky said.

"I'm just tellin' you like it is."

The waitress brought their drinks and Cheeks shot his Stoli like water.

"How about you just tell us where the girl is?" Via said. "Then we don't need to worry about the rest."

"See what I mean? You get the girl, problem solved. It's a lot for ten grand."

"Stick with the deal, Sonny."

"Where is she?" Nicky asked.

"The money first."

"Look, Sonny, I've got your dough right here," Via said, patting his jacket. "Nobody's welshing on the deal. But we need to be sure you know where she is."

Cheeks put his hand on his chest and smirked. "What, you don't trust me?"

"Where is she, Sonny?"

Cheeks lit a cigarette. His fingernails reminded Via of a crab. "You know I could be killed for telling you this."

"It's a little late to worry about that," Via said. "The way I see it, you get burned either way. If I tell Brassi you know where the kid is and won't tell us . . . well, figure it out."

Cheeks was clicking his lighter open and closed, a subtle grin on his lips. "I ain't worried about Tony Brassi."

"Yeah? Neither was Tommy Getti."

"Yeah, I heard that was Brassi."

"You heard right."

"Well, everybody gets what's coming to him, don't he?" Cheeks said.

"You should hope not."

The waitress came back again. Via told her they were done and asked for the check and she went back toward the bar.

"Sonny?" Nicky asked.

Cheeks blew smoke at him. "I was you, I'd look in the most obvious place."

Via studied Cheeks playing with the lighter, trying to be cool. "If it was obvious, we wouldn't need you," he said.

"That's what I'm sayin'."

"I know what you're saying and I'm telling you forget about it."

"Your boy here's a real ballbreaker," Cheeks said to Nicky.

"Why don't you just tell us where she is?" Nicky said.

Cheeks sucked on his smoke and pretended to be interested in the Sox game on the TV across the room.

Via glanced around, wondering how the hard hats might react if he grabbed Cheeks by the hair and introduced his face to the tabletop.

"Where is she?" he asked again.

"If you sold crystal, where would you hide a diamond?" Cheeks asked, still staring at the TV.

"We don't have time for riddles, Sonny," Nicky said.

"I think he means she's with some other girls. Right, Sonny?" Cheeks sneered at Via. "Ain't you teacher's pet."

"Just get to it."

"There's this place in Cicero. Belongs to our friends."

"This place?"

"The Tuna Club. Ask around, it's the biggest cathouse out there."

"A goddamn whorehouse?" Nicky nearly shouted.

"Where are they keeping her?" Via demanded.

"I just told you."

"I said *where*?"

Cheeks didn't look at him. "I still ain't seen no money."

Via showed him the envelope and counted out some cash and laid it in front of Cheeks, who immediately riffled through the bills.

"The fuck? This is only half!" Cheeks shouted.

Via noticed the hard hats look their way. He waited until they went back to their beers, then grasped Cheeks by the wrist and twisted it sharply beneath the table, making him drop his smoke.

"Where is she being kept at this club?"

"In the wine cellar, the wine cellar."

"You get the other half if this checks out," Via said, putting the envelope back into his pocket.

He released Cheeks, who jumped up just as the waitress came back with the check, knocking a tray of glasses from her hands.

"Fuck this!" Cheeks shouted.

The crash turned the bar in their direction and one of the hard hats got off his bar stool and moved toward them. Cheeks saw him coming and stepped over the mess and hurried toward the door. Nicky got up to go after him but Via pulled him back into his seat. The waitress was on her knees picking up the broken glass.

The hard hat came over, a bulky guy wearing a leather tool belt below a big belly.

"You all right, Wendy?" he asked, looking down at her.

Over the guy's shoulder, Via saw two more men walking toward them. He tapped Nicky and they both stood. He reached into his pocket and put a hundred-dollar bill on the table.

"Sorry about the mess."

They stepped around the waitress and the guy with the tool belt and headed toward the door. The other two men stepped in front of them.

"You're in the wrong bar," one of them said.

"Who says—" Nicky started, but Via backhanded him on the arm.

"You're right," Via said.

He maneuvered Nicky around the men, but the one who spoke put his hand on him. Via stepped back and opened his jacket to show the .38, and the guy jerked his hand back like he had touched a hot stove. He and his friend moved aside.

Outside there was no sign of Sonny Cheeks.

"Sonofabitch!"

"What's the problem? We got what we needed," Nicky said.

"I wasn't done talking to him."

They walked toward the parking lot, Via quiet, Nicky chattering to get rid of the nerves the hard hats gave him. "You think he's telling the truth?"

"Hey, he's your friend."

"So this doesn't work out, it's my fault?"

"This doesn't work out, won't matter whose fault it is."

The parking lot was behind the bar, just off an alley that served as the service conduit for the businesses that backed to it. It was seldom used except for that and as they walked into it, Via realized they had made a mistake.

At first, he thought it was the hard hats. Then he heard Ziggy's flinty voice. "Out for a stroll with your boyfriend?"

Before either of them could move, Ziggy struck Nicky on the head with the butt of a gun and he fell to the ground.

"Don't move," Jolly said to Via.

His face was a skull and cross bones. The bandages crisscrossing his nose formed a large white X and both eyes were blackened. He noticed Via looking and snarled, "You think I look bad? Wait'll I get done with you."

When he reached in to take Via's gun, Via rammed his head into the middle of the X. Jolly let out a cry and dropped his weapon and Via pulled him close so Ziggy couldn't get a shot.

"Goddamnit!" Ziggy screamed.

Via squeezed his hand inside his jacket and brought up his .38, but Jolly knocked it away and began pounding his face. He caught Via with a solid right and Via's knees went slack and then Ziggy was on him, too. Via felt a sharp kick in his side and then both men started on him with their feet. He curled into a ball, wondering where his gun had landed, but they had him against a brick wall and he couldn't roll free enough to do anything but try to protect his body.

He took a hard kick to the head and things began going gray when he felt Ziggy's body suddenly yanked away and heard Jolly give out another yelp. Through an enveloping haze he heard scraping and grunting and something like wood snapping. Then gravel kicked up around him and he thought the men were kicking at him again as he lost consciousness.

When Via came to, there was a distinct and familiar smell, salty and metallic. He ran a mental inventory of his body and was surprised the blood wasn't his. Then he sensed something large looming over him.

"Pretty soon there ain't gonna be enough left for me," Lucci said.

Via sat up and rested his back against the wall. "Still tailing me, huh? How long you been here?"

"Long enough."

"Couldn't stop it any sooner, huh?"

"Lucky I stopped it at all."

Lucci tossed something that bounced off Via's chest and fell onto his lap. It was Ziggy's finger, still wearing the star-shaped ring. "Souvenir."

Via brushed it off his jeans and rose slowly, bracing himself against the wall. He was badly bruised but nothing was broken.

"You ready now?" Lucci sneered.

They went over and pulled Nicky to his feet. Nicky looked

around and saw Jolly's and Ziggy's twisted bodies. He sat down again and put his head between his knees.

"So, you learn anything?" Lucci asked Via.

"Salerno's got her stashed in Cicero."

"So, when're we goin' to get her?"

"Tonight," Via said.

CHAPTER 17

Sonny Cheeks was right; the Tuna Club was easy to find. At the first gas station in Cicero they pulled into, a pimple-faced kid gave them precise directions.

"Best little whorehouse in town," the kid said, pushing out his chest.

Lucci glared at him and the kid stopped grinning. Five minutes later, the big Excursion turned into the club's parking lot.

"Pretty crowded for a week night," Nicky said, as they found a spot in the back row. "A lot of windshields with Chicago city stickers."

The building was an old hotel, dating back to the days when the area was a country getaway for Chicago's rich and infamous. It was set back from the roadway and surrounded by trees, and if not for the large lighted signs advertising LIVE NAKED NUDES and TOPLESS LAP DANCING, you might drive right by without noticing it.

The club was named in honor of Tony "Big Tuna" Accardo, who ran Cicero in the 1940s, making it into what the papers called "The Walled City of the Syndicate." After Accardo, Sam "Momo" Giancana moved in, bringing with him the so-called Forty-Two Gang, a bunch of vicious youngbloods out of an area called the Patch on Chicago's West Side. Nothing grew in the Patch but thugs, and Via's father was one of them. He remembered the stories his old man used to tell about the

Walled City, which, as a kid, sounded to him like some exotic place in a faraway land. Now, sitting in the parking lot of the Tuna Club, he wished it were.

"This place looks like the devil's own playground," Nicky said, chattering as usual to dispel his nerves.

"Looks okay to me," Lucci said.

"Yeah, that's what I mean."

The three of them checked their weapons, Via his S&W .38 Special, Lucci a chrome Colt .45 Commander, and Nicky the .32 S&W revolver he usually kept at the office.

"Hope you don't have to use that," Lucci said, "only good for cappin' mice."

"Listen," Via said, "all we have to do is get to the wine cellar without arousing suspicion. Shouldn't be any trouble. Just act like customers, guys out for a little T 'n A."

"You pass, you could win an Oscar," Lucci said to Nicky.

"Just keep your eyes open," Via said.

"You trust this fag?"

Nicky leaned forward from the back seat. "Fuck you, okay?"

Lucci put his hands up and grinned like the schoolyard bully. "Hey, I mean the other fag."

"Anyone ever tell you you have issues?" Nicky snapped. "You ever question your own lifestyle, what you do? Beating up people? Ever consider maybe it's not the best use of your time?"

"How 'bout I beat *you* up?"

"See, you're a very angry person. Believe me, it's not good for you. I know. I used to be into self-destructive behavior, too. But I couldn't see it for myself. No one wants to think he might be wrong. Change is hard. Changing yourself is the hardest thing of all. I just couldn't see it for myself. This is what I'm trying to tell you. I couldn't see it for myself, so I couldn't stop myself."

"I can stop you," Lucci grunted.

"That's exactly what—"

Via reached back and slapped Nicky on the knee. "He means it."

"I was just saying."

"Trust me, you're being self-destructive," Via said.

They got out and tucked their guns away and walked toward the club, the gravel lot crunching beneath their shoes like shattered glass.

At the entrance, a melon-headed bouncer with cauliflowered ears looked up to give Lucci the evil eye but opened the door when Lucci gave it back to him.

Inside, a redhead wrapped in a green sequined dress as tight as a tattoo greeted them. They followed her into the main bar, a large open area dominated by a thrust stage where several women in various stages of undress were doing just that. "Proud Mary" blared from a booth overhead where a string-haired DJ pretended he was on MTV. The pole dancers looked more bored than proud.

Surrounding the stage were dozens of dimly lit tables, waitresses flitting about in transparent blouses and silver hot pants, topless lap-dancers gyrating in G-strings sprouting money. Over all, there was a thick cloud of smoke and noise.

Via gave the hostess a sawbuck and she led them to a booth against a far wall. As soon as they were settled, a waitress came for their orders, her breasts pressing against her sheer blouse like loaves of Pannetone. Lucci was staring at them like a catatonic until he caught Nicky smirking at him.

"We gonna drink, or find the girl?" the big man huffed.

"Don't get excited," Via said and Nicky burst out laughing. Lucci gave Nicky the Reaper's eye and he stopped.

Via perused the crowd, thinking about Brassi's daughter. Salerno was smart to hide her here. No one would notice another girl stuck in one of the back rooms. Or in the cellar, if Cheeks was right. She was probably drugged, which no one would notice either, and which was probably good since it would make it easier to get her out. If they could do that without getting killed. No telling how many guards might be watching her. Thinking that, he suddenly realized they would be watching the crowd, too, and the doors, and felt chilled realizing how easy it was to get in.

"You boys can't see very well from back here," the waitress said, delivering their drinks. "Would you like something a bit more close up? Like a table dance?"

"Well," Via said, "we were hoping to get a little closer than that."

"Really?" she chirped, like it was the first time she had heard such a thing. "How close?"

"As close as possible."

She smiled broadly and left them and a few minutes later the woman in green sequins re-appeared.

"I hear you gentlemen are hoping to get a closer view."

"Up close and personal," Nicky said, his voice an octave lower than normal.

"Well, that might be possible, but we do have rules."

"Rules," Lucci grumbled.

"Just a question. You gentlemen wouldn't be police officers, would you?" she asked, straight out. "You know, you have to say so if you are."

"No, we're just here looking for some fun," Via said.

"I think we can help you, then," she said. "Follow me."

They filed out of the booth, Lucci last, and she looked up at him wide-eyed. "You that big all over?"

She led them back across the room toward a door behind the stage. On the other side of it was a hallway lined with dressing rooms where half-naked women tried on costumes, flipped through magazines, or talked on the phone. It looked like a backstage scene from one of those old Hollywood musicals.

"These the girls?" Lucci asked.

"These are the performers," the woman said. "The girls are this way."

Following her down the hall, Via noticed one of the girls, short and petite, walking toward them. She was wearing a kid's school uniform, except the skirt was too short and the blouse was open to her navel. On impulse, he grasped her by the shoulders and crouched to look at her face, which was heavily made-up to look younger than her age.

"I've been a bad girl," she said flatly. "I should be spanked." Her eyes were hazy and vacant.

The woman in green sequins came and stood over her. "Honey, you know you're not supposed to wander the halls."

The girl blinked at her and then went back the way she came.

"If you will follow me, Gentlemen," the woman directed, and they continued along the hall.

She led them to a red room and settled them on a large sofa that matched the color of the walls. Before them was an ornate gold table stacked with several thick leather-bound books.

"Just look through these. I think you'll be able to find something you like."

Lucci began leafing through the books, which were actually photo albums neatly indexed by body type, race, and fetish.

"Madonn'," he said.

"Yes, we have quite a varied menu, so take your time," the woman said. "I'll be back shortly."

Before she went out the door, Via asked, "You have a wine cellar?"

"I think we can provide just about any vintage you like. Why don't you make a selection from the portfolio first?"

She went out through yet another door across from the one they'd entered through.

"You see this?" Lucci said, waving an album in his huge hand. "Some of these are just kids!"

"You're real quick," Nicky said.

"You upset because there ain't no little boys in here for you?"

"Hey," Via interrupted. "Does this seem a little too easy to you?"

"What do you mean?" Nicky asked.

"Getting in here. If Salerno has the girl stashed here, seems like someone would have noticed us by now."

Lucci glanced up from the book he was paging through.

"Maybe they did," Nicky said, his voice a bit shaky.

Via got to his feet. "Let's get out of this room and do what we came here for."

They went back through the door they'd entered, filed back past the dressing rooms, and stopped where two women in bathrobes sat passing a joint back and forth. Via stuck his head through the doorway.

"You know where the wine cellar is?"

"In the *cellar*. Duh," one of the women giggled, and the other threw a cackling fit.

Nicky handed her a twenty and she said: "Door at the far end of the hall marked Employees Only. But don't mention I told you, only employees are supposed to go down there."

"No shit?" the other stripper cracked, and they both broke up again.

The three men hustled along the hallway, checking more dressing rooms as they did, half expecting to find a gun pointing out at them along the way. The cellar door was unlocked and Via eased it open and listened for a moment, but heard nothing. He put a hand on Nicky's shoulder and told him to stay upstairs and keep watch.

"Let the big man stay. I'll watch your back," Nicky whispered.

"He's too conspicuous. You'll be better here."

"And what if someone asks what I'm doing here?"

"Pretend you're the costume designer," Lucci said. "They'll believe that."

Via slapped Nicky on the back—"You know, that's not half bad."—and went through the door with Lucci.

Guns drawn, they descended a long, dimly lit flight of stairs enclosed on both sides by brick walls that gave back a rufous dust when touched. Via wiped it on his jeans and was surprised to find his hand was sweaty. This *was* feeling too easy. Behind him, a stair creaked under Lucci and he motioned for him to stop. He listened again for sound from below, but still there was silence.

He continued down, Lucci following. The air grew cooler and he could sense the weight of subterranean earth and rock and realized he could hear nothing of the raucous music and catcalls from the stage above. At the bottom was a dusty concrete room stocked with hundreds of boxes of canned goods and crates of wine. The light from the stairway cast a feeble glow.

"The fuck?" Lucci said, looking around. "Some wine cellar, no wine racks."

"No guards, either."

"Somethin' ain't right."

"See if you can find a light switch."

There was one on the wall next to Lucci, but when he tried it, nothing happened. The two men looked at each other and pointed their weapons into the dark. They started forward but stopped abruptly when they heard a muffled noise from a corner of the room.

Lucci flicked his lighter and they moved in the direction of the sound. Via spied a worn wooden door secured by a large padlock. He found a crowbar atop one of the crates and handed it to Lucci, who snapped the lock like a pretzel. The door creaked open and the distinctive smell of urine filled the air.

The small room seemed to be used for storing tools and Via accidentally kicked over a shovel in the dark. Someone moaned. Lucci held his lighter closer to the floor and they saw a young girl curled inside a filthy sheet.

"It's her," Lucci said.

She was bound, gagged, and blindfolded. Via knelt to undo the knots, but Lucci pushed him aside.

"Get her outta here first." Lucci put his gun back in his jacket and lifted her like a rag doll.

She came awake then, just as they stepped back through the door into the larger cellar, and began struggling and trying to talk. Via slipped the gag from her mouth and she cried out:

"Nyet! Nyet!"

He realized it then, the way you know you're going to fall and can't do anything about it, and he ran back toward the stairs just as the shooting started.

He returned fire in the direction of the shots and pulled Lucci behind a stack of canned vegetables. The girl began screaming and kicking furiously.

"I'm gettin her out!" Lucci yelled.

But before he could move, a bullet punched through one of the boxes with a dull *thwack* and the girl went limp in his arms. Via looked over and saw a wet, red hole punched through her blindfold.

Lucci let out a roar. He yanked out his .45 and began firing wildly into the shadows, the big gun echoing like thunder against the surrounding stone.

Via began moving toward the stairs but Lucci was still holding the dead girl.

"She's gone!" Via yelled.

Lucci seemed confused by the blood blooming on her blindfold.

"It's not Brassi's daughter!"

Lucci looked at him and then at the girl again.

"It's not her!" Via shouted.

Gunfire rang out above them and a body tumbled down the stairs. The guy was still moving when he reached the bottom, so Via shot him in the brain.

Bullets were exploding through cartons all around them and red wine was spurting on the floor. Lucci set the body on the ground and shoved a new clip into his gun. Then they ran, firing wildly, Lucci pushing Via up the stairs.

Nicky was heading down, so Via spun him and the three of them burst through the door and slammed it closed behind. Startled faces gaped from the dressing rooms along the hall and Nicky yelled to them, looking for a back door. One of the strippers pointed frantically and seconds later they were outside running in the cool night air.

There was a stand of trees behind the place and Nicky started for it.

"No! Get to the truck! The truck!" Via shouted.

Two of the ambushers pushed through the back door, shooting. Nicky swiveled around to fire back. One of the shooters fell and Nicky let out a cheer; then he folded up suddenly and crumpled to the ground. Bullets kicked up gravel around Via's feet. The moon was full and low, defining him like a cardboard target.

Lucci shouted, "Come on!"

Via ran over and knelt next to Nicky, who was sucking air and exhaling blood.

"I got him, didn't I?" Nicky coughed.

"Yeah, slid down the stairs like a sled."

"I forgot where we parked," Nicky said. He managed a small smile and then died.

A bullet whistled past. Via got up on one knee to return fire but another bullet ripped through his left shoulder, knocking him back. Lucci fired from somewhere behind him and the shooter went over. Via heard Lucci's truck start and he began running, emptying his gun into the dark behind him. He jumped into the passenger seat just as Lucci jammed the truck into gear, kicking gravel into the air. Via looked back over his shoulder and saw a gun barrel flash and heard the muffled pop. The bullet pinged through the lift gate and punched into the center console between the front bucket seats. Lucci gunned the truck and they sped out of the lot. He kept his eyes in the rearview for about half a mile and then slowed and took the Eisenhower Expressway ramp back toward the city.

Via could smell his own blood wicking through his shirt. He put his hand over the wound and carefully tried to lift his arm, which still seemed to work. He rested back against the seat, feeling lightheaded. Lucci opened the center floor console and took out a pack of Camels, which had a hole through it. He cursed and threw the pack out into the night.

"Cheeks set us up," he said.

"No shit."

"Sent your boy to fag heaven."

Via jerked toward him but the pain in his shoulder forced him back again.

"You should be thinkin' what we're gonna do," Lucci said.

"I know what we're going to do. Get me sewn up first."

"Then what?"

"Then we're going to kill him."

Dr. Pervez Khouri was not happy to see them. He lived forty minutes from his office and didn't like leaving the comfort of his suburban home to drive back at night into the city, which he considered a hostile, predatory place where animals roamed after dark. The emergency work he did for the Mob convinced him he was right.

"Can't you guys get shot during daylight hours?" he said, bending over Via. "It looks like it went straight through. A fraction lower, it would have taken out your clavicle. Lucky for you."

"You call this lucky?"

"Fix him up, Doc. We got work to do," Lucci said.

"Work," Khouri snorted.

"Just get him on his feet."

"I will do what I can. Wait outside, please."

While Lucci read magazines in the waiting room, Khouri numbed Via's shoulder and began to clean the wound.

"Work," he scoffed again. "If I were you, I would find a different job."

Via drifted off while the doctor worked, dreaming about his childhood again, his past following him like a hungry dog. He saw his father coming home from work, stripping off his blood-stained shirt, his mother soaking it in the bathroom, the water dying red in the sink where he brushed his teeth. He heard his parents whispering, then shouting, his father slamming a door, his mother coming into his room, kissing his cheek, smoothing back his hair. He heard his father pick up the phone, the clicking of the rotary dial, his father's voice: "It's done."

He heard it again, louder, and opened his eyes to Khouri standing over him, pulling off his surgical gloves, repeating, "It's done."

CHAPTER 18

Sonny Cheeks's place was part of an old warehouse recently converted to condominium apartments and lofts. It was just one more new box built over an old box in an old neighborhood, which now had new problems, like a lack of parking space. Lucci had to circle the block twice before a spot opened up near Cheeks's building, which was wedged in on both sides by other condo conversions still too early into rehab to have tenants. Perfect for what they were about to do.

Looking around, Via felt a flare of déjà vu. "Christ, I know this place. I negotiated the contract on this property years ago for your boss."

"Yeah, and now you're back to sweep up," Lucci sneered.

The rash of renovations around the city was good news for the Outfit. It got a piece of pretty much every union and construction contract handed out. It was good for the Mayor, too, who not only got healthy kickbacks from the developers, but also a rush of new, young white voters who would keep him in office for another couple of decades.

It had been good for Via, too. He had handled all of the contracts in the neighborhood and made a killing. Another perk for being mobbed up. Of course, that was before Monkey Wrench, before he lost his law license and Brassi had no use for him anymore and decided he was too high profile to keep around. Hell, he might have been rich by now, maybe be ordering some other poor sonofabitch to find Brassi's daughter, instead of taking orders from a Neanderthal like Lucci. Everywhere he went he was reminded of things he'd lost.

Lucci parked and shut off the engine. He reached into his jacket, took out his gun, and screwed a silencer onto the barrel like a union plumber threading pipe. They got out and went around and opened the hatch. Inside was a large blue and orange Chicago Bears duffel bag containing a knife, a length of rope, an ice pick, and Lucci's red toolbox, which he opened. From it, he removed a thin crowbar—a jimmy bar—and two pairs of brown leather gloves, which they both pulled on.

"You're a real Boy Scout," Via said. "Always prepared."

"Fuck you."

They strode briskly to the entrance, jimmied the inner security door, and checked the mailboxes for Cheeks's name. They went up the fire stairs to avoid accidentally meeting someone on the elevator, went through the door marked 2, and followed a helpful little sign pointing the way to *2D*.

The hallway smelled of fresh paint and the floor was still plywood. Lucci stumbled on a raised nail and the crowbar slipped from his hand. They stopped and waited to see if anyone heard and then went on ahead.

"Give it to me," Via whispered when they got to *2D*, but the door was already ajar.

From inside, they heard scuffling and then something hard hit the wood floor. Lucci tucked the crowbar into his jacket and pulled out his .45.

Edging inside, they found Sonny Cheeks hanging from an exposed cross beam, kicking furiously, his eyes bugging out. Someone was clanking down the fire escape and Lucci started after him through the open window but Via shouted for help with Cheeks. They held him around the thighs and pushed up to slacken the rope.

"Hold him!" Via shouted, feeling the stitches in his shoulder giving way. He righted the chair that had gone over and stood on it. Then he undid the crude knot and Cheeks folded into Lucci's arms. Lucci tossed him roughly on the bed and Via bent over him. Cheeks's breathing was strangled and his head was wrenched at an unnatural angle.

"The girl. Where is she?"

Cheeks gasped for air. He opened his eyes, but Via knew he wasn't seeing anything.

"Sonny, you want help, you have to tell me about Brassi's kid."

Cheeks blinked. He gagged and moved his lips, but no words came out.

"The girl, Sonny. Where is she?"

"Maybe he needs to be choked some more," Lucci said.

"Sonny?" Via urged. "You want to live, tell me. Where does Salerno have Brassi's kid?"

Cheeks tried to move his head to look at him.

"What was that?" Lucci asked.

"Where, Sonny?"

Cheeks coughed and tried to speak. Via put his ear next to his mouth and listened. Then he stood and watched Cheeks struggling to breathe.

"What'd he say?" Lucci asked.

"It was one of Salerno's men."

"His own boss? I don't get it."

"Tighten the knot. Help me hang him up again."

Cheeks gasped and tried to move his head again.

"What for?" Lucci asked.

"So Salerno doesn't know we found him."

Lucci stared over the steering wheel, a frown on his simian brow.

"I don't get it," he said again.

Via looked out at the passing buildings, thinking aloud.

"Cheeks wouldn't have set up the ambush at the Tuna Club without Salerno's okay. So maybe this was punishment for botching the job. Or, maybe it's because Cheeks knew Salerno had Brassi's kid and Salerno didn't trust him to keep it quiet."

All of that seemed to Via to make some sense. Or maybe just as much sense as he could make of it.

"So why'd Salerno hang him up?"

"To make it look like suicide, so it wouldn't draw suspicion to himself. Been too many killings already."

"Gonna be some more," Lucci said. "So now what?"

"I figure Salerno will want a meet."

" 'Bout fuckin' time. What the hell've we been doin' here?"

Via and Lucci arrived at Brassi's as the young woman they had seen before in the emerald sheet was leaving. Brassi showed them into his living room, anxious for a report.

He was in gray Armani, his Bruno Magli shoes like mirrors, his diamond pinky ring glinting as he tugged his silk shirt collar to make sure it was flat. Another would-be John Gotti, Via thought, another Dapper Don flaunting his money. Stupid. Just made him a bigger target, pissed the Feds off even more, civil servants making maybe sixty thousand a year getting their noses rubbed in it by a lowlife like Tony Brassi. Everyone knew that was why Gotti received special attention. Nobody likes a big shot. Those working-class cops just couldn't wait to scuff his shiny shoes.

"What do you have for me?" Brassi asked, smoothing back his hair.

Via filled him in, while Lucci squeezed into a loveseat and watched a soccer game on cable.

"So Salerno killed him?" Brassi asked when Via finished.

"He fucked up the ambush. What would you do?"

"I'd have killed him just for being a fag."

Lucci chuckled.

"What the fuck you laughin' at?" Brassi barked. "You know Salerno contacted me? You two are runnin' around like Dumb and Dumber and I'm dealin' with that fuckin' scumbag. Now he wants to meet because of this shit."

Lucci snapped off the TV. "You gonna talk to him?"

"I'll do what I have to do. Then, he's dead."

"You whack Salerno, there's going to be war," Via said.

Brassi grinned. "With who? Salerno's guy, Marcelli, skipped town. And Jimmy Razor, well, he's out of the picture, too. It ain't like the old days, Via. Things don't work that way no more."

"So, your kid gets snatched and you get an opportunity to take over the city?"

"Funny, ain't it? Maybe the best thing she ever done for me, starting this. Because when I finish, no one's ever gonna forget it. And no one's ever gonna blackmail me again."

"He's gonna cap you, Boss," Lucci said.

"What, you finally finish your G.E.D.? No shit he's gonna cap me. That's why you two are goin' with me. It's all arranged. Two of Salerno's boys, the two of you. A place called Pino's on Western Avenue. Tomorrow night. We run some of our illegals through there. Everyone comes heavy. This way everybody feels safe."

"Take Albanese," Via said, "I'm not one of your boys."

Brassi got in his face. "You're whatever I want you to be! You got a stake in this, so I figure you'll be on your toes. But, just in case your heart ain't in it, I'm leavin' Bobby Bat to look after your wife and kid."

A cold rain plinked on Nicky Fratelli's casket as Via and his fellow pallbearers carried it to the graveside. There were few mourners, maybe twenty, but the important ones were there:

Nicky's mother, Grace, who refused to look at Via; Nicky's partner, Craig, whose last name he couldn't remember; his ex-wife, Karen, who shot him daggers; Meggie, who was crying; and Dee, who grasped his arm when he stepped back from the grave.

A priest from Nicky's church said some perfunctory prayers, the casket was lowered, Craig stepped forward and threw a flower into the hole, and it was done.

As the mourners shuffled about, Via left Dee to talk with Nicky's partner, while he went over to Meggie and Karen.

"You happy now," his ex snapped as he walked up.

Via ignored her and hugged Meggie. "I've missed you. Everything okay?"

"No, everything is not okay," Karen said too loudly, and some of the mourners turned her way.

"Mom, it's a funeral," Meggie reminded her.

"Your daughter's afraid to go to school. And you got Nicky killed."

Meggie touched her arm. "Mom. I haven't seen Dad for—"

"And you're not going to."

Via touched his daughter's hand. "That might be best for awhile. In fact, I'd feel better if you hadn't come here."

"I had to, Dad."

"I know, and Nicky would have appreciated it. But I'd better take you both home now."

"Harry will take us home," Karen huffed, gesturing toward Soltis's Town Car, parked next to a blue-and-white at the edge of the grass about fifty yards away.

"Bodyguards, huh?"

"Thanks to you."

"Mom!"

Standing there shivering beneath her umbrella, Meggie seemed frail and childlike. Not the budding sophisticate now, but the little girl he barely knew growing up. He reached out and touched her hair.

"Go ahead now."

Meggie stretched up and kissed him on the cheek and then went off toward Soltis's car. Via watched her go, then fixed on his ex.

"You always have to put me down in front of her?"

"Don't kid yourself. She knows who you are."

"I'm her father, that's who I am!"

"And that's a burden she has to live with the rest of her life."

Via stopped himself. "Look, I'm not going to do this here."

"What's the matter, afraid your girlfriend over there might learn something about you?"

"Maybe about you, too."

Karen stomped off to join Meggie, pausing on the way to say something to Soltis, who was coming across the lawn.

"Not a happy reunion, huh?" Soltis said, strutting up.

"You here checking the headstones for voters' names?"

"Pretty funny for a guy who just got his cousin killed."

"Nicky knew the risks," Via said, but it sounded hollow even to him.

Soltis wiped the rain from his glasses with a silk handkerchief. "And did he know you'd be connected again?"

"I told you, I'm not connected."

"So you say. But ever since you got involved with Brassi again, people been turning up dead."

"Like Billy Carlyle?"

"Don't fuck with me, Via! I've got enough on you to put you away."

"You've got nothing."

"I've got three men shot dead in Cicero. One of which happens to be your late bitchboy here. You trying to tell me you weren't at some joint called the Tuna Club?"

"Never heard of the place."

"So, what, your fag friend went by himself to some strip joint in Cicero to see what he's been missing?" Soltis put his glasses back on and hiked his pants. "I got at least two women who can put you there, asshole. You think they won't pick you out of a line-up?"

"I think you've got a couple of junkie whores who work in a Mob joint, who couldn't I.D. their own fathers."

"Where were you Wednesday night?"

"I'll have to check my calendar."

"You'd better have an alibi, smart guy."

"I was with a friend."

"I know your friends."

"She's over by the grave, you want to ask her."

"A woman. Figures. I hope you told her what she's getting herself into."

"You know, Harry, you ought to give that up, sitting around with my ex replaying past disappointments. You think that makes you look better?"

"I don't need you to make me look good, Via. I'm going to nail you. I'm going to nail Brassi, too, and any other scum you're involved with. You fucking wops. Think you're above the law? I'm going to put you away, Via, off the streets and out of Karen's and Megan's lives."

"You're a real guardian of the downtrodden, Harry. A real fucking saint. Save it for the voters."

"Listen, asshole, I'm going to put you in Cicero, and I'm going to tie you to the death of Sonny Cicci, too."

"Sonny Cheeks? I heard he hung himself. Another Mob-connected junkie. You're running in the wrong social circles, Harry. You'll never get elected like that."

Soltis stuck a bony finger in Via's chest. "You need to think about something, Via. The cops need to pin this mess on someone. If I can't nail Brassi, I'll give them you."

Via bent forward and whispered into Soltis's ear. "Say hello to Billy Carlyle's folks for me."

Dee suddenly appeared next to him and slipped her arm into his, sheltering him with her umbrella.

"Come on, Frank, take me home, will you?" she said, pulling him away.

"Remember what I said!" Soltis called after him. "Remember what I said!"

Dee gripped Via's arm tighter as they walked across the wet lawn. "I see you're still pissing people off."

"He was born pissed off."

"Who is he? Looks like an accountant."

"Nobody special."

"Special enough to have a police escort."

Via peered at her, liking her intelligence, and knowing it was trouble, too.

"He might ask if I was with you two nights ago."

"Were you?"

"Sure, you remember, we fell asleep on your couch watching Home Shopping Network."

She didn't laugh and he reached over and touched her hand.

"Listen, this is going to get worse before it gets better," he told her.

"Is it going to get better?"

Maybe she was too smart to be with him. They came to the car and he opened the door for her. "Maybe you shouldn't see me for awhile," he said.

"Awhile?"

"I'm not sure."

"Well, at least you're not bullshitting me," she said.

He went around and climbed in next to her. She was silent, staring into space. He stared into the rearview, watching Soltis drive off past the graves, his ex-wife and daughter in the back seat, moving away from him in the rain.

CHAPTER 19

Pino's Restaurant was just north of downtown. It was family-owned and empty, the owner having sent the staff home for the night, and small enough for Lucci to check out thoroughly before bringing Brassi through the door. Via found the owner in the small kitchen watching TV and sent him out to the alley to wait.

The place had two doors, a back one near the kitchen, where two of Salerno's soldiers stood watch, and the front entrance, where Via and Lucci took up their stations.

Brassi stood in the entryway, hands on his hips and contempt on his face, looking like General Patton surveying a battlefield. Al Salerno sat at a small table in the middle of the dining room, his hands on the tabletop, showing he was there to talk. His men, like Via and Lucci, also kept their hands in view.

"Still looks like he buys his clothes at Sears," Brassi sneered.

He smoothed his lapels and strolled slowly toward the table, keeping Salerno fixed in his sights. Salerno glared back, then tried to look disinterested when Brassi sat across from him and demanded, "Where is she?"

"What, not even a hello?"

"Where is she?"

"She's safe. Nobody's touched her."

"Except when you snatched her off the street?"

"Take it easy. We work this out, everything goes back to normal."

"Things *was* normal. Now we're sittin' here."

Salerno smiled coldly and called to his men at the back door. "See if you can find some wine back there."

"Forget the wine," Brassi said. "This ain't a goddamn social visit. You have her, we deal. You don't, go fuck yourself."

"I told you I have her."

"I know what you told me."

"Hey, what proof can I give you?"

"I ain't got time for games."

Salerno spread his arms and smiled again. "You want I should deliver her ear?"

Via saw Brassi tense, restraining himself.

"No proof, no deal," Brassi said.

"You always was a hard-headed sonofabitch."

"We done talkin' then?"

"Hey, you ain't even heard what I want. I thought we was here to discuss terms."

"I want my kid. That's the terms."

Salerno hunched his shoulders and leaned into the table. "You know, you gotta understand somethin'. We each got our problems. Me, I got *tizzuns* spillin into my territory like a oil slick. Everything's turnin' black. What the fuck I'm supposed to do? I'm losin' money every day, while you're chargin' fees to handle what little I got left."

"So discuss it at the sitdown."

"This is the sitdown. You and me."

"You got nothin' to discuss."

"I knew you'd be like this."

"We're done," Brassi said.

"Hey, you ain't givin' the orders here!"

Brassi pushed back from the table.

"The fuck you goin'?" Salerno thundered. "You don't leave 'til I say so." He moved the palm of his hand across the tabletop and glanced over at his guards.

Via saw one of them unbutton his coat and he reached back and quietly locked the door behind him.

"I should kill you right now," Brassi shouted.

Salerno's right hand left the table. "You ain't killin' nobody!" He brought a gun up from his lap.

Brassi shoved the table into his chest, knocking him back onto the floor. Lucci had his cannon out and shot one of Salerno's men in the heart just as he showed his gun. The other gunman dropped to one knee and got off a shot that hit Lucci high on the right thigh. Via fired back but missed. Something struck the door behind him and he knew it was more of Salerno's men. The shooter in the back fired again, but the bullet missed Via and went through the door. Whoever was on the other side suddenly backed off.

Lucci shot the shooter and he collapsed, spurting blood from his neck like a garden hose. Brassi was hammering Salerno with a chair. Via ran over and pulled Brassi off and dragged him toward the back. Lucci limped behind, turning back to put more holes through the front door. The three of them climbed over Salerno's downed men and pushed through the back exit, out into a narrow alley.

The restaurant's owner was hiding behind some discarded boxes and jumped up with his hands in the air. Lucci nearly shot him. Via looked around frantically, searching for an escape. He pointed at a door across the alley.

"What is it?" he shouted at the owner.

"The bakery."

Via shoved his .38 in the guy's nose. "You want to stay alive, keep your mouth shut," he said, but it didn't matter any. The guy's eyes went white and he fell over into the trash, a black hole in the back of his head. Four more of Salerno's men were charging up the alley.

Lucci put his shoulder to the bakery door and Via and Brassi followed him in. The security alarm went off and they ran to the front door and out onto the street. A Chevy Impala was parked at the curb and Lucci shattered the window and got in. He hotwired the car like a pro. Via and Brassi jumped in back and Lucci peeled away.

"Why'd you pull me off him?" Brassi yelled at Via. "I coulda killed that prick!"

Lucci spoke into the rearview. "It was a set-up."

"You figure that out all by yourself?"

"Looks like Salerno doesn't have her, and he doesn't know about the books," Via said.

"No shit."

"Salerno hears you're desperate to find your kid, he sees it's an opportunity to get you where he wants you."

"Dead," Lucci added.

"With Rizzo out, you're the only one between him and control of the whole city," Via said. "I guess great minds think alike."

Brassi slammed a fist against the car door. "Who's got my fuckin' books?"

Via was asking himself the same thing. If Salerno didn't have Brassi's kid, she could be anywhere. Finding her might be impossible. Who would he start with now? Who the hell would risk kidnapping Tony Brassi's kid?

"If she's not shopping the books to one of the families, what the fuck she's gonna do with them?" Brassi asked.

Lucci jerked around in his seat. "Boss, where we goin'?"

"Watch where you're drivin'."

"Uh, Boss, I think I better see the doc. My shoe's fulla blood."

Brassi leaned over the seat to look at the wet red stain on Lucci's leg.

"Can't you do anything right?" he said.

Headlights swept across the City Medical Associates parking lot and the three men reached for their guns while a dark-colored Lexus swung past and parked directly in front of the building. Dr. Pervez Khouri got out and shuffled with the weight of the world toward the entrance. When Lucci cannon-balled the car up beside him, he nearly jumped out of his shoes.

"Take it easy, Doc. It's just your favorite patients again," Lucci said, exiting the car.

"What is it this time?"

"Godzilla here thinks he's got a bullet in his leg," Via said.

"Another gunshot? The NRA must be in town."

"Just fix him up," Brassi said. "And do it fast."

The three men followed Khouri through the door. Lucci limped into his office, while Via and Brassi stayed in the waiting room. Via sat on an orange vinyl chair Khouri must have bought right after med school. Brassi, as usual, was pacing, trying to get some perspective on things.

"Goddamn it, who's got my books?"

"You mean your kid."

Brassi stopped pacing and hissed through his teeth, "I told you. I don't give a shit about that kid."

"Yeah, but she's the only one knows for sure where your books are."

"Little bitch."

"Let me ask you something," Via said. "If one of the dons didn't nab her, who else has something to gain?"

"Only thing they're gonna gain is a bullet in the brain."

"That's what I mean. Who would take the risk? There haven't been any demands, no threats, nothing."

"Well, somebody's fuckin' got her! What about this!" He took the hostage note from his pocket and threw it in Via's face. "You're so fuckin' smart, answer that!" He stomped over to the window and stared out at the dark parking lot. "Somebody's got my fuckin' books."

Via stared at the note on his lap and picked it up and unfolded it. Something caught his eye. He laid the note on the chair next to him and ran his finger across the letters, which were cockeyed like alphabet soup. He reached into his jacket and took out the class schedule Tina Brassi had given him. He unfolded it and spread it out next to the hostage note, looking back and forth between them, seeing the same misaligned characters on both. Then he held each of them up to the overhead light and saw the same watermark.

It was a minute before he truly grasped it. "Sonofabitch," he said.

Brassi turned back into the room.

"Look at this," Via said, pointing at the papers.

Brassi came over and stood with his hands on his hips squinting at the two pages.

"You see it?" Via asked.

"See what?"

"Look again."

"What's this, Where's Waldo?"

"Look closer."

Brassi picked up the papers and held them in front of him for what seemed a long time, his eyes bouncing over the pages like a ping-pong ball.

"Now hold them up to the light," Via told him, a subtle smile forming on his lips.

Brassi held the papers up like an x-ray, red slowly rising in his face.

"See it yet?"

"Where did this school schedule come from?" Brassi demanded, shaking the paper at Via.

"Tina. From your kid's computer printer."

Brassi glanced at the papers again. "Can't be. It ain't possible."

"Two separate sheets of paper with identical misprints and identical watermarks, printed at different times by different people on different printers? That's what's impossible."

"You're out of your fuckin' mind." Brassi threw the papers at Via. "She ain't that fuckin' smart."

"Not smart enough to use different printers, maybe."

Brassi went over and lowered himself slowly into a chair.

"She's been playing us off each other," Via said. "To keep you busy, keep you from suspecting her."

Brassi stared at the floor, one hand clenched inside the other, a rapid pulse blinking in his temples.

"You get it yet?" Via taunted.

The door to Khouri's office opened and the good doctor came out with Lucci, who was limping behind him.

"I got the bullet out. Just like a pea in a mattress," Khouri said. "Average-size man would not be walking." He went to the front door. "If you gentlemen are done getting shot this evening, I am going back to bed. Turn off the lights when you leave, please. The door will lock behind you." He went out.

"We goin' to get Salerno now?" Lucci asked.

"Something's come up," Via said.

"What the fuck?"

"Looks like your boss's ex is smarter than he thought."

Lucci looked over at Brassi. "What the fuck? He tried to cap you, Boss."

"Goddamn bitch! I'll kill her!" Brassi suddenly bellowed. He jumped up, startling Lucci, who lurched backward.

"I'll do it for you, Boss."

"Better find out where she stashed the books first," Via said.

"You bring her here," Brassi seethed. "She'll tell me."

"What are you going to do, have Bronco work on her?"

"Might work on you, too," Lucci said.

Brassi cursed again and ran his hands through his hair.

"You ever consider," Via said, "Tina might have someone else working with her?"

Brassi had a crazed look in his eyes. "How do I know you ain't? You always had the hots for her, didn't you, Via?"

Via got to his feet. "I refused to work for her, remember? You think I'd put my daughter at risk? I'm in this because you forced me into it."

Brassi thrust a finger at him. "And don't forget it. You remember what you got at stake here."

"Once I find your kid, you leave my daughter alone."

"You bring my ex and that little bitch here, your kid's out of the picture. But you'd better be right about this."

"I'm right," Via said, trying to sound convinced, finding it hard to believe he could be so stupid, letting Tina Brassi play him like some amateur.

"Fuckin' bitch!" Brassi shouted. He gathered up his jacket and barked at Lucci, "You walkin' now?"

"Ah, it was a small slug."

"Then drop him where he tells you," Brassi said, jerking a thumb at Via. "I've got somethin' for you to do."

"Ain't I goin' with him?"

"I got another job for you. Somethin' don't take brain work. Got somethin' for Bobby Bat, too."

"When am I goin' to kill Salerno?" Lucci asked.

Chapter 20

Rose Piccoli could not find the ricotta cheese. She studied the dairy case for several minutes, but couldn't seem to locate it. Her spells were getting worse. One moment she was fine, the next she couldn't remember where she was. Now she couldn't find the ricotta she needed to make the lasagna she had promised her husband.

Sammy loved her lasagna and she had made it for him at least once a week for forty-four years. She once made over twenty pounds of it, back in the sixties, she thought it was, when Sammy had the Salerno Family's soldiers sleeping in their basement. It was a good life. And good lasagna, too. But how was she going to make it without the cheese?

She stood before the dairy case awhile longer, until she forgot what she was doing there, and finally pushed her cart to the cashier and then out into the parking lot.

Bronco Lucci watched her coming to her car, a small, frail woman who reminded him of the mother he left long ago in Palermo. He waited until she loaded the groceries into the trunk and then came up beside her. She didn't resist when he took the keys from her and moved her around to the passenger seat.

"What do you want?" she asked.

"We need your husband to do something for us."

She raised her hand to her mouth. "Should I make a lasagna?"

★   ★   ★   ★   ★

The President of the United States had just killed two men when the phone rang. Bobby Albanese lunged across the couch, hoping to get it before it woke his wife, but he was too late and she called out to him from the bedroom.

"Who the hell calls this time of night? Somebody die?"

"I got it. Go back to sleep."

He pressed the mute button on the TV remote and listened to Tony Brassi while he watched Harrison Ford flying Air Force One and mouthing something to some guy with a gun. After he got his orders, he hung up and clicked off the DVD player, slipped his suspenders up on his shoulders, and went in to tell his wife.

"I gotta go out."

"This time a night?"

"It's business, what do you want?" he said, going into the bathroom.

"They can't send one of the young guys, somebody doesn't have a family. They got to treat you like some *cugine*?"

"What family? It's only you. Or ain't you noticed Franny don't live here no more?"

"Whose fault is that?"

He came back into the bedroom, his hair combed—"Don't start that shit"—and went over to the dresser and took a gun out of the sock drawer.

"Where you going?"

She pushed herself up out of the sheets, hair curlers scraping against the headboard. He thought of a whale breaching.

"Downtown. I gotta pick somethin' up."

"You comb your hair to run errands now?"

He checked the gun and stuck it in his waistband. "I'm supposed to look like Don King now?"

"You bastard. You're gonna see that Polock *puttana*."

"I told you, it's work. Why you always gotta be like this?"

"You like your whore better, why don't you just stay there?"

He went out to the hall closet and put on his overcoat and opened the front door.

"Bobby?" she called to him.

He didn't answer.

"Bobby? Bring back some butter pecan ice cream, will you? You know the kind I like."

Jimmy Rizzo couldn't feel his foot anymore. That was the good thing about the drugs they gave him. The bad thing was, he didn't know how much was in him, or how long he'd been there. He remembered being brought to this room and tied to this chair, but what had happened since, he wasn't sure. He was only certain he wanted it to be over soon. So when he recognized Bobby Albanese's voice at the door, he was almost glad.

His babysitter, a ropey guy named Pauli, let Albanese in and lit what seemed to be his millionth Kool.

"Christ, it stinks in here," Albanese said, unbuttoning his coat. "Open a window, why don't ya."

"Hey, it ain't my fault Jimmy here can't hold his water."

"That right, Jimmy?" Albanese asked. "You piss yourself?"

"Whatta you think," Rizzo slurred. "This *stronzo* wouldn't untie me to go to the can. Lucky I ain't shit my pants."

Albanese raised an eyebrow at Pauli, who told him, "He's still stoned."

"Hey, Bobby," Rizzo pleaded, "untie me so I can go to the john."

"You gonna do him here?" Pauli asked.

"And haul his dead ass down the stairs and past the desk clerk? What're you, stupid? Jimmy's gonna take a ride with us."

"Bobby, come on. At least let me clean up. I don't want to go out like this."

The last of the drugs were still snaking through Rizzo's bloodstream, keeping him inordinately calm.

Pauli was jittering around, trying to find his shoes. "So how we gonna do this?" he asked, retrieving a white patent leather loafer from beneath the bed.

"Was up to me, it'd already be done," Albanese said. "Fast and clean. But Tony's pissed about his kid."

"Ah, shit," Pauli complained. "I shoulda worn old clothes."

"The fuck," Rizzo said, his speech clearer now, "we known each other twenty years. Have some respect, Bobby."

Pauli slipped his shoes on and snagged his jacket off a doorknob. "We gonna do this, let's go. I been cooped up here too long." He went around and untied Rizzo's ropes.

"Let's go," Albanese said, pulling Rizzo up by his arm.

Rizzo stood there, unsteady, getting his bearings. "Come on, Bobby, let me take a crap, huh? You don't want me stinkin' up your car."

"I ain't sittin' next to him," Pauli said.

Albanese sighed. "You emptied his pockets, right?"

Pauli waved him off.

"There a window in there?"

"We're on the fourth fuckin' floor. Besides, it's painted shut."

"Nice place." Albanese removed his coat. "All right," he said to Rizzo, "make it fast."

Rizzo shuffled to the bathroom, dragging his wounded foot behind. Once inside, he closed the door and turned on the water in the sink. Then he opened the medicine cabinet. The empty syringe was where he had seen Pauli leave it. He heard Albanese yell at him to hurry. He jammed the needle into his neck and pushed ten c.c.'s of air into his jugular vein.

★ ★ ★ ★ ★

Via sat in Nicky's Honda staring at the green awning on the front of Tina Brassi's building. He wore large black sunglasses and a Cubs cap pulled low over his brow. Three empty Starbucks cups littered the floor, but the coffee was barely keeping him awake. He had been there over two hours and was beginning to think he might have missed her.

He wasn't good at stakeouts, impatient and easily bored. Which was a problem, because boredom led to fatigue and fatigue led to carelessness and carelessness led to doubt. Now he was thinking maybe he was wrong. What if the Brassi girl was really missing? How would he find her then? How could he protect Meggie?

On his left, a police patrol car passed for the second time, slowing as it did. More trouble. He started the car, figuring to drive around the block a few times so the cops wouldn't see him here on their next pass, but it was already too late. They reversed into a driveway near the end of the block and headed back. Pulling away now would look even more suspicious, so he waited while the cruiser stopped next to him and the cop on the passenger side got out and ambled over.

"Afternoon."

Via put both hands on the steering wheel where the cop could see them.

"Waiting for someone?" the cop asked, sun flashing off his badge like a warning light.

"Something like that."

The cop pushed out his lower lip and nodded like he'd heard it all before.

"Something like that?"

"There a problem?"

"A problem?" the cop echoed. "Hey, Gil, he wants to know if there's a problem," he yelled over to his partner, who was still behind the wheel.

"Don't know. He think there's a problem?" the partner shouted back.

The cop cocked his head at Via, who opened his hands and showed his palms.

"No problem here."

"So why'd you ask?"

Up the street, Tina Brassi came out and stood in front of her building.

"You live around here?" the cop asked.

"Yeah, nearby."

The cop studied him over his aviator sunglasses like he was examining a mug shot. "Those your coffee cups?" He looked like he probably wore his uniform to bed.

"Coffee illegal now?"

"Don't I know you from somewheres?"

"I've been around."

"Yeah, looks like it."

Tina Brassi was smoking a cigarette and looking back and forth down the street.

"So, what'd you say you're doing here?"

"Like you said, waiting for someone."

"Like I said?" the cop sighed. He put his hands on the car door. "Okay, let me see your license and registration."

"Look, I'm a private investigator. I'm on a stakeout."

"A stakeout? Just like the movies?"

"I'm just going to take out my wallet," Via said, reaching into his jacket with two fingers.

The cop stepped backward and rested his hand near his holster. Via brought out the investigator's license and held it up to the cop's sunglasses. He removed his own, so the cop could get a look at him. He glanced out the windshield and saw Tina Brassi pacing.

"Via? Where do I know that name from?"

The cop looked back toward the cruiser again just as a limo came up beside it, unable to get around. Via realized it was what Tina Brassi was waiting for.

"Hey, Gil, you run plates on this guy?" the cop yelled.

Gil motioned to the limo and waved him back to the patrol car. The cop leaned in again.

"So, where have I seen you, huh?"

Before Via had to answer, the limo driver laid on his horn and the cop whirled around. "What's your hurry?" he shouted and marched over to have words with the driver.

Via hoped Gabe Court wouldn't notice him.

While the cop and Court argued, Via saw Tina Brassi looking their way. Then she started walking in their direction. Via put his sunglasses back on and slumped down in the seat. The coppers got a radio call and the cop named Gil shouted for his partner to get in. The cop shouted some parting words to Court and got back into the cruiser.

As they sped off, Tina Brassi stopped walking and waved the limo forward. Gabe Court moved past Via and picked up Tina Brassi, who flipped her cigarette into the gutter and got in. Via pulled out to follow them.

For the first hour, he thought it was a waste of time. She seemed to be merely running errands—the cleaners, post office, drug store—but when the limo stopped at an American Airlines ticket office on Michigan Avenue, he thought maybe he was right after all.

There was no place to park without being seen, so he drove past and into a city parking garage up the block. Then he stood inside a Banana Republic storefront across from the ticket office and watched kids not much older than Meggie buying fifty-dollar shirts made in twenty-cents-an-hour South American sweat shops. He wondered if that was how the company got its name.

When Tina Brassi came out and rode off in the limo with Gabe Court, he went across the street. There were three agents behind the counter in matching blue uniforms and blonde hair. They smiled at him like synchronized swimmers, until he asked to see the manager.

"Is there something I can do for you, sir?" one of them asked while the other two busied themselves at their computer consoles.

"I need some information."

"Where are you going to?" The smile back on again.

"Are you the manager?"

"Uh, no, sir. We don't have a manager at this office. May I help you?"

"There was a woman in here a minute ago. Name of Tina Brassi. Did you wait on her?"

The smile went out again and the agent glanced nervously at her associates. Via took out his P.I. license and showed it to her.

"Are you a policeman?"

"I'm a licensed representative of the Cook County Sheriff's Office," he lied. "I'm here on official business." He let her see the .38 beneath his jacket.

"I . . . I don't know, we're not supposed to." She looked over at the other agents and asked, "Do you know what the policy is on this kind of thing?"

Via pulled his sunglasses down on his nose and eyeballed her.

"Ma'am, Mrs. Brassi is a known fugitive, restrained by the Cook County Sheriff's Office from leaving the state. Anyone, Miss Douglas," he said, looking at her nameplate, "including American Airlines, or its employees, who knowingly aids her in doing so is subject to prosecution under the laws of the State of Illinois."

The agent's eyes were on her associates again. She gave them a look that said, *What do I do?*

"We are losing valuable time," Via said.

"Girls, you're witnesses," Miss Douglas said, already working her keyboard like a court stenographer. "The passenger's name again?"

"Brassi. Tina Brassi. B-r-a—"

"Yes, I remember now. Going to . . . Paris. Yes, two first-class seats, O'Hare to Roissy Charles de Gaulle."

"Two seats?"

"Yes. Tina Brassi and an Annette Brassi. Leaving tonight, at eleven-twenty p.m."

Al Salerno had big plans. Sure, he blew it by not killing Brassi at their meeting, but these things didn't always go as expected. It was a mistake trying to trap him, put him on his guard. Now that everything was out in the open, he would have to finish it fast, while Brassi was still distracted trying to find his precious kid. This time Brassi wouldn't see it coming. Then things would be put right.

First, he would consolidate Brassi's family under his regime. Then he'd move against Delacante and bring his gang into the fold. There would be a little killing, of course—this wasn't an election, after all—but not like the old days. Everyone now had too much to lose. He'd keep the capos in place and maybe even increase their piece of the action, do the same for the cops and politicians, too, just to calm everyone's fears, let them know things would continue just the same.

In the old days, the underbosses would have been trouble, but Jimmy Rizzo was already dead, found cold in some one-star hotel. And Brassi's mob was like a corporation with a bunch of vice-presidents with no real power. No, this was going to be easy. Once Brassi was gone, everything else would fall into place.

And Brassi would be easy, too. Stupid fuck. Too worried about his kid to realize what was really happening. Like everyone else, Brassi had gotten too complacent. Everyone, Salerno thought, except him.

He went out front and his driver brought his Lincoln around the circular driveway and he climbed in. Another car pulled up tight behind and when they got to the front gate, still another car positioned itself in front of them.

"Like the President's motorcade," Salerno said to his driver, a guy named Sammy Piccoli, whom he had known for over thirty years.

Piccoli twisted around pointing a 10mm Glock.

"They said they'll take care of my wife," he whimpered, and put a round in Al Salerno's forehead.

Then he put his own lips around the gun barrel and squeezed the trigger one more time.

CHAPTER 21

Tina Brassi was busy packing when the intercom buzzed. She glanced at the clock: 7:10 p.m. She wasn't expecting anyone. She closed the suitcase and slipped it under the bed. She pushed two more into the closet. The intercom buzzed again and she went out into the hallway and hurried over to it.

"Yes?"

"There's this Mr. Via here to see you again."

She hesitated, mentally looking for an exit. There wasn't one. "It's okay, Willis."

Downstairs, the security guard peered warily at Via and hung up the phone.

"Your friends gonna meet you here again?" he cracked.

Via had no prejudice; he would just as soon hit a black man as a white one. He slugged the guy with his .38 and dragged him by the collar over to the janitor's closet. He appropriated the key ring from the guy's belt and fiddled with the door until it opened. Then he put him inside and threw the lock.

Upstairs, Tina Brassi was wearing the same white robe as before, but he could see she was fully dressed beneath it now. He didn't wait for her to invite him inside.

"What is it? I was about to take a bath," she said, following him anxiously down the hallway into the living room. "You can't just barge in here."

He grabbed her by the shoulders and pushed her onto the black sofa. "You know why I'm here."

"Know what?"

"Don't."

"What's wrong?"

It seemed a long time since he had first found her waiting in his office. He knew then it meant trouble so he wasn't surprised when trouble came. But he never expected it to involve his daughter, or hers, for that matter. He looked at Tina Brassi trying to play dumb and wanted to hit her, wanted to hurt someone, all of the Brassies, his ex-wife too, and Harry Soltis. They could all go to hell and he would be happy to send them.

"You think this is worth your kid's life?" he shouted.

"I don't know what—"

He slammed his fist on the coffee table, making her recoil.

"I'm trying to save her life," she whimpered.

"By helping her blackmail Tony?"

"That was all her idea. Her and that shitbag Getti. I didn't know until she came here looking for help, after he was killed."

"She had the books then?"

"Yes."

"And you decided the best thing was to be her new partner."

"What could I do? You think Tony would forgive her? Besides, what was done was done."

"And you heard opportunity knocking."

She spoke through clenched teeth. "You think I don't owe that prick? The years I put up with him? I had his books. What would you do?"

"That doesn't excuse involving my daughter."

"You'd do anything to keep her safe, wouldn't you? It's no different for me."

"Tell me, did you decide to do this before, or after you came to see me?"

"Before."

"So that was all part of the plan."

"I figured hiring you to look for Annette would make her disappearance look legit."

He went over and sat in a chair across from her so he wouldn't hit her. "And to hell with what might happen to me or my daughter?"

"I'm sorry about your daughter. I didn't plan on that."

"You think that matters?"

"No."

"How'd you know about the big sitdown?"

"I didn't. It was just luck."

"No, not just luck. When you found out, you sent the hostage note to make Tony think one of the dons had your daughter."

She reached into her robe for a pack of cigarettes. She patted one loose and tapped the end of it on the side of the package, stalling for time. He reached over and snatched the smokes and tossed them onto the coffee table with the *Town & Country* magazines. "Do you know all that's happened?"

"I told you, I had no choice."

"Neither do I. I'm taking you and your kid to Tony."

"He'll kill us both."

"Think I care?"

"You can't—"

"I can and I'm going to. You got me into this and now you're going to get me out. Where's your kid?"

"Frank, wait."

"Shut up."

"Wait, wait." She reached out and touched his hand. "We once had something, didn't we? It's not that long ago. We could get the money for the books and go."

"Where, Paris? Are we going to take my daughter, too? Maybe my ex-wife? I don't think my kid will go without her. And we can't leave her mother behind to be used to bring us back, now can we?"

"Frank—"

"Shut the fuck up. Where is she?"

"I'm begging you."

"Where?"

"Can't you and me—"

"There is no you and me. Where is she?"

Tina Brassi lowered her head and began to cry. Via was unmoved.

"The Hyatt downtown, under a different name," she sobbed. "I enrolled her in a school in France, under another alias. I thought we'd be gone by now, but Getti was murdered and everything got more complicated."

"You haven't seen complicated. Get your coat."

She was startled suddenly by a noise at the door and she looked down the hallway, which Via couldn't see from his chair. Her expression changed to fear, and then his did, too. Bronco Lucci was pointing a gun at him.

"Nice place like this, you got no security downstairs?" Lucci said.

He went over to Via and took his gun from him. "Where's the books?"

"Ask her."

Lucci swung the gun to Tina Brassi. "What about it? I don't ask twice."

Via rose from the chair. "What the fuck are you doing here? You couldn't wait until I brought her?"

"You're just hired help."

"You think you're not?"

Lucci hit him with the .45 and Via went to the floor on one knee.

"You don't want to piss me off," the big man said. He turned back to look at Tina Brassi.

"I don't have them," she said.

Lucci stepped toward her and she put her hands up in front of her face.

"Don't," she pleaded.

He grabbed her by the hair and bent her head back. "You think Tony cares what I do to you?"

"Please. Don't. My daughter. They're with her."

"Get her."

"She's downtown. At a hotel."

"Then we're goin' for a ride."

"Yes, okay, but can I just finish getting dressed?" she asked gesturing toward her bedroom door.

Lucci looked her over. "Fuck with me, it just gets harder." He waved her away with the .45.

Via pulled himself up onto the sofa, blood seeping from a gash on his left cheek. "You want the credit for finding her, huh? Make your boss happy."

Lucci stood like a monument staring after Tina Brassi.

"Still the good soldier? What do you think you're going to get out of this?"

"Shut the fuck up."

"You can take the books, take control, be Brassi's boss."

"I told you."

"You don't need us. You just need the books."

Lucci turned and seized Via by the throat and jammed the gun against his forehead. "Shut your fuckin' mouth!" He raised the .45 to strike him again, but Tina Brassi came back from the bedroom and shouted, "Stop it!" and for some reason Lucci did.

"Come here," he ordered. He ran his big hands up and over her, across her breasts, between her legs, under her beige silk jacket, taking his time.

"What's this?" he said, finding a .22 pistol tucked into the small of her back. "You're as fuckin' dumb as he is."

He slipped the pistol into his jacket pocket and pushed them down the hall.

CHAPTER 22

In the parking garage, Lucci's truck was parked at the end of the first row of spaces. A maroon Buick Park Avenue, vaguely familiar to Via, was parked in the next row over.

If Via had been more watchful, he might have seen it coming. He might have seen Charlie Pignotti waddle up behind them, might have seen the gun in his hand, the sweat running off his nose, the small crazy black eyes in that big porcine face. He might have seen him pull the trigger, seen the pulpy red explosion. But he wasn't watching, he was thinking, trying to figure out what to do next.

And then the gun went off and he jerked around to see Lucci come down like Goliath, and the answer land suddenly at his feet.

Tina Brassi jumped back screaming, clutching herself with both arms.

Pignotti, wild-eyed, was waving the gun around. "You see that? You see that? I been following this fuckin' freak of nature all over town."

"My God! My God!" Tina Brassi screamed. There was blood splattered on her suit.

"Motherfucker killed Jolly and Ziggy."

"Jesus Christ! Are you out of your fucking mind?" Via yelled.

Pignotti stared at Lucci, looking surprised at himself for doing it.

"Fuckin' ay!" he crowed.

"You know who this guy is?"

"Fucker killed my boys. I saw what he did."

"You were in the alley that night?" Via asked, trying not to look at Lucci's .45, which had landed under the bumper of one of the parked cars.

"I saw what that fuck did."

"You were there, but didn't stop it?"

Pignotti seemed fascinated by the pool of blood growing beneath what was left of Lucci's head. "You see the size of this cocksucker? But I got him, I got him."

Via realized Pignotti was stoned. "Yeah, yeah, you got him, but what are you going to do now?"

"Like fuckin' King Kong," Pignotti crowed again.

"You'd better get out of here, Pig. That gun sounded like a bomb went off."

The fat man's foggy eyes fixed on Tina Brassi. "Who's this?"

"Brassi's wife."

"His wife?"

"Don't worry. He was going to kill her."

"The fuck you talkin' about?"

"The dead man. He was going to kill her."

"Brassi's wife?" Pignotti looked her up and down and then at Via again. "What's this shit? What the fuck's goin' on?"

"You just killed yourself, that's what."

Pignotti waved the gun at the two of them. "Maybe I should kill the both of you."

"Listen to me, you just whacked Brassi's main man," Via said. "Think it through."

"Shut the fuck up!" Pignotti began walking around, talking to the air. "Wait a minute. Wait a minute."

Via inched over to the .45, but Pignotti caught him and waved him backward. "You prick. You owe me five grand."

"That's all you can think about?"

The Pig wagged the gun at him and Via put his hands up.

"Listen, listen. I have something better," Via said. "Something that will save your ass with Brassi and get you a lot more than five gees."

Tina Brassi took a step closer to him. "Are you crazy?"

"I have Brassi's books," Via told Pignotti.

"What books?"

"His books. Records. Everything. Every deal, every payoff."

"His books?"

"He'll pay big to get them back." Via flicked his head at Tina Brassi. "That's where Lucci was taking us. She stole them."

Pignotti gawked at Tina Brassi as if she had just appeared.

"Look, it's on a computer drive. Mrs. Brassi here was going to use it to blackmail her husband. It's in Lucci's pocket."

"You think I'm stupid?"

"You're stupid if you don't take it."

"I nailed that motherfucker, didn't I?" Pignotti bent over Lucci and yelled, "I rocked your world, motherfucker!"

Via crouched in slow motion, keeping his eyes on The Pig while he moved his hand over Lucci's body. "Brassi's books are right here. In his pocket." He slipped his hand into Lucci's jacket.

Pignotti was trying to focus. "You really Tony Brassi's wife?" he asked, looking over at Tina.

When he did, Via pulled Tina Brassi's .22 out of Lucci's pocket and fired four bullets into Pignotti's chest. The Pig's short legs went limp and he melted to the floor.

"You shot me," he squealed, trying to stop the bleeding with his fingers.

"I'm surprised the slugs got through all that fat."

Pignotti began to shake, eyes going white, the bullets and drugs and loss of blood too much for his heart to handle. He closed his black eyes and died.

Via heard Tina Brassi moving behind him. He turned to see her pointing Lucci's .45.

"Give me my gun," she said.

"You fucking kidding me?" Tires squealed on one of the upper floors. "Your neighbors are coming home."

He reached in and got the truck keys from Lucci's jacket, keeping his eyes on Tina Brassi. He could see the tension in her face, her mouth taut like a rubber band about to snap.

"You're not in enough shit already?" he said.

Her hand began to shake and tears welled in her eyes. He went over and yanked the gun from her, then hurried her into the truck. He headed down the exit ramp, his heart like a hummingbird. She sat next to him, silent, sobbing to herself, her pear perfume mixing with the stale smoke, the air smelling like something sweet gone bad.

"You can't take her," she pleaded when Via pulled into the Hyatt's turnaround.

"I can and I am."

"He'll kill her. I know him."

"You should've thought of that before."

"She's just a child."

"So is my kid. Go up and get her. It's your only chance. You don't come down with her, I'll help him find you."

CHAPTER 23

Via sat in the truck and watched Tina Brassi go through the revolving door, head down, walking slowly across the hotel lobby, knowing her plans were unraveling just as his were suddenly knitting together, an unintended gift from Charlie Pignotti. The Pig had rocked the world all right, and it was turning again. The trick now was to turn it in the right direction. All it required was the proper lever.

He was thinking about that when his cell phone jolted him.

"Dad?"

That word always gave him a twinge of guilt. It was pretty much the only thing that did.

"Meggie? You okay?"

"I just wanted to see if you're okay. You haven't called for awhile."

"Sure I am."

"I heard Mom and Harry talking. Are you in trouble?"

"Don't believe everything you hear from Soltis. Isn't it about your bedtime?"

"I'm fourteen, Dad. I'm studying for a history test tomorrow."

"Listen, I never told you I'm sorry for what happened."

"I know."

"It won't happen again," he said, wondering if he would live long enough to keep that promise.

"Will you come and see me soon?"

250

He watched Tina Brassi come back into the hotel lobby, looking back over her shoulder.

"Sure I will. Soon," he said. "Go back to studying. Everything's fine."

Tina Brassi came back through the revolving door, her daughter Annette shuffling behind her, eyes on the ground, shoulders hunched into a navy blue hoodie. She looked like a prisoner on her way to the gallows.

Via knew she was feeling her world turning, too, realizing she couldn't do anything about it now. She was just a kid, like Meggie, caught up in something she couldn't really comprehend. He found himself beginning to feel sorry for her. But then Tina Brassi brought her around and put her in the back seat.

"You're turning us over to that bastard?" the kid spat at him.

She didn't look much like her photo. Her hair was short and limp and dark circles rimmed her solemn eyes. She had obviously been crying.

"You're as big a prick as he is," she said.

Her mother came around and climbed into the shotgun seat and Via pressed the lockout for the doors. "Sweet kid," he cracked.

"What do you expect? She's going quietly?"

"Forget it, Mom. He's chicken shit. Everybody's afraid of Tony."

Via looked into the rearview. "You screwed up, kid, it's no one's fault but your own."

"Go ahead, take me to him. I don't care. I'll tell him to his face."

"Where is it?" Via asked.

"Fuck you."

He pivoted in his seat. "Listen, you little shit. Don't be stupid. Those books are the only thing that can help you now, but not the way you think."

"I already made a hundred copies."

"Sure you did. Hand it over."

"Fuck you."

If he didn't have a daughter of his own, he might have hit her.

"What do you mean, help us?" Tina Brassi asked.

"Look, we want the same thing here. You want your daughter safe and I want mine. You have two choices: you give the books to me and go on to Paris, or you give them to him and take the chance he doesn't kill you."

"You'd let us go?"

"If I have the books, I don't need you."

Tina Brassi flicked a hand at him. "Now who's being stupid? You think you can deal with him? He'll kill you and your daughter, too."

"Who gives a shit, Mom," Annette said.

"You need to think about what happens to you two," Via said to Tina Brassi. "This is the best offer you're going to get."

"He's a fucking asshole, Mom. He works for Tony."

Tina Brassi glanced back at her daughter and then back at Via with eyes that were red and weary. "You'll let us go?"

"I told you, I don't need you for what I'm going to do."

"She's my only child, Frank."

"So get her out of here."

Tina Brassi hesitated, staring at him for a long moment, then leaned over the back of her seat. "Give it to him," she told her daughter.

"You crazy? He's going to kill us. He'll take the books and get rich. That's all he cares about."

"And how much were you hoping to get for them?" Via asked.

"I didn't do it for the money," Annette said. "That was Tommy's idea. I just wanted people to know."

"Know what?"

"The kind of man he is."

"Everyone knows the kind of man he is."

"No. They don't. At school they think he's just some rich businessman. The priests think he's great because he gives them money, pays for the band instruments, pays for the new furnace, gives Father Kochinsky a new Lincoln. No wonder they want to name a goddamn building after him. It's all a fucking joke. Do you know the whole Mafia culture is based on the Catholic priesthood? It's a fact. Jesus Christ, the nuns keep him in their evening prayers. Can you believe it? He's a murderer, a fucking murderer, and they think he's a saint. That's what I wanted everyone to know."

"Yeah? Well, now the nuns can pray for you. Hand it over," Via said.

"You're no better than he is."

"Just give it to him," Tina Brassi ordered.

"Fuck you, too."

Tina Brassi reached over the seat and pried the flash drive from Annette's clenched fist. Annette began flailing, pounding the back of the seat and shouting.

"Go ahead, go ahead. I don't care anymore. He killed Tommy and he's going to kill you and he's going to kill me. It's what he does. That's what I wanted people to know."

Tina slapped her and the shock stopped her. She put her head in her hands and began to weep.

"It's finished," Tina Brassi told her daughter. "Finished."

She turned back around and thrust the small silver cylinder at Via. "Take it. Go ahead, take it. It's your problem now."

"You'll be sorry, you'll be sorry," Annette whimpered. "You're as bad as he is."

Via started the truck and drove out into traffic, rolling the flash drive in his hand like a bullet.

CHAPTER 24

Dee frowned as she watched Via come up the stairs with two women, a mother and daughter by the look of it, the way the older one held the younger by the elbow, guiding her up the stairs, both moving like mourners, Via behind them, looking up at her, trying to read her expression, Dee wondering if she should just close the door and go back inside.

"I need another favor," he said when they reached her door.

"No kidding. I thought you were Jehovah's Witnesses." She stepped aside slowly and let them in.

"Sit in there," Via told the Brassi women, pointing toward the kitchen, then caught himself and said to Dee, "Okay?"

She threw her arms in the air and stomped down the hall to her bedroom.

"Remember, you have nowhere to go," Via told the Brassi women.

He left them there and followed after Dee, who was sitting on the edge of her bed, fists clenched at her side. He sat next to her and tried to explain the situation, watching her listening, seeing the questions forming on her lips, which were pressed tight, the color forced out of them.

"She's the wife of Tony Brassi?" she asked when he was done. "The gangster?"

"Ex-wife."

"That supposed to make a difference? Your face is cut and there's blood on her blouse, for Christ's sake."

254

"Look, I know it's a lot to ask."

"A lot? No. 'Will you hide some stolen money in your safe?' is a lot. 'Will you hide some vicious mobster's wife and kid from him?' is way beyond a lot."

"It's not stolen."

"Jesus, you don't get it, do you?"

"Look, you can keep it."

"What?"

"The money. You can—"

She slapped him hard enough to make his eyes water.

"Jesus Christ! You know, it's not like I didn't think about it. I knew I was tempting the devil but I didn't care. After I thought about it, I didn't care. I knew you were trouble, but I've had trouble before. I don't know why, but I think I see something in you that maybe you see in me. But I've felt this way before, so I could be wrong."

Via ran his hand across his cheek. "What can I tell you?"

She stood and walked over to close the door, her back to him. "You don't tell me anything, so how do I know?"

"It's not that simple. I can't just turn them over to him."

"Why not? You said yourself, they brought it on themselves."

"That's right. And Brassi brought it on me. It's not them he wants, it's his books. If I give them up, he's off the hook, but I'm left hanging. Somebody has to pay for what's happened. If the cops can't get him, they'll want me. The prosecutor's already dangling me in front of them. I gave up one life for Tony Brassi; I'm not going to prison for him."

She spun toward him. "And I'm not going for you. I'll make a lot of sacrifices for a man, but that's not one of them."

"All I'm asking you is to take them to the airport, make sure they get on a plane to Paris. Stay with them until they take off. They already have tickets. You'll be safe; no one knows you or knows they're here."

"And what happens after?"

"You're about forty grand richer. You buy the bar."

"That's it? I'm paid off and that's it?"

"What do you want from me?"

"I want you to be here when I get back so I can remind you what an asshole you are."

"Tell you what. I'm not here, you can have it engraved on my headstone."

She didn't smile. "Don't look for me at your funeral," she snapped.

"Look . . ." he started, but she turned her back to him.

He went out and told the women to get ready. Annette continued to curse him, still not getting it, still arguing with her mother.

"It's not fair. It's not fucking fair. My whole life is fucked up and he gets away with everything."

"You're lucky he hasn't found you," her mother said.

"Am I lucky you married him? Am I? You knew what he was."

Dee came out of the bedroom wearing her coat and scowled at Tina Brassi. "I have to listen to this all the way to the airport?"

"She won't stop," Tina Brassi said.

Dee went over and got in Annette's face.

"Listen, you spoiled little bitch. You're done talking, you're done whining, you're done crying. You walked into my apartment on my time and screwed up my life. I don't have to save your ass, and I don't really want to. I don't owe you anything except maybe a good beating. I don't like you, or your mother, and I don't care what happens to you. I'm doing a favor for someone who I don't even know if it's worth doing for. One word in the car and I'll toss your asses out onto the street. Understand?"

The kid didn't answer, so Dee clutched her by the jaw. "Understand?"

Annette gave a grudging nod and Dee let her go. There were deep purple imprints beside her mouth.

Dee went over and grabbed the women's coats and tossed them at them, then pushed Tina and her daughter out the door. She turned back on the stairs and pointed at Via. "You'd better be here when I get back!" Her words hung like ice in the air.

Via went to the window and watched them go, Dee marching them along the sidewalk, giving orders, Tina Brassi dragging Annette by the wrist.

He watched the car pull out from the curb and move silently down the street, then went back into the kitchen, glad to be rid of them. He needed time to think. He found a bottle of Absolut on the counter and a glass in a cabinet and carried them over to the table. He put the flash drive next to them and stared at it awhile. He downed some vodka and thought about what had transpired: Pignotti dead in a cold parking garage, Bronco Lucci lying next to him without a face, Tommy Getti, whose face he had never seen and no one would ever see again. He thought about Vito Tessa floating with his friends, his neck broken like Sonny Cicci's. He thought of Nicky decaying like the roses on his casket in his grave.

Those roses made him think of Carmine Delacante then.

"Watch I don't have to send flowers for you," the old Don had said to him.

"Maybe you'll have to send them for Brassi," he had replied. He poured another drink and stared at the flash drive some more. After he had stared at it enough, he picked up his cell phone and began searching through the stored numbers.

When he found the numbers he was looking for, he swallowed the booze and began making calls. *If you ain't connected, you ain't protected, he said to himself.*

CHAPTER 25

Tony Brassi stared out at Lake Michigan and sipped his brandy, wondering what the hell was taking Lucci so long. Dumb fuck couldn't do anything right. He should have gone himself. It never paid to rely on other people. Not even family. His own wife and kid, for Christ's sake. He should've never trusted the little bitch. Nothing but trouble from the moment he opened his door to her. What did she think, she could blackmail him? Her and her traitorous mother? The two of them did nothing but cost him money.

Well, it would be over soon. Once he had his books back, Tina and Annette would be over, too. It would have to be staged properly. An accident of some kind. He would have to plan it himself. Sure as hell couldn't depend on Lucci to do it. Where was that dumb fuck? He couldn't trust anyone.

He pivoted in his chair and looked over at Caesar Augustus, tribune, statesman, consul, and first emperor of Rome. So beloved by the Romans they declared him a god upon his death, a death caused from poisoning by his wife. Another goddamn traitorous woman. That sculpture had been custom-made and it cost a small fortune. Now, Brassi thought he might tie his ex-wife to it when he tossed her off his boat into the lake.

He heard the outer door open and finished what was left of his drink and went over and settled into the red leather chair behind his desk. He was going to enjoy seeing the looks on their faces.

"So bring them in," he said when Via came through the inner door.

"They won't be joining us."

"What the fuck you talkin' about?"

"They're not coming."

"Get Bronco in here."

"He won't be joining us, either."

"Don't piss me off, Via."

"Your big man's dead."

Brassi started to laugh but stopped when he saw the look on Via's face.

"That's right. Charlie Pignotti killed him. Surprised him in Tina's parking garage."

"Don't mess with me."

"The Pig put a bullet in his brain."

"Who the fuck you kiddin'?"

Via almost smiled, waiting for it to sink in.

It took Brassi another moment. Then lines began forming on his forehead. "Bronco? You telling me Pignotti clipped him? Fuckin' Pignotti? He let that fat ass piece of shit ambush him? The fuck? Now I gotta kill Pignotti, too?"

"You don't need to worry about that."

Brassi massaged the back of his neck and twisted his head from side to side. "This shit is out of hand. That *stronza* is gonna pay for this."

"Somebody has to," Via said

"Goddamnit! Where's my fuckin' books?"

The outer door opened again and Brassi's eyebrows went up.

"It gets worse," Via told him.

He went over and opened the inner door. Two men came into the room and split off on either side of it. Then Carmine Delacante shambled in.

"Some place you got up here in the clouds, Brassi. Now I see where those fees I pay you are goin'. You like being up so high? Me it would make nervous. Too far to fall."

Brassi rose from his chair. "What the fuck is this now?"

"Relax. You're gonna find out soon." The old man shuffled to a chair in front of the desk. "Sit," he told Brassi.

"Fuck yourself."

Delacante grinned at Via. "I told you, a goddamn hardhead."

The old man motioned to one of his guards who came over and pushed Brassi back down.

"You gotta pay for Jimmy Razor, Tony," Delacante said.

"I don't gotta do nothin'. Jimmy offed himself."

"Let's say he was persuaded."

"Say whatever, but he got himself killed."

"You gotta pay, Tony. You know the rules. Think they don't apply to you?"

"Rules? There ain't no fuckin' rules no more. There ain't no Outfit no more. Everyone's dead."

"Not yet," Delacante said.

"You sayin' you're gonna miss him? Rizzo was a dickless fuck."

"Yeah, sure, but he was my biggest earner. And he was *my* responsibility."

"He was planning to whack you. Me, too. Ask Via here."

"You nabbed him because you thought he stole your books," Via said. "Turned out you were wrong."

Brassi spread his arms and grinned like a wolf. "Hey, honest mistake. I'm willing to pay for it. How much you think the little prick was worth?"

"Money can't fix this," Delacante said.

"Money can fix anything. How much?"

"You caused a lot of trouble. Bodies turnin' up everywhere. Cops turnin' up everywhere. Now the Feds are turnin' up. It's bad for business."

"You're missin' the big picture here, Carmine. I did you a favor. Business is better than ever. With Salerno gone, there's just us two to cut it up."

The old man leaned forward on his cane. "I prefer to eat alone," he hissed.

Brassi glanced over at Delacante's men. Via saw apprehension in his eyes, but his voice didn't betray it.

"The cops are watchin', the Feds are watchin'," Brassi said, taunting the old man. "And you're gonna take me out? Even you ain't that stupid."

Delacante rubbed a finger across his pale lips, hiding a slight smile. "That's why I'm gonna let the Feds do it for me." He tipped his head toward Via, who dangled the flash drive in his fingers like a charm.

Brassi shrugged his shoulders. "So, you got my books. What're you gonna do, blackmail me? I go down, Carmine, you go with me. Those books got your name in there too, you know."

"You're right, I ain't stupid. That's why I worked a deal with the Feds."

"The Feds again? Who you kiddin'?" Brassi scoffed, but there was a glint of sweat on his upper lip. "They got enough on you they don't need to deal. They been tryin' to nail your ass for twenty-five years for whackin' Johnny Fischetti. So what the fuck you got to deal with?"

"Ask Frank here, he set it up."

"Fuck him."

"You should show some respect. This is a smart guy here."

"Fuck the both of you."

"You know, it's a funny thing. You get a good lawyer, the cops might need more than these books to put you away. Just to be sure, I'm gonna give 'em . . . What'd you call it Frankie?"

"A corroborating witness."

Delacante grinned at Brassi. "Still knows how to lawyer, this guy." He laughed and that started him coughing.

"You know nothin'," Brassi barked. "Witness to what?"

"To whatever the Feds need," Via said. "Don Delacante is going to tell them whatever they want to hear about your past sins. In return, they're going to turn a deaf ear to his."

"Whatta you think, we're gangbangers?" Brassi blustered. "Nobody knows nothin'."

"You think it matters?" Via said. "Like the Don said, too many bodies floating around. The cops need someone to tie them to. Can't look bad in front of the FBI. They just need testimony that can do it for them. Don Carmine already gave them a statement."

Delacante ran the back of his hand across his mouth and tapped his cane against the desk. "You shouldn't of killed this Getti kid, Tony."

"Who says I did?"

"I say so. I say we was havin' dinner and you was braggin' about how you did him. You was drinkin' and you was braggin'. Said you killed that loan shark, too. What's his name?"

"Charlie Pignotti," Via offered, and Brassi shot him a glance.

"Yeah, Pignotti. And, you know, I think hard enough," Delacante said, "I think maybe I say you admitted you did Johnny Fish, too, way back then."

Brassi was scarlet. "Fuck you, the Feds ain't gonna buy this bullshit."

"Haven't you been listening?" Via said. "They already have."

Brassi slammed his palm on the desk and Delacante's men reached into their jackets.

"You're fuckin' selling me out?" Brassi thundered.

Delacante smiled coldly. "You break the rules, this is what happens." He scratched the stubble on his chin. "Think of it as payback for Jimmy."

"You're dead, Carmine, you're fuckin' dead. The both of

you. You're fuckin' dead. And your daughter—" Brassi started to say to Via, but he stopped when the outer door opened again and the sound of footsteps came toward them.

"I told you it gets worse," Via said, checking his watch. He went over and opened the inner door again.

Brassi's eyes saucered as Harry Soltis marched in, followed by a platoon of uniformed cops who spread around the room like Marines taking Baghdad.

"Anthony Brazzini," Soltis recited, "you are under arrest for racketeering, extortion, and murder, and too many other crimes to list. Read him his rights, Sergeant."

The cops went over and yanked Brassi up and cuffed him.

"You motherfuckers," he yelled. "You're fuckin' rats. You're both fuckin' rats!"

"Get him out of here," Soltis ordered, and the cops dragged Brassi to the door.

Soltis stood watching the doorway after Brassi left, smiling to himself and cleaning his glasses with his tie. He held them up to the light and put them back on his bird-like nose and turned back to Delacante.

"Copy of your signed statement," he said, taking an envelope from his jacket and handing it to the old man. "Your lawyer is going to need this."

"Give it to Frankie. He's my lawyer now. You forget that's part of the deal?"

Delacante gestured over his shoulder and his bodyguards came over and helped him stand.

"Ain't this nice, Mr. Prosecutor, the way it all worked out," the old Don said. "Everyone gets what they want. You get the Mob bust you need to get elected. Frankie gets his license back, so he can represent me when I give you Brassi in court. And I get to sit back in my garden and smell the roses." He nodded at

Via. "You done good, Frankie."

"I'll be in touch," Via said.

"Sure, sure. You're on the clock now. Gonna cost me whenever we talk." Delacante hobbled to the door, his men like mountains on either side. "See you in court, Mr. State's Attorney," he said, and went out.

Soltis strutted over to Brassi's desk, plucked a Cohiba from the humidor, rolled it under his nose, and hiked his hip up on the desktop.

"You think you got a good deal here?" he said, lighting up, blowing smoke out through smug lips. "Don't bet on Delacante looking out for you. When I re-negotiate the old man's deal and leave you out, you think he's going to go to prison to save your ass?"

"Wake up, Soltis," Via said. "You're not going to do that."

Soltis admired the cigar in his hand and smirked. "As far as you're concerned, Via, I can do whatever the hell I want."

"Sure. But what you really want is a seat at the grown-ups' table, and I can help you get it."

Soltis snorted. "You already did, asshole. Isn't that what this is all about? You just gave me the bust that's going to put me in state office."

"Yeah, it'll get you on the front page. But the election's a long way off and the voters have short memories. Not to mention you're dating a mobster's ex-wife. You're talking about the big time here. Face it, no one knows you, Soltis. You're going to have to run a high-profile campaign. And you're going to need political and financial backing to do it."

"What do you know about it?"

"I know someone who can deliver all of that to you in a nice, neat package. Someone who spins in high circles, knows your buddy the Mayor, knows lots of big names with big money. And

I happen to know he'd be willing to use his influence to get you what you need."

Soltis clenched the cigar in his teeth and sneered. "Who you kidding? I know the kind of people you associate with."

"Then you must know Richard Bitberg."

"The investment banker?" Soltis flicked his wrist. "Everyone knows him."

"That's right. And he knows you. He's waiting for your call."

"Still the goddamn joker, huh? You're in no position."

"See if this is funny." Via took out his cell phone and began dialing. "I did a job for him a little while back. He owes me a favor."

"You really think I'm fucking stupid?"

When the number was ringing, Via held the phone out to him.

Soltis stared at it skeptically and pulled the cigar from his mouth: "What the hell is this?"

Via pushed the phone at him. "Don't screw it up."

Soltis grasped it like a hot iron and put it cautiously to his ear.

"Who is this?" he barked.

Slowly, his face changed, eyes wide and white, and he slipped off the desk and began walking around the room, rubbing the back of his neck, scratching his head and peering at Via from the corner of his eye.

Via imagined Bitberg at the other end, pacing across his office, enjoying the opportunity to play kingmaker before he had to go home for an evening of kowtowing to his wife. Soltis listened intently, nodding now and then and making noises as if afraid to speak. When he finally did, Via could hear apprehension in his voice and knew Soltis was finally beginning to realize what he was selling himself into.

When the conversation ended, the new candidate for State's

Attorney handed back the phone, looking like a guy whose mother-in-law just drove off a cliff in his new Bentley.

"A good-news-bad-news kind of thing, ain't it?" Via said, smiling through his teeth. He put the phone to his ear and listened for a moment, then said, "When I'm done with it, Dickie. When I'm done with it," and clicked off.

Soltis pointed the Cohiba at him. "You've got something on him, don't you?"

"Got something on you, too. Don't I?"

Soltis lifted his chin and looked down his long nose when he spoke, but his voice sounded hollow and tinny, like he was speaking through a soup can.

"You think you're smart?"

"Smart enough to know what makes the world turn."

"You think you own me now? Is that it?"

"Nah, Bitberg owns you." Via grinned like the devil. "Thing is, I own Bitberg."

"You're still nothing but a goddamn gangster," Soltis sneered.

"That's right, Mr. State's Attorney, and guess what—we're practically related."

The Cohiba had lost its taste and Soltis crushed it out on Brassi's desktop. "Give me Brassi's books," he demanded.

He held out his hand and Via slapped the flash drive into his palm.

"We're done now," Soltis said. "I don't want to see you again."

"You'd better get used to it. We're going to see each other often."

"Not if I can help it."

"But that's just it, Harry. You can't. Can you?"

Via started toward the door, then paused and looked around again. "Cheer up. We've both gotten what we wanted. And now Karen will get what she wants, too."

"She wants you out of her life."

"Well, then you had better explain things to her, Harry. Because I'm coming by to see Meggie for Sunday dinner. In fact, I'm coming next Sunday, too."

He turned back toward the door and said over his shoulder, "Yep, I'm dropping by any time I please. Any time I damn well please."

ABOUT THE AUTHOR

Dan Doeden grew up in Chicago on the streets where this novel takes place. An army veteran, he attended college on the G.I. Bill, where he learned to love books, and went on to earn a Ph.D. from Northwestern University. He still lives and writes in the Chicago area.

Doeden is also the author of the detective novel *The Crux Ansata,* available in the Kindle bookstore. You can contact him at www.dandoeden.net.